D0927423

4/2019
PA

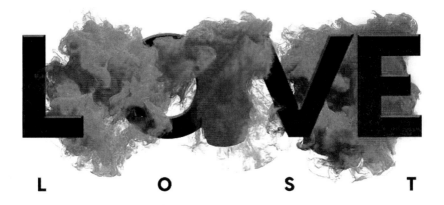

CONTENTS

Chapter 1

"I never really knew something so beautiful, could bring so much pain." Aiden 'Kidd Brewing said to me. I'm Ray, I am his best friend. We've gone through everything together. With all the things that Kidd has seen and been through, I would have never guessed that he could be so hurt over a girl. A girl that he knows he can't be with.

I've known Aiden for about 15 years now. We first met at this ghetto-ass park on the westside of Las Vegas. On a normal day, you would have never seen someone like me down there. But some of my friends who lived on MLK St heard that Kidd was running the court. So they called the top players in the city to come see, which was my crew.

I lived in Angel Springs, this little suburb up North. I knew that no 'Kidd' from this area was better than me. Right when we walked up all I heard was, "I'm Kidd! I'll be here all night!" His eyes then scanned the court and looked me dead in my eyes, "You lost or you taking a number too?"

I looked around and said, "Who me?"

Kidd yelled out, "Yeah that little boy is definitely lost!" Him and his friends laughed. This was the point when I probably shouldn't have let my pride get the best of me.

I then said, "No, I'm the boy that is going to send you home with a loss!"

He started a new a game and we were up next. He blew right by the guy holding him, went right down the middle of the lane and dunked it so hard I thought the rim was brake. He pointed at me, "I'll make this game fast since you think you're going to send me home with a loss."

I was puzzled. Was he talking shit to me and I was on the sideline?

"Game time! Get the fuck off the court," he yelled at the guy he was playing against.

And just like that the game was over.

Kidd then pointed at me and said, "You, Mr. Give me L's, y'all next! Get on!"

Now it was our time to pull up and do what we came to do. I mean after all it's just basketball and nobody in this city was better than us. When it comes to one on one, I'm the man.

"I got the one running his mouth," I said as I picked up Kidd. I should have let someone else play defense on him. He grabbed the ball and said, "Check, ball in."

His first shot was a step back three pointer right in my face. I had my hands up and everything. Then I had the ball.

"So what you going to do with it little man?" He just kept talking shit to me.

"Thank you!"

What! He just stole the ball that easy? After that I didn't say anything. I had something to prove now.

It came down to game point both ways, I was still playing tight defense on him. He ran over to get the ball. "Move! Move! Move! This boy really thinks he can hold me," he laughed. "Everyone! Anyone! Someone!"

He was doing all this yelling as I was playing defense on him. He then put the ball in between his legs, drove right, put the ball in front of me to steal. As I reached for it, he made the fastest spin move I have ever seen. It was like he was there for a second and then he was gone.

All I heard was, "Tell this little boy who I AM!"

I walked off and asked everyone I saw who this Kidd was. Several of the players told me that, he just moved here and has been on the court every day since. This was my first meeting with Mr. Kidd. We sat there as he won game after game, talking shit to each person. He made each point look easy, a smile stayed on his face. It was as if he was having fun beating everyone. I wondered who was this mysteriously guy and why everyone called him 'Kidd,' because he looked pretty damn old to me.

I was just about to be a freshman at one of the top basketball high schools in the city. Walking into high school for the first time, was everything. It was way bigger and had more people than I have ever seen at a school. My first class, was Freshmen Orientation. Walking to class and seeing all the pretty girls this school had to offer, made me happy I was there. English class was next. I walked in, sat down and started talking to my friend Nick.

"Aye, what up Mr. Give out L's haha" I knew that voice, it was Kidd.

"Hey, what's up man? I didn't know you went to school here."

Was he really talking to me? I should say something. "Hey, what's up man?" We took out seats next to each other.

"Hey man you seen any fine girls?" He asked me.

I said "Hell yeah I seen all of them".

"No, you haven't. There's this girl named Carol and boy is she a sight to see.

We had first lunch together and I saw this girl walking to lunch. She looked like an angel.

"Kidd, who is that?" I asked with my mouth open.

He really wasn't paying too much attention to me, he was busy waving and saying "what up" to everyone as we walked down the hallway to the cafe.

"Yo, Kidd you missed the prettiest girl I ever seen".

He looked around and said "Yeah? Who? Point her out".

As I scanned the cafe looking for this pretty face, she walked right behind us. I tapped Kidd.

"There she goes right there".

"Oh yeah that's Carol, the girl I was telling you about." She was everything a boy could dream of.

"Yeah man she is fine as hell" I told him smiling, as he looked her way.

"Yeah I know, I told you she was the prettiest girl in our class," he said to me.

Kidd then started talking to the upper class-men that were on the basketball team, laughing and pointing out girl to get at. This is when I found Kidd to be as smooth as butter, not just on the court but with the ladies also.

He ran up to me and said, "Yo, you see that girl right there"

I replied, "Which one? There's a group of girls!" This had to be the most heartfelt description I have ever heard, but I later found he was good with his words. He described her as if he never wanted to look at anyone else, it was special.

"The girl right there to the right, the one with breathtaking beauty, eyelashes that butterfly so gracefully. Look at her hair run wild with those highlights, almost if we're were staring at the sunset," he said "Right Ray?" As he put his hand on my head.

"Yeah right", I replied, "I mean I wouldn't have put it so much like that but I get your point she is fine as hell that's for sure". I could hear him tell all of our friends that he would be able to get her.

"Stop lying she's upper-class, she wouldn't give you a second look and I heard she dating Dub the captain of the basketball team. So tell me Kidd, how you plan on getting her?" I asked. He turned to look me in my eye and said, "Look at me". He licked his lips. "I'm Kidd, meaning that I'm that Kidd everyone wants to be and every girl wants to know… don't worry Ray, just watch me work."

He walked up to Dub I could see them go back and forth for a while. They pointed at "Sam", Samantha was her real name. I watched Aiden walk up to the girl he said he could get. They talked for a while then the bell rang. Luckily for me, I had Aiden in the next class.

8

"So what did she say?" I asked.

"What do you think she said?" Kidd replied as he was laughing at me.

"She didn't say anything, I did all the talking."

I looked at him wondering what he could have said.

"Well what did you day?" I asked. With a smile on his face, Kidd bit his lip and replied, "Said whatever I had to say, to keep a smile on her face."

Aiden was a real smooth guy then and even smoother now. This is partly why I can't believe him when he says "she really hurt me." He has been through what I like to call hell and back, so how does this little pretty girl from sunny California hurt this man to his soul? If I knew the answer to love, I guess I would be more than just this Dispensary owner. Which happens to be the best Dispensary store in America. Okay top five for sure. I am only the owner because of Aiden and the move he made. He is a great businessman. After a couple years overseas playing ball, he puts his money into cannabis dispensaries and other business stores he had. We own a few storefronts in different states, Kidd and I still get high to this day. After all this was the plan that made he believe in life again.

I remember the first time we got high, thinking we are way too young to be doing anything, let alone smoking weed. It was Friday night, I was spending the night at Kidd's house. I practically lived there. We were still freshmen and Sam, the pretty upper classmen, had invited us to her party and everyone was going to be there.

This is when Kidd asked me, "Have you ever smoked weed?"

"No." I replied.

Shocked that he would even ask me that. I'm a mixed boy from the suburbs, I have never seen weed before. He talked me into trying it for the first time.

"Ray come here!" He yelled at me from the kitchen.

I walked down the hall from his room. He showed me what he liked to call "tangerine kush". The smell was strong and almost smelled like tangerines.

"Hey, let's get high before we go to that party." I didn't really know how to answer that.

Without a pause I said, "Come on with it, let's get it."

I then asked him, "Is this your first time smoking?"

He turned, looked at me and said, "Life is a mystery Ray and I want to be the best question mark, you have."

He then proceeded to try and roll a joint. When he was done, I asked, "Is it supposed to look like that?"

"Yeah I think so."

He didn't sound too sure. Maybe he hadn't smoked before like I thought he did. We lit it and got high for the very first time.

Smoking was everything I thought it was going to be. It made everything around me so great. Food tasted better, the music sounded better and it made it way easier for me to speak to girls at the party.

The party was something you see in movies. Just to think, we were the only freshmen there. As I was dancing, Sam's pretty self walked over to me.

"Your Kidd's friend right?"

I replied, "Yeah, that's my boy, how did you know?" I asked.

"I saw you with him the other day"

"So if you saw me with him, why did you ask me if I knew him?"

"Because Kidd doesn't have many friends, you didn't know that?" She replied. I thought to myself, we can't be talking about the same Kidd. Is she talking about Aiden? He knows everyone and everyone loves him. Kidd not have friends, yeah right.

Just as I went to ask Sam, why she said that Kidd doesn't have any friends, Kidd walked up. "Ray, I see you met the beautiful Samantha. Oh I mean Sam."

She laughed and looked around, "Real funny Kidd, or maybe I should use your full name also?"

"Hey hey!!!" He said as he put his hands up in a joking manner. Okay, you win Sam. But Sam, I didn't know you talked to freshmen now?"

As she laughed, she said, "I talked to you, didn't I?"

Kidd smiled and said, "look at me?" As she stared him up and down. He said, "Exactly! As you can see, I'm someone you want to talk to, pretty lady." He winked and walked away. He then grabbed me and said, "That's how you do it Ray."

I was puzzled, then I asked him, "How you do what?"

"How you make her fall in love with you," he said.

I was confused because we just left her standing there and now there was another guy talking to her. Shortly after that, I couldn't find Kidd anywhere, until I walked into the kitchen. He was sitting down on the stove looking at the refrigerator.

I walked up to him and asked him, "What are you doing?" He looked at me, his eyes were bloodshot red. I could tell he was higher than I was. I knew that because I only took like two hits of the joint and he finished the rest of it alone. "Kidd you okay?"

"Yeah can you open the fridge?" He asked me. "Ray, look in there and see if they got something good, because that subzero fridge looks way too good." He just looked at me with a funny look.

I laughed and told him let's go and get something to eat and drink.

We left, were on our way to this place called N Da Cut. That was next to these run-down public living apartments. It was obvious that I didn't belong there. I was well-dressed, half white, half black kid from Angels Springs, with a soft spoken voice. But I was with Kidd. He was a little bit taller than me and was from this area. He was also so half black and half Native American. Which was cool with me because I never had a Native American friend or a friend from the hood. He also was a little darker than I was but not by much. The way he talked, I knew he had my back if anything was to happen.

The next day we decided to go to his old middle school to put some shots up. As we were walking I asked, "Why do you like hanging out with me so much?" This is when I found out, why he was the way he was.

"Ray, can I trust you?"

I replied, Yeah, why wouldn't you be able to trust me?"

He said, "Because I only trust few, and if I trust you, that's a big deal." He squinted, his eyes looked at me and Kidd went on to say, "But Ray I feel like I can trust you. And I can be who I'm meant to be rather than who the world wants me to be."

I was in awe, I didn't really know how to respond. "Don't worry man I got you, the same way you got me." I responded.

He looked at me and said, "I got you for life Ray." He slowed down and was looking at the ground.

I could tell he was in deep thought. I could've sworn I saw what looked to be tears forming in his eyes. I put my hand on his shoulder just as he turned to look at me. He looked up and I felt a raindrop. I heard him say thank you as he was looking up at the sky. I just stood there confused.

"Thank you…. for what?" I thought he was talking to me.

He smiled and said "No Ray, not you, I'm thanking God for allowing my brother to come back to me for a little."

He didn't seem as strong as before. It was easy to tell he was hurting on the inside. I couldn't watch him look like this, it was starting to make me sad. "Aye Kidd you good?" I lightly asked as I stared at him.

He said, "Ray I told you, I'm good," as he wiped his eyes. I told him, "I'm not going anywhere, anytime soon."

I went on to ask him, "What was this about your brother?" As far as I knew, he had two little brothers, one that lived with him, which is the one I knew. Another brother with his father, who lived on the East coast, but Kidd didn't really know him because he wasn't really fond of his father. As I went to grab him, he stopped and sat down on the curb. It was still raining, Kidd didn't care about getting wet I could see that. He then looked up at me, "What are you doing Ray?"

I could tell he wanted me to sit down next to him.

"You gonna sit down, or keep pushing it?"

The way that sentence came out his mouth sounded like he was testing me. Seems like he wanted to see if I would stay with him when it was raining. It was easy to stay by someone's side when the sun was shining outside. Thinking to myself, damn, why does it have to be raining?

He then put his head down on his arms in between his legs, I just stayed next to him. "Kidd, it's okay, you can tell me anything, I got you for life A…"

He slowly started to open his mouth to speak.

"Somethings you can't know about me Ray." I could see tears hit the floor as he said that.

"Kidd, what are you talking about?" His voice got a little louder,

"Ray I choose to live my life alone because everyone leaves and no matter what, I will be alone in due time."

I was lost for words. Was he implying I was going to leave him? I looked at him with my hand turned to the side,

"Kidd, I ain't gonna leave you bro, no matter what, I will always be here for you."

I might have gotten a little carried away on explaining how he didn't need to worry because I wasn't going anywhere anytime soon. It wasn't until I said,

"No matter if it is raining and lighting is striking down, I will be by your side Kidd." He looked at me, tears still in his eyes and said something that I will never forget.

"I knew there was a reason, I felt so close to you."

There he goes again confusing the shit out of me. I wondered what is he talking about now? I asked,

"And that reason is what?"

As I put my hands up in confusion. He then went on to tell me a story that I will never forget.

"Ray, the reason I said my brother is because I had a older brother when I was a child but he was taken by a bullet when I was young. The reason, this is my first time talking about him is because my mother and I promised we wouldn't bring it up. Brings back to much pain."

This was something I would have never guessed. If you knew Kidd, he was always smiling and joking around. I didn't want to ask, but the unknown was killing me. Slowly the question,

"How did he die?" Came out my mouth. I then said, "If you don't want to tell me then, its fine." In a calm voice he said,

"Nah, it's okay".

Kidd began to tell me about the last time seeing his brother.

"We were walking to go get something to eat, at this mini market on the corner. We had to hop this wall, but it was broken and had red tagging all over it. We jumped the wall anyway. This was a store that we've gone to a lot but this time he stopped and looked at me and said, "Aiden, stay right here, I'll be right back."

Kidd then said with rain pouring down his face,

"I was lost as I was looking at him," I asked,

"Why can't I come?"

He turned and looked at me and said,

"Aiden them D-Boyz are on the block and I don't need you over by none of that nonsense, so just wait here."

"So I didn't do anything, I just sat on the broken wall and watched him go in the store."

Kidd finished the story almost crying.

"It was like clockwork, The D-Boyz were right in front of the store and they knew my brother. So as he walked out they yelled, putting their hands up and said, "Ight A get wit us later". They called him A because his name was Angelo, which stood for the Angel in their Native American tribe. My brother put one hand up with the bag in the other and what looked to be a brown old Lincoln pulled up real slow and all I heard was gunshots. I jump behind the wall I was sitting on and looked up to see Angelo laying on the ground. I was only a little Kidd, so I didn't know what to do, I just kept telling him to get up and he just laid there."

With tears in his eyes he looked at me and said,

"One bullet pierced his lung and he died on scene."

I tried to comfort him,

"Kidd I'm sorry."

"You don't have to be sorry for anything, its life, shit happens". He went on to say, "I've seen a lot at a very young age Ray. I know people don't stay, so don't tell me you gonna be here for life and not mean that shit. I'm okay with being by myself."

"Kidd, I got you not matter what," I replied.

After hearing the story of how he lost his brother and just seeing life he was living. It made it easier for me to be happy for the things I had at home. I have everything a kid could really dream of. I have both of my parents in my life. They buy me anything I want and always make sure I'm okay. Being over at Kidd's house was always great, even though it was in the hood and what not. His family did things together, while my parents were too busy with their careers. I had everything I needed at my house. However, Kidd's mother gave me more than a house, she gave me a place I could call home. His mother treated me like family. I even had to clean the house. I once asked her,

"You know I don't live here right?" She looked me in my eyes and said,

"Yeah, I know, but you eat right?" I replied

"Yeah, I eat over here all the time."

Mary Jane was was her name, but everyone called her Mom, including me.

"Okay so if you eat here, play here, and sleep here then guess what? You also clean up here too. So get to cleaning or leave but when you leave, you are no long welcome back." Aiden just looked at me and said,

"Yeah she's right if you can't help ya boy clean up the house, how I know you got my back out there on the street."

I didn't say anything just kept cleaning because if I lost Aiden as a friend I wouldn't know what really to do with myself. He was always straightforward. What you saw is what you got and I admired that so much.

He prides himself on being a man of his word. So if he said something, he was going to do just what he said. I didn't find this out until the day I came to school and Kidd wasn't there. I walked everywhere looking for Kidd. I was asking everyone if they had seen him. I could tell the people I was asking knew something just by the look on their face. I went over to Sam, tapped her to get her attention.

"Have you seen Kidd?" She looked at me and said,

"You didn't hear what happen to Kidd?"

I was looking around because I didn't hear anything, nobody told me anything.

"No, what happened?!"

She shook her head and told me,

"Don't worry Ray, Kidd is fine."

She then made this look, I could tell she was surprised about something. I looked in the same direction she was looking in and I could see all the kids from lunch running over to see. It looked like they were about to fight, I ran over thinking it was Kidd, but he was not there. I just watched everyone arguing with each other but it was separated. It was crazy, all the athletes and hood people Kidd knew were on one side. That just happened to be the side I was on. On the other side, were the Mexicans from this Mexican gang at school. Just by listening to what was going on, I found out what happened to Kidd and why he wasn't at school.

From what I heard, Kidd got in a fight with one of the guys from the Mexican gang. Now that gang wanted to jump Kidd. The story was that the gang was beating up this boy at the bus stop and Kidd's neighbor stepped in and wouldn't let them finish. The gang members tried to jump this neighbor and Kidd stepped up to end it. Kidd told his neighbor to go home and he would handle it. Kidd walked up and the oldest guy who was a Junior, stepped up. Then Junior said,

"What the fuck are you doing Kidd? You with them?" Kidd responded,

"I ain't wit nobody, you know what it is over here." He kept running his mouth, this is how Kidd was, Kidd then said,

"Y'all some bitches, trying to jump somebody," Junior told Kidd

"We never liked yo ass anyways." Kidd stepped closer and said,

"You ain't gotta like me to get yo ass whooped." He followed that with,

"I ain't one of these little ni**as, I'm going to knock yo ass out."

Junior pushes Kidd. Kidd's backpack slides off and Kidd punched him right in the mouth. He didn't stop swinging until everyone had to pull him of the Junior. Kidd looked at the rest of the guys and asked,

"Who's next? Run up, all y'all can get it."

The others just helped their friend up and put their hands up in the air saying they were coming back shooting. Kidd got his phone out and made a call. By the time he hung up this car was pulling up and Kidd's homeboy Jay hopped out with his gun in the air, yelling out "Oh so who got a problem?! Because I heard someone was talking about shooting." The others were scared and it was showing, they got back in their car and sped off. As they were doing that, the cops came and Kidd was gone by then. When I heard of what happened it kind of made me think, maybe Aiden isn't someone to be messing with. Maybe all the stories of him being ready to fight were true.

The next time I saw Aiden was at his house. He didn't have any marks on him or anything. I asked if he was okay. He smiled, looked at me and said,

"I'm always okay. You don't have to worry about me Ray, I handle my own."

I laughed and told him.

"But you don't have to handle it by yourself." He looked me up and down. I had on some blue jeans and a white V-neck shirt.

He asked, "Ray have you ever been in a fight?"

I couldn't lie to Kidd, I put my hand down and said, "No". Then told him, "But I know if it came down to it, I would get out there and throw them thangs."

Kidd looked around and laughed, "Who you trying to fool, Ray?"

"Nobody, I'm serious," I said as I stood up.

As he was laughing he said "Ray, Ray, calm down as long as you with me, nobody is going to fight you."

I looked at him with my head turned to the side and asked, "What does that mean?"

I was confused once again.

He then shook his head and said, "Ray, I'm Kidd, everyone knows me and if you with me ain't nobody going to mess with you, just trust me."

As he put his hands on his hips he said,

"Don't nobody want problems with the Kidd."

At that moment, I knew Kidd would always have my back.

It was the end of freshman year, basketball season. The season that seemed to go by so fast. I guess that's what happens when you're the best freshmen class in the city. Even though we weren't on varsity, everyone loved watching us because we put on a show. Kidd was always talking and trying to do something big so everyone could go crazy. The funny thing is nobody knew Kidd was thinking about quitting when the season first started. He wasn't starting and felt like he was getting overlooked, but it was because he wasn't really playing at his full potential.

It wasn't until this one practice where he just went off, like he did in the park. Although this wasn't exactly the same. The night before the practice, Kidd was going off, talking to Mom about how he was better and the coach wasn't starting him and that he wanted to quit the team. Mom told him,

"I didn't raise no quitter, and you're not about to quit because you're not starting."

Kidd bit his lip, I could tell he was mad, he said,

"If I don't start next game I'm done playing."

Kidd was about to storm off to his room, Mom said,

"Go to practice this week and if you don't start then you can quit but don't quit, if you didn't leave it all on the court."

Kidd didn't say anything just kept walking to his room. I walked right behind him,

"Kidd you okay?"

As I put my hand on his shoulder.

"Yeah! I'm alright" he said.

As he fall on his bed, then bounced up, looked at me and asked,

"Do you really think Dom is better than me?"

Dom was the guy starting over Kidd.

I said, "Hell no."

I wasn't lying, Kidd really was better than him, Kidd just wasn't playing for real. I told Kidd,

"If you want that spot, you got to go get it straight up!" I yelled as I banged my fist in my hand.

He got up and said, "You right Ray, watch yo boy work!"

He got up and went outside and started shooting in front of his house, working on different moves.

It was getting late, about two o'clock in the morning now. What I saw next blew my mind. We're shooting one shot, it rimmed off and was now rolling down the road. In mid spin, the ball just stopped and what looked like a cloud or a shadow just stood there. This tall white shadow person looked at Kidd and pointed to his house. Kidd ran over, grabbed the ball and we dashed inside. I was freaking out, I have never seen anything like that. I went to grab Kidd to ask him what the fuck just happen. As I was grabbing him, we heard a car peel out. The gunshot came one after another. We both jumped onto the floor. Kidd just told me to keep my head down and everything was going to be cool. That definitely woke everyone in the house but everyone was fine. Come to find out, it was a drive by shooting right down the street from Kidd's house. Even though we could have just been shot I was still freaking out that we might have seen a ghost.

Now that everything was back to normal and we were about to sleep, I asked Kidd,

"Yo what was that outside?" I asked loudly.

He looked at me, "You wouldn't believe me if I told you,"

I got up, to look at him and asked,

"Kidd why wouldn't I believe you?"

He replied "Because that was my brother. He said it wasn't safe no more and we needed to get in the house."

I was looking at him like he was out of his mind.

"Your brother?" I asked as I put my hand on my head in confusion.

He closed his eyes and said, "Yeah it was my older brother Angelo."

Then he put his hands in prayer position and said,

"Thank you A, you got me." I was still kind of confused. I didn't say anything except,

"Okay,"

and closed my eyes. I mean that was better than getting a bullet in my chest.

The next practice Kidd went off, I mean he was everywhere playing super defensive and getting every rebound. He went to the cup trying to dunk on everyone. I mean just watching him play was amazing. He was playing so hard, that when I looked at him it looked like he had tears in his eyes. He was now crying and letting everyone see as he was still going off. Coach ended practice because he wanted to talk to Kidd. Kidd walked in the locker room.

I asked, "Kidd, you good man?"

He said, "Yeah."

I asked him, "Then what was up with all those tears?" As I chuckled.

He then made me feel bad that I was laughing as he said,

"My brother was in the gym with us, he was in the corner." He then put both hands on his head.

"He reminded me that I wasn't doing this for me, but for us."

I was blown away, because Kidd was so real with me, I then told him, "Make him proud."

He said his famous words, "Don't worry Ray," and finished with, "I got this, I got us Ray."

As he put his arm around me.

"So what did coach say?" I asked as Kidd started to walk out of the door. "Coach just told me to tell Angelo I'm starting and I better not let him down."

The next game was a blow out with Kidd starting it was too easy playing any other team. We even blew the top team out by 40 points.

Our next year was coming up and Kidd was being recruited to play at these other high schools in the city. I knew he was thinking about going to another school because the school we were at wanted him on JV. Our school just had a lot of good players that were older than us, but Kidd felt he was better than them. And that it shouldn't matter about class standing but who was actually is better. In the summer we had a tournament and coach decided to move Kidd and I up to varsity. Kidd had his opportunity to show why he should be playing on varsity and he definitely put on a show. Passing like crazy, getting players open and nobody could really hold him, he was scoring at will. We both thought he should be playing up and didn't need to be on JV but our coach still said no. He wasn't moving him up and he had to shine on JV this year and next year kill it on varsity. Kidd didn't like that, he wanted to play against the best and he felt like if he wasn't playing up against the older guys then he wasn't playing the best.

Kidd started talking to this high school on the East side, which was a different hood from the one he lived in now. Coach Van, the other coach wanted to better Kidd every way so he let Kidd play on varsity. The best thing is that, at that time the assistant coach was real close to Kidd's family. I guess he had coach Kidd when he was child. Until this day Coach V and Kidd are really good friends and Coach V still works Kidd out whenever he needs it. I went with Kidd to the new school on the East side because that school was closer to my house. My parents felt that with Kidd and the upcoming class at this new school, we would be super good. They were right, we ended up finding out that Kidd's cousin Jake and one of his childhood friend's. Wright, was going to school with us too. We were by far the best team on the East side in almost every sport. Kidd and I played football, basketball and volleyball. We also lettered in all three sports. Even though we were at a new school, Kidd was still the same with the girls. He was a guy everyone loved to hate.

Being at this new school allowed me to really see what Kidd was capable of and why people showed him so much respect. Not only that, but it showed me that he was a man of his word and what he said he was going to do he would do always. I remember this one time Kidd was getting at this one girl, who was upper class. I don't know what was up with Kidd always trying to get at older girls. Kidd was now talking to this pretty Junior named Kate. She would come over to his house, with her sister and her friends so that was cool for me because I always had a girl to get at also. Kate didn't text Kidd back for about two weeks and that wasn't like her, they talked all the time. Kidd asked me,

"Ray you think I should text Kate again, she didn't text me back all day?"

I mean she was pretty and I wanted Kidd to hit that so I said,

"Yeah, hit her up one more time she might have been busy."

I probably shouldn't have said that because Kidd texted her.

Kidd: What up pretty lady?

Kate: Aye bitch-ass ni**a this Kate's boyfriend, don't text my girl phone again or I'm going to beat yo little ass think I'm play.

Kidd sat up on the couch and looked at me, showed me what this dude had said. Kidd was hot that someone would even talk to him like that. Before I knew it, Kidd was texting back.

Kidd: Ni**a you sound real hard over a text message. When I see you, we gonna see if that mouth gonna work afterwards.

Kate: Yeah we gonna see and watch me knock yo ass out.

Kidd was getting even angrier as he was telling me,

"He must not know who I am." He was cracking his neck saying, "He gonna find out, don't worry."

I was thinking to myself, is Kidd for real right now? Even though I had never seen Kidd fight or anything, I heard stories. It sounded like Kidd turned into a whole different person.

Three weeks after those texts were sent, Kidd ran into Kate's boyfriend. We were walking through the gym after football practice. We had a game the next day. As we were walking though, the girls volleyball team was in the middle of a game. Right before we got to the door Kidd turned and asked one of our teammates.

"Who is that with Kate?"

As he pointed at her in the stands with some guy. Our teammate put his hand up said,

"Oh that's Kate's boyfriend, Jim."

Kidd just looked and told him,

"Go tell him to come outside and let me holla at him."

I watched out, as teammate go up and talk to Jim. Kate and Jim got up and started to walk outside. Kidd pointed at Jim and yelled out,

"Aye little ni**a let me holla at you real quick."

Jim turned and said,

"Ni**a you don't know me."

Kidd then walked over, his voice just got harder as he said,

"But you texting my phone like you know me."

Kidd was putting his football gloves on.

"I told you it was on sight, when I saw you."

Kidd then swung, Jim stepped back and started to run behind cars. Kidd was going off, telling him to stop being a bitch and catch his hands. Kidd was ready to fight. Some friends and I were grabbing him, trying to hold Kidd back.

Jim was on the phone and within five minutes a black car pulled up and four guys hopped out of the car. Kidd was telling me,

"Ray, you better have my back if this shit goes south."

I was now standing behind Kidd and told him,

"I got yo back for life, let's get it."

What we didn't know is that one of those guys knew Kidd and told everyone to get back in the car. That is when Jim was going to have to handle this on his own. As this was going on, Kidd was on the phone and from what I heard, Kidd was telling people to come and be ready. Jim then yelled out,

"Meet me at Kate's house if you really about getting yo ass whooped."

At this point Kidd was on fire with with anger and I could tell he just wanted to beat this guy up.

Kidd said, "Don't trip we gonn be there."

I was looking around. Did Kidd mean, just him and I? asked Kidd,

"What are we waiting on? Let's push to her house."

Even though Kidd was mad, he seemed calm as he said,

"Ray calm down and wait." He then explained why we were waiting.

"We can't go over there, with just you. No offense." He said as he looked me up and down.

"Don't worry he's going to get it."

Within the next ten minutes, the person he was on the phone with showed and it was Pop. One of Kidd's oldest homeboys that he grew up with. Pop walked up,

"Kidd what's good, who gotta problem?" He asked as he looked around. Kidd answered

"This little bitch made ass ni**a name Jim. He's Kate's boyfriend, and he was running his mouth like he was hard, but that ni**a called somebody and a car pulled up."

30

Kidd was telling Pop what happened as we were walking to Kate's house. A car pulled up and it was more of Kidd's hood homeboys. That's when Pop said, "I put the word out."

We ended up getting to Kate's house with eleven people, all waiting to fight. This is how I knew Pop was legit and didn't really care about getting into trouble. Pop walked up to Kate's door, banged on it countless times. Kate stepped out and said,

"My man ain't bout to come out here and fight."

Pop said, "Bitch shut up! And tell yo bitch boy to come out here and catch his issue!"

Jim heard all of that and came out saying,

"I ain't fighting in front of wifey's house."

Kidd was just standing out in the middle of the road with his football gloves on signaling Jim to step into the road. I was just amazed at what I was watching, Kidd didn't say anything, just standing there head down ready to fight. It was something you see in the movies, we were standing in the middle of the road, forming a circle around Kidd, waiting for Jim to walk in the road. The street lights were dim and Jim walked in the middle of the road running his mouth saying,

"You ain't bout shit, Kidd!"

As he got closer he said,

"Kidd, more like bitc…"

and Kidd just took off with a right hook straight to the mouth. All I saw was Kidd firing off on all cylinders, every punch connected he didn't miss one. I didn't understand how he could take a beating like this, I wanted to stop it. Then Kidd had him on the gate just beating the shit out of this guy. Pop came in and grabbed Jim's hands and said.

"You better not try no shit," then looked at Kidd and told him,

"Get back in the street and handle it."

Kidd fixed his gloves walking back in the street. Pop let Jim go and said,

"Catch yo issue, bitch boy."

Kidd then fired off again just one punch right after another Jim was down and I guess broke Kidd's chin because all I know was Kidd looked down and screamed out.

"YOU BROKE MY CHIN, IT'S OVER FOR YO ASS!"

Kidd just got to beating Jim down until we had to pull him off Jim. Kidd was looking at Kate and said,

"Come get yo bitch of a boyfriend and tell him when he text me make sure he know who I am."

Kate just walked out and helped Jim up to the house. We all just followed Kidd, walking back to our school which was only a couple of blocks away. I was still amazed that Kidd was capable of something like that. Everyone was talking about each hit Kidd landed and how he whooped his ass. Kidd didn't say a word, he just kept walking like nothing happened, he was just so smooth and he knew it.

We were still in football season but it was not coming to an end. Playoffs were coming up and we honestly only got there because of Kidd. He was a hell of a football player. It was coming up on Halloween and I was going to spend halloween with Kidd. We were going to this big Halloween party. When I got to his house Mom said.

"Aiden hasn't come out of his room all morning."

I was looking down the hall and asked,

"Why?"

As I put my hands up. She said,

"I don't know, he just locked the door and said to leave him alone."

Mom was really concerned. This is when she got a call from Kidd's father and they were on the phone for about five minutes. Mom started to cry and said,

"Kidd's grandma passed away in her sleep."

I didn't know what to do or how to feel I just put my head down, walked to Kidd's door. I sat right in front of it, all I could hear was music and what sounded like Kidd crying. I said,

"Kidd, I'm sorry bro. Just know I'm here for you".

Mom walked up and said,

"Ray, he's going to be okay,"

as she was wiping her eyes. She put her hand on the door and said,

"Aiden, let me in," with a light voice.

Kidd opened the door and went straight back to his bed. I just stayed by the door and watched as mom spoke to Kidd telling him,

"It's okay, everything will be fine," as she rubbed his back.

Kidd turned and hugged her,

"It's not okay!" Rang out of his mouth.

He was crying and his voice weak,

"I didn't get to tell her goodbye. All I wanted to do was tell her goodbye!"

My heart was breaking watching Kidd, who I always knew to be strong and fearless. It made me forget that he was just a kid like me. But life hit him harder, Kidd stayed in his room for the next three days. He didn't come out once for anything; food, bathroom, shower, nothing. I couldn't believe it. He missed our playoff game that we ended up winning and going to the second round. When Kidd came back coach asked,

"Where were you Kidd? You don't come to practice or anything what the hell!?"

Kidd went off saying,

"I don't give a fuck about this team or anything."

He stormed to his locker and threw all of his football gear out. Coach went over,

"Kidd what's wrong?"

At this point Kidd was crying,

"My grandma died", he said as he cleared his face.

"I didn't get tell her goodbye or that I love her."

His head dropped. Coach told me to get out as they talked. They were in the locker room for a little while. Kidd was wiping his eyes making a mean face trying to show that he wasn't crying, but I knew he was. That's Kidd he was always trying to hide his pain.

Chapter 2

It blows my mind how fast time has gone. Now here we are, moving Kidd's things into his new house in the trees. It is breathtaking, Kidd's real dream house. As I sort through boxes I find this glass jar with a lot of what looks like to be note. I grabbed one and seen it was written to Cherilyn, his high school sweetheart, the one he always said, "got away". I sit down and put the jar in my backpack, I take a note and open it:

Hey, so today I thought about you because it was beautiful outside and I thought about you wearing your red and black cheerleading sandals. You were so beautiful and I remember how time stood still when our eyes locked. I just thought about you laughing and watching you enjoy life. Telling myself this is how life should be lived, right next to you. I also remember telling saying this is what happiness looks like. I stood there and felt the fall as I looked at you and every time I closed my eyes I saw your smile and fell a little more. I just hope you're showing the world your beautiful smile because it's something that belongs in a art gallery...

Love. Kidd – xo

I can't believe what I'm reading, I almost forgot Kidd was so in love with Cherilyn. She was the best thing for him, a girl who made Kidd better in every way.

He walked back in the room. "Ray! What the hell you doing?"

His voice scared me I was in deep thought, thinking about them together. I put the letter in my pocket and said, "Waiting for you to help me with this dresser."

We got everything packed and are now heading to his new house in the trees. As we drive, I ask,

"Now that you got everything, you gonna settle down?"

We pulled up to a red light, Kidd looked at me and said what he lived by,

"You know me Ray, I don't do relationships."

Looking at him, I can tell he said that enough that he now believed that statement.

The drive to his house was needed. Just wanted to see what he had planned for the future. I asked,

"Do you ever think about Cherilyn?" He paused the music and clearly went into a thought, "Ray, I've always been honest with you and honestly there's not a day that goes by that I don't think about her."

I am lost for words, I just said,

"It's been like nine years, don't you think you should give it up?"

He was shaking his head as he said,

"I'm not waiting for her or anything."

Kidd tries to turn up the music but I lower it again.

"This is why I didn't want to tell you," he said, "I knew you would look at me like that."

I try saying saying that sounds good.

"Kidd it's cool, I know she was your true lover but everything happens for a reason."

We are now pulling up to his house. Kidd asked,

"What are all these cars doing here?"

As he was looking at all the cars. He could recognize all the people that was in the house.

"Wait, wait, you knew this was going on, didn't you?" Kidd asked me as he pointed at the house with a little laugh.

We walk in and everyone yells, "Surprise!" There was sign put up that reads "New House Same Love." Kidd was in shock, everyone is here. All of our old friends from college are here and all of Kidd's childhood friends as well.

Money walks up, "Oh so this must be what getting away feels like," as he grabs Kidd. Money was Kidd's oldest friend they go back to before I met Kidd. I just knew they always looked out for each other growing up. Kidd turns around. "I mean couldn't live in the hood forever, so why not get something with a beautiful view?" They shake hands and hug.

I walk to the backyard to see who is all here and to see if the true potheads found the stoner room Kidd had in the back. I walk into the clubhouse Kidd had outside. I saw video games, two seventy-inch televisions and the stoner room in the back. I walk right past the 2k games that were going on and went straight to the room. There was already a cloud of smoke that hit me, right as I walk in. The smell was just what I am looking for. "I'm glad Kidd put the right guys in place to run the dispensaries", I thought to myself. I'm still standing in the doorway trying to find a seat when I hear, "Ray how the hell you been?" I look around trying to figure out who is talking to me. I think I may be contact high just from walking in here because all I can say is, "Jesus, is that you?" It is so cloudy in here I think I might be in heaven now. A voice out of the smoke starts laughing and replies, "No stupid, it's Dre," as he hands me a blunt.

Dre and Kidd were first roommates when he was at junior college in Oregon. I take the blunt and sit next to Dre.

"I been good, just living life," as I blow the smoke out. I ask "How you been running these dispensaries?" He replies

"It's been treating me great, I got two more that are about to open up in Florida."

I think, I may have hit the blunt too hard.

"Florida? Who you know in Florida?"

Dre is rolling another blunt saying,

"You know me and Kidd, always meeting people, trying to do this and that. I'm just enjoying the ride."

I knew the business was booming but with Kidd's ideas, I never really know what he is doing. Me and Dre keep the blunts in rotation. As we smoke our third, I know this is the seat you could find me in.

Kidd is in the backyard looking at the sunset, smoking what looks to be a joint. To my surprise, Kidd is alone. Everyone is enjoying themselves and happy to see Kidd so successful. I walk over to Kidd,

"Glad everyone is here?"

He turns with a smile on his face,

"My whole life I just wanted the ones I love to not struggle. Now that they don't have to, I just want to be the best part of people's memories. Watching everybody enjoy life is how life should be."

He always made sure the people he cared about didn't have to worry about anything and he did a great job of that.

As we talk, more people start to walk over. Kidd only wants to talk to close friends. He starts to walk towards the built-in fire pit he had put in. It had beach sand around it and places to sit.

Me, Dre, Money, Pop, Trunk and Shev follows. It is just us seven and Kidd sitting. We talk for hours, reminiscing about all the things we went through growing up. Thinking, damn we been through some shit and to think just because of Kidd, we're all friends now and successful.

Money, laughing asks,

"Kidd, remember when we had to come up with two dollars and fifty cent"

Kidd busts out laughing without letting Money finish says,

"To get a five dollar pizza. Those were the good old days."

We are all rolling up joints and blunts smiling and enjoying each other's presence. Nothing too serious about life or business, just living in the moment.

Pop asks Kidd,

"So what pretty girl inside is off limits?" We all look at him, also wanting to know who Kidd has his eyes on. Kidd makes a face and says,

"Y'all know me and y'all know I don't do relationships. I'm just chilling, so what if it's alone, I'll get there one day."

He puffs the joint and blows the smoke in the air. Pop laughs and looks at us,

"So you mean to tell me "Mr. Love" don't got no girl or girls?

"You know Kidd got some fine ass girl somewhere," Dre added.

"Nah for real, I been riding it solo dolo." Kidd blurts back to Dre.

"Nah nah I know what it is, Kidd still stuck on Cherilyn."

We all keep sitting here, as smoke goes up into the sky from the pits, blunts and joints.

Money laughs,

"Kidd really, you still want Cherilyn?" Kidd is smiling, I can tell he is thinking of her.

"Nah I don't want her, all I ever wanted was her to be happy. I just hope wherever she is or whoever she's with he, is making her happy."

Shev finally speaks up,

"There she go right there," pointing towards the house.

Kidd head spins around so quick,

"Yeah that ni**a still wants her." Said Shev as he laughed at Kidd.

We are all laughing because nobody was there. I can tell Kidd is getting a little frustrated,

"That shit ain't funny." He smiles, "Pass me that shit, no mo smoke for you," as he points at Shev.

"That shit ain't so funny now."

Kidd laughs and finally passes the joint to Shev. We can tell he still misses her, no matter how he jokes and tries not to show it, it is still clear as day.

The night is coming to an end everyone is now leaving. Mom walks up,

"Aiden where my room at?"

As she puts her hand up. Kidd looked around laughing,

"Mom, why you need a room when I already bought you a house?" He asks shaking his head.

"If you really want to stay, any room with a bed, you can call yours."

He thinks about it for a second and says,

"Not my room, so don't think about it," laughing.

Mom replies,

"No, I'm not staying just was trying to say you need a woman's feel in here"

Kidd shrugs his shoulders,

"Maybe one day we'll get there Mom."

Kidd looks at me,

"Ray, what the hell you doing?"

I am honestly too high to do anything but sleep. I had planned on staying in the guest room. I looked at Kidd,

"I got some rolled up, I'll leave after that."

We sit down by the pool side and chat about what life had ahead of us.

A couple of days have gone by and Kidd has been off somewhere either writing, taking pictures or something. I am now on my way to meet my fiancé at our dispensary/coffee shop in the valley. The best environment to be in, the lighting is dim, it is the best place for the best vibes. As I arrive I find a table. I order a chai tea and joint then text Jasmine my fiancé.

Ray: Hey baby, I'm sitting in the back at our table do you want me to order you something?

Jasmine: Oh my god I'm sorry babe, I forgot can I make it up to you?

Ray: Yeah, don't worry about it babe I'll just chill or go to the gym or something.

Jasmine: super, sorry again babe.

Now, that my girl wasn't going to the shop. I decide to go into my backpack to pull out my laptop. I see the glass jar with the notes. This is the perfect time to read them. I'm alone, the lighting is great and the vibe is right. I know I shouldn't read them but I want to remember when his happiness meant something in his life.

I remember when he wrote these. Mom had just made us dinner and made us sit and watch <u>The Notebook</u>, a movie she was trying to make us watch for the longest. After the movie was over I asked Kidd, "man you miss Cherilyn don't you?"

Kidd replied, "Yeah I do, she was my best friend."

I then said, "Did this movie give you hope?"

He smiled, "Yeah it kinda does, but I'm damn sure not writing her 375 letters, if she don't reply after the first one I'm call it quits."

I looked up at him,

"Kidd you ain't going to write her nothing, ni**a you barely can spell."

I remember him saying,

"Ni**a shut up, but you right I probably ain't gon' write her shit. She ain't thinking about me,"

he then let out a little laugh.

Now as I sit here with this jar, I realize he really did write her and just didn't tell anyone. For someone to be such a social butterfly, he sure did keep to himself a lot.

It was raining today, it reminded me of the first time you spent a night at the house. I remember telling myself as you laid on my chest, that nothing else in the world mattered as long as you were with me. Then you looked up at me and those big brown eyes were the key to my heart. I knew I didn't have to feel alone no more because I had the one I looked for my whole life. Until this day Cherilyn, you're my smile, my heart beat and the reason to wake up in the morning...

Love. Kidd – xo

I wonder what Kidd would do if he knew I was reading these notes, to the woman of his dreams. I still remember the first time they met. It was our Junior year in high school, we were still attending the school on the east side. It was Halloween night and after last year when Kidd found out about his grandmother, he no longer celebrated Halloween. This was a time when I saw Kidd at his lowest, his only regret was that he didn't get a chance to tell her goodbye. I could tell he was going through depression. His cousin and I spent the day with him. He didn't want to do anything and he really didn't care about his appearance.

We were at his house, Kidd went to the bathroom and when he came out we were going around the block to smoke to try to make him happy. Kidd was freaking out after we were finish smoking, so he ran into the garage. When we got back in his room I said,

"Kidd, you need to relax, you're gonna get us in trouble."

Kidd began to jump up and down, dropped to the floor and looked at us.

"Ray, I'm cold,"

he told both of us,

"Come touch me."

When I put my hand on him, his skin was frozen like a block of ice, it was like he was dead or something.

We got him up and put him in the bed.

"Kidd go to sleep bro you'll be fine,"

I told him, as I gave him a blanket to try and get him warm. He went to sleep but he was laying on his back, arms folded across his chest, it looked like he was in a coffin. When he woke up, he scared all of us. He woke up with a yell,

"OOH SHIT RAY, TAY!!"

We both looked at him and Tay said,

"Shhh keep it down before you wake someone up."

Kidd then told us why he was tripping,

"Yo, I had the craziest dream ever."

I was looking at him all types of crazy then asked,

"What was this dream?"

He then began to tell his dream,

"This guy came to me out of the dark and reached for me, I stepped back and he said "don't worry everything will be okay." He then waved his hand, my life but only the bad things appeared. With is other hand he waved it and said, "if you take my hand, this can will be your life and it was me walking into a party and everyone was showing me mad love."

We both just looked at him,

"Then what happen next?" Tay asked,

"I closed my eyes and said I don't fear anyone but God and I woke up." Kidd said.

That story gave me the chills. I hid my own fear and said

"Kidd you tripping, you need to chill bro."

Kidd was back to being his self after that crazy nap he had. I was wondering why he was the only one tripping if we all smoked the same thing. I asked him,

"Why were you tripping, is there something you ain't telling us? Because I know tree does make you like that."

I put my hands up looking at him. He said,

"Remember when I went to the bathroom, well I took some pills."

Me and Tay just looked at each other until Tay said,
"Ni**a only white people do shit like that."

Kidd put his hands up,

"Okay, I was low and wanted to ended it all."

I couldn't believe it, he was always strong didn't like to show any weak emotions. I never would have thought anything was wrong with him. The way he hides his feelings was something I couldn't fathom.

That night a couple of girls texted Kidd's phone and wanted to hang out with us. Kidd didn't really want to be around anybody but Tay and I were bored and playing the game was getting old. Kidd asked us,

"Do you guys want these girls to come over and kick it?"

We looked at each other and said,

"Hell yeah!"

I then looked at Kidd,

"You think I want to be around y'all all night, I'm trying to see some beauty."

Kidd laughed,

"Okay, I'll tell them to come over".

Within ten minutes they pulled up, but none of the girls that were hanging out with us were driving. We walked outside as they pulling up to Kidd's house. We were walking out, telling one another which girl was going to be ours tonight. Kidd didn't care that much; he came out of the house, hair wild as can be with a grey ripped hoodie, some basketball shorts that had a hole in them and some Jordan slippers. Kidd looked a mess but Tay and I didn't say anything, just let him be him.

Right when the car pulled up Kidd asked,

"Yo, who is that driving?

I never seen her before, so I couldn't say anything. She was a little light skin girl with a gorgeous smile, eyes big and brown, hair that came down so peacefully; she was truly beautiful in every meaning of the word. After all the girls got out the car I asked Nat,

"Who is your friend that dropped you off?"

She made a little smile,

"Oh that's Cherilyn, she a cheerleader, at the Upper East Side school." She then asked me.

"You think she's cute or something?"

I said, "No," then continued saying, "If I wanted her, why am I here with you?"

she laughed and we headed to the house.

Kidd then walked over to the car and just left Bev there by herself.

"Hey pretty lady, where you going?" He asked before she could leave. Cherilyn looked him up and down, "Oh, wouldn't you want to know." Kidd looked around then, smiling at her he relied,

"Yeah, I would wanna know, because next to you is where I'm trying to be. Just give me five minutes and if you still want to leave, you can go."

It was only Cherilyn in the car everyone else was already waiting to go in and hang out.

Cherilyn ended up staying for that five minutes. Kidd looked at us and said

"Go ahead inside, I'm going to stay out here and get to know this angel."

Cherilyn, laughing and smiling, asked,

"We're not going inside with them?"

Kidd still had a smile on his face said,

"Why go in there, when we can stay out here under the stars and get to know each other, with no interruptions?"

She looked at him,

"But what if I want to be with my friends?"

Kidd was so smooth he then said,

"Then you can be with your friends."

She stood up, to start walking and he followed that sentence with,

"So what do you want me to tell the stars that came out to see the prettiest thing on this earth?"

She stood there and told her girls,
"Go in, I'll be right there."

Kidd still had a smile on his face; we totally forgot he just tried to kill himself twenty minutes ago.

They sat on the wall outside of his house for way longer than five minutes. As we were in the house, I asked about Cherilyn.

"How do you girls know her?"

They told us she was messing with some senior who was the big brother to Qunn who played at her school. Qunn was pretty good at basketball in the city also, so that's how we knew of his brother. Bev was kinda mad and we could tell because she came to be with Kidd and as soon as Kidd laid his eyes on Cherilyn, everything was a rap.

He came back inside, and I asked,

"Where's Cherilyn?"

I thought for sure he gamed her up and she would walk in with him. He just said,
"I guess she had other plans before she dropped off the girls."

Bev was a little jealous, she said,

"Oh yeah, she going to see her upper class boo."

Kidd made this face and said,

"I know, and I ain't tripping."

Tay and I looked at each other, and Tay said,

"Ni**a, she going to be with some other ni**a and you cool with that?"

Kidd shrugged his shoulders.

"She not going to be with him, I can feel it. Don't worry, just watch me work, boys."

The girls then said

"She doesn't date anything but older upper class men."

Kidd had a smirk on his face,

"I bet you girls are right."

They said,

"Yeah, we are, that's our girl, we know her."

Kidd smiled and said,

"You're right; she might date upper class men, but she'll fall in love with me."

The way Kidd said it, he sounded so sure of that statement. We all just looked at him and Tay said,

"Yeah right, you don't see how fine that girl was."

I said,

"Yeah, Kidd, I don't think you gonna get her bro."

Kidd said,

"I love when people doubt me. It creates something in my body, where I have to prove you wrong now."

It was getting even later, it was two in the morning. Kidd wasn't showing Bev any attention. We could tell all he was thinking about was Cherilyn. They were texting back and forth, until she came back. About 2:45am, and Kidd went outside and they sat on the wall again talking to one another for hours. It was now about six in the morning and they were still going at it, laughing and making each other smile like it was the only thing they could do. Cherilyn told him,

"As much as I love sitting here with you, I have to get home it's way to late."

Kidd then asked,

"Too late?"

Cherilyn replied,

"Yeah, the sun is about to come up."

Kidd said,

"So it's not late, it's just really early in the morning."

She laughed,

"Okay, you're good Kidd, I can see that."

He put his hand on his face,

"You're right I should let you go home."

Smiling she said,

"Yes, you should Kidd."

As they walked to her car Cherilyn said,

"I did have a good time with you Kidd."

Kidd looked around and pointed at himself,

"You had a good time with me?"

She giggled,

"I mean yeah if I'm still here and the sun is coming."

Kidd smiled at her,

"Good because I just wanted to make sure you were the reason for the sun rising in the morning."

Cherilyn got to her car,

"Oh is that right Kidd, and how many girls have you said that to?"

Kidd walking closer to her car,

"Only you."

She then opened the door to get in,

"Yeah right Kidd. You must take me as a fool."

Kidd was now leaning on the car,

"Come over tomorrow let me prove it to you."

She sat there thinking about it.Kidd then said,

"Okay if you're not going to come over then let me get a hug."

She got out the car to give him a hug, he then asked,

"How about a kiss?"

She was blushing,

"No Kidd, I just met you."

He had this disappointed look on his face.

"Okay you're right, one one the cheek at least?"

She was now in the car with the window down talking to Kidd.

"Okay come here but just one on the cheek."

He smiled,

"Okay deal,"

As he leaned in the window, she slowly leaned closer to him, about to kiss him on the cheek. When he turned his head and kissed her on the lips and they kissed for at least ten seconds. He came up eyes open in shock that she kissed him back,

"Okay sorry, I had to feel what your lips felt like." He then said, "I know, I probably messed everything up for myself but I had to."

She was in shock also that he even did that.

"Nobody would ever think of doing something like that, you have balls Kidd and that's cute and who knows I might have wanted to kiss you also. But I guess you never know."

Kidd said,

"Let me make it up to you."

She started her car

"I don't know, I'll think about it."

then she drove off.

Kidd with a super big smile on his face came in and said,

"Yo I think I found the girl of my dreams,"

He then kept going on,

"Y'all don't understand how amazing she is."

I was half asleep,

"Yeah Kidd I bet, go to sleep bro."

Kidd laid down and just stared at her name on his phone.

Next morning came and Kidd was up cleaning the whole house, living room, Kitchen and his room. I got up,

"Yo Kidd, what you doing bro?"

Kidd, with a smile on his face showed me his phone,

"Read the texts," he ordered me to as he handed me his phone.

Kidd: Good morning beautiful text me when you wake up.

Cherilyn: Hey Kidd, how did you sleep?

Kidd: Dreamed about you and smiled all night.

Cherilyn: haha yeah I bet.

Kidd: No really dreamed about you coming over today. So can we make this dream come true?

Cherilyn: I don't know Kidd, I made Pat mad going back to your house last night.

Kidd: Is he your boyfriend?

Cherilyn: Not but I been talking to him for a min now.

Kidd: Just come over so I see your beautiful face one more time and then we can go back to no knowing each other.

Cherilyn: Okay, Kidd I'll come over don't make me regret it.

Kidd: When?

Cherilyn: I guess you just have to be ready.

I was smiling now too,

"Aye okay Kidd, you in there,"

as I was giving him high five.

He looked at me,

"I don't know bro"

I looked at him sideways,

"Ni**a don't know what?"

He was rubbing his face,

"Ray, there's just something different about her."

I just looked at him,

"What's different?"

He smiled.

"When I'm with her time slows down and I feel alive, like my life is meaningful or something."

I couldn't believe what Kidd was telling me, he just met this girl and he's already head over heels for her.

It was the middle of the day, I looked at Kidd as I laid on the couch.

"Maybe she ain't coming."

Kidd was walking into the kitchen,

"She coming, all you need you need to do is believe in da Kidd."

I just looked at him,

"Yeah okay we'll see."

Kidd was even making her something sweet, for her to have after she had some of his step dad's BBQ. It was the best BBQ in town for sure. I watched Kidd plan everything, I didn't know what it about her but whatever it was it had Kidd falling and fast.

Mom walked in the kitchen and looked at me and Tay then asked us,

"What the hell got into Aiden?"

We looked at each other and said,

"He met this girl last night and basically fell in love."

Kidd walked up,

"I ain't in love just think this girl is mad cool and she the prettiest thing I have ever seen."

as he was smiling thinking about her.

Mom looked at the house, seen how clean it was and asked,

"Aiden did you do this?"

She then looked on the counter

"Oh you even made your famous banana pudding."

She looked at him and finished saying,

"Yeah, I definitely need to meet this girl."

Kidd then said,

"You're going to meet her, she's coming to the house."

His phone went off and he looked down,he then began to walk back and forth.

"Everybody just be cool, don't mess this up for me."

We all looked at him sideways. I said,

"Boy if you don't sit down, you gonna mess it up for your damn self."

Kidd looked around,

"You're right, I gotta be cool."

Tay then said,

"Yeah be cool, be Kidd right now not Aiden."

Kidd was walking to the door and out he went. I was guessing she had just pulled up to the house. Kidd walked in with her and she looked even prettier than she did last night. Kidd introduced Cherilyn to everyone and saved Mom for last, walked over,

"Mom this is Cherilyn."

Mom took a pause and looked her up and down.

"So this is the girl that you're madly in love with?"

Kidd started to blush, "Shhh, she don't need to know everything just yet." Kidd went on to say, "I have to know she's going to stay first."

Cherilyn was turning red but she kept her cool just like Kidd does and responded by saying, "Oh thank you so much, but I'm really not that pretty and Kidd that's only if you want me to stay," as she winked at him.

I was looking at Tay and he was looking at me I then said, "Shit I don't know who she trying to lie to."

Me and Tay were laughing and Tay said, "Shit if Kidd don't want her to stay I do."

I realized we said that louder than what I thought. Kidd looked at me and told Cherilyn, "Don't mind those two dick heads over there, they don't see beauty like your every day."

She was laughing and walking to the kitchen to sit down, she smelled the food then looked at the pudding, "This looks good." She then looked at Mom, "I know, I haven't tried anything but your cooking looks and smells amazing."

Mom looked at her and said, "I did no cooking or cleaning today, thanks to you Cherilyn."

She was puzzled, lost for words and didn't know what to say but she asked "Thanks to me?" Making a face, "I don't know what I did but you're welcome."

Kidd walked over into the kitchen by the food and said, "She's thanking you because I did all the cleaning and cooking."

Cherilyn was lost for words once again but somehow said, "So you're almost like the perfect guy?"

He looked at her with one eyebrow raised, "Almost, more like for sure or definitely"

She smiled then said, "I look forward to finding that out."

We all sat in the living room watching the football game, clowning around and laughing. Cherilyn was definitely more than just a pretty face. The way she interacted with everyone like she knew us her whole life. He really surprised when she knew so much about sports, not just football or basketball but everything. The way Kidd looked at her was something magical. Every time she looked at him, she smiled and it was like they were in their own world.

The night was coming to an end and we were now sitting in the dining room playing this card game Kidd's family played all the time.

"After this game, it's a wrap, y'all ain't gotta go home but y'all gotta get the hell out my house."

Kidd's step father JJ yelled out. Kidd said,

"Okay let's make a bet since this is our last game."

as he was looking at Cherilyn.

"But we're already playing for money," she replied.

He then said,

"No, no, not for money. If I win, you have to let me fall in love with you."

Mouths dropped to the table. Did I just hear what I thought I heard? Cherilyn looked him in the eyes and asked,

"What did you ask me Kidd?"

He looked her right back in the eyes,

"I said if I win all you have to do is let me fall in love with you."

She slowly squinted her eyes,

"Deal, but if I win you gotta be in my life forever."

Once again mouths dropped to the table. I was thinking this game is going to be interesting.

The game was getting started and right off the back the game started good. Everyone else besides Kidd and Cherilyn were making jokes. I could tell Kidd wanted to win bad. I played the King of Clubs, with a big smile Kidd yelled out,

"Game time!"

As he slammed down the King of Hearts. The goal in the card game is to get all a pair of the cards you have in your hand and then you win. Kidd putting down that King of Hearts won him the game.

He looked at Cherilyn,

"So I guess that means you have to let me fall in love with you."

She smiled at him,

"I guess we'll just have to see if your really going to fall for me or not."

They both got up and walked to the door and Cherilyn said goodbye to everyone.

Chapter 3

As I sit here reading letter after letter, I notice that I didn't realize Kidd was this in love with Cherilyn. The way he talks about her is incredible. To this day I still haven't heard him talk about any girl the way he talked about Cherilyn.

I remember the third day after they met, it was the first time I heard Kidd say he loved a girl. We just got out of school and were walking to Kidd's house, I looked at him smiling so hard at his phone. This is when I asked,

"Yo what you smiling so hard for?"

Kidd looked at me still smiling,

"Damn I can't smile and be happy?"

I shook my head,

"Let me guess, Cherilyn is the reason for the smile isn't she?"

Kidd was texting,

"Yeah, she just said when she gets out of school she's going to come over."

I was happy for Kidd, he was always talking about meeting the right girl, and now he found her. I asked him,

"You ain't gonna hit that?"

in a joke manner, Kidd said,

"That's just it Ray, you know me, after I hit I'm not going to want her no more."

I then made this weird face, was he going to hit and stop talking to her like the other girls? I asked him,

"So after you hit that you don't think you'll still mess with her?"

Kidd stopped walking,

"She's everything I've been looking for in a girl, she's funny, smart, athletic, beyond gorgeous and that's my fear Ray."

He grabbed me,

"That I'm going to hit and everything will go out the window."

I started to walk again,

"Kidd who knows this girl could be the one."

We were coming up to his house,

"I know, that's why I haven't tried to make any move yet,"

Kidd said as we walked in the door to his house. I was making a side face, I hope he didn't expect me to believe that bullshit.

She pulled up to the house, me and our teammate Jolt were in the living room playing a game when she came in. We looked at her.

"What up, Cherilyn?"

She waved her hand,

"Oh hey Ray, I thought Kidd was going to be home alone today?"

I responded,

"Shit he was but he told me you was coming, so I had to come over to see if you brought a friend."

She laughed and said,

"Ray, my friends want a man not a boy."

I quickly responded,

"So what you want a boy? Because you're with Aiden and he goes by Kidd so now."

She laughed again, this time a little hard and said,

"The reason I'm giving Aiden a chance is because he has potential and sometimes potential is cute.

Shortly after she said that Kidd came out of his room, they hugged each other tight. They slowly made their way to Kidd's room when Jolt grabbed Kidd.

"I bet you ain't gonn hit that."

Kidd stood there contemplating, then said

"Bet!"

Jolt's eyes got big,

"Okay how much?"

Kidd looked at his door, then shook his head slowly,

"A bill."

Jolt looked at him,

"So I'm guessing you're confident."

Kidd turned around and walked into his room where Cherilyn was waiting. Cherilyn was looking at everything in his room, newspaper articles on the wall next to his jerseys, she looked at his close.

"You have a whole lot of shoes Mr. Kidd."

Kidd replied,

"What can I say, I'm a sneakerhead."

She kept looking around his room,

"Wow, how many trophies have you won?"

She pointed at his stand which had two levels full with things Kidd has won and accomplished. He smiled,

"I don't know, would you like to count them for me?"

She laughed a little,

"So I see you got jokes, that would take a lifetime to count."

Kidd stood there smiling,

"At least that means I would have you for a lifetime."

She brushed it off like she didn't hear him and jumped on the bed. Kidd then said,

"Don't get too comfortable, pretty lady."

She laid there grabbing the bed sheets and blanket,

"So what did you say earlier ? You wanted to be with me for a lifetime?"

Kidd looked at her eyebrow raised,

"Not just a lifetime but for every lifetime we live."

Grabbing the sheets again,

"So then why aren't you laying down with me?"

Kidd sat on the end of the bed looking her up and down,

"So let me ask you Kidd, how many girls have you had in this bed?"

She was getting closer to him. He answered with,

"It doesn't matter how many girls seen the bed. The real question should be, how many girls have seen my heart and the true Aiden, not just Kidd."

She put her hand on his back,

"Kidd you must think you're real good or something don't you?"

He moved towards her,

"No, I don't think I'm nothing but I can tell you what I'm trying to be and that's the reason you're able to show off that beautiful smile,"

as he lightly rubbed his hand on her chin. They were now looking each other in the eyes.

"Kidd, I heard about you and how you do girls."

She then asked,

"So, what makes me different?"

Kidd was biting his bottom lip,

"I don't know, I just feel complete when I'm next to you."

He kinda shook his head,

"Did I say that out loud?

He then laughed a little.

"I meant to say, I just love how easy it is to talk to you and the fact that you can make me laugh all the time is the best thing ever, and you're hands down the prettiest, most down to earth woman I have ever met and…"

She pulled him in and kissed him mid-sentence. Me and Jolt were still out in the living room now watching *How High.* The music in his room got louder and all I could hear was what sounded like her screaming and just the wall banging over and over again.

Then it stopped and Kidd came out the room with a magical look on his face. His hair messed up, shirt was off, sweating, and he even had scratches on his back bleeding and all. I looked at him and asked,

"What happened?"

I put my hand up, he took a deep breath and said,

"I think I'm in love."

We busted out laughing. He stood there,

"Nah for real I think I love that girl."

He came in a little closer and said,

"Jolt I'm going to need my money, and it was the best I ever had Ray."

He ended with,

"You know I been with a lot of girls but she's the one no doubt."

I remember looking at him as he went back in the room, he really had found the one.

Chapter 4

I was in the shop so long, it was now closing time, one of the works came up to me.

"Hello, Mr. Ray are you staying?"

She went on to ask,

"If you are, is it okay if we close up?"

I honestly wanted to stay and keep reading but I said,

"No ladies, it's okay, you guys can close up and go home."

Then told them,

"I'm going to leave here soon."

Right when I said that, my phone started to ring, it was Kidd. I picked up,

"Yo, what up boy."

Kidd asked,

"What are you doing?"

I told him,

"I'm about to leave the shop. What's good you need me?"

I can hear him laughing and a girl in the background. He was still laughing,

"Nah just wanted to see if you could meet me at the view in a couple of minutes?"

I was going to go home but I wanted to asks Kidd about Cherilyn and if he remembered writing these notes, So I said,

"Okay I'll head that way right now."

Kidd replied,

"Okay see you in a minute."

I could still hear the girl in the background.

Driving there, I turned the radio on to see what they were playing because I haven't listened to the radio in a long time. The first song that came on was *There Goes My Baby by Usher*. I shook my head. How is it right after I get done reading and reminiscing about Kidd and Cherilyn their song comes on? I was just pulling up to the view where Kidd told me to meet him. The view is on top of this hill overlooking the city, the way the lights shine up here was always breathtaking. I got out of the car, it was kind of dark and I could see Kidd standing with someone but I couldn't see her face. I thought it was Cherilyn. I mean why else would Kidd call me up here when he's with a girl? Kidd walked up to me,

"Ray, took you long enough."

We shook hands and he pulled me close,

"Yo Ray this might just be the one."

I stepped back and looked at him with a side face. I then asked,

"Who is she?"

as he called her name.

"Sherilyn!"

I started to smile so big, Kidd is really getting back with Cherilyn! I saw her legs walking, and they were just like they were in high school. She put her hand out,

"Hey, I'm Sherilyn."

My eyes were now big because it wasn't the Cherilyn I was thinking about, but I just shook her hand,

"What's up? I'm Ray."

This Sherilyn was shining, body out of this world, teeth pearly white, and her eyes blue like the ocean. She then said,

"Yeah, I heard so much about you."

I looked at Kidd,

"Oh really?"

Then replied to her,

"I hope you haven't heard everything."

She giggled,

"I don't think so."

Making a little smile.

"I just know you and Kidd go way back and you're his best friend and business partner."

I smiled,

"That's all you really need to know then."

Kidd laughed and said,

"Ray, I just brought you up here to meet my future, not to try and take her from me."

We all laughed. Sherilyn then grabbed Kidd and kissed him,

"Nobody's going to take me from you."

Kidd now had his arm around her.

"Yeah I know,"

as he gave her a kiss on the head. I just stood there shaking my head. Kidd seen me shake my head,

"What the hell you shaking your head for Ray?"

I replied,

"I'm just thinking about how far we came, to where we are not. Who would have thought the struggle would take us here, on top of the city."

He looked at me then looked at the view of the city,

"A kid from nothing, made a life he dreamed about."

Pulled Sherilyn in closer and kissed her yet again. After they kissed I said,

"I'm not trying to stay up here and watch y'all kiss and make out all night."

I then began to walk back to my car, Kidd then said,

"My bad bro, I just wanted you to meet her."

I smiled and said,

"I'm glad I was able to meet her but just know you don't have everything you dreamed about just yet. But we can talk about that later, I gotta get home to wifey."

Kidd looked at Sherilyn,

"You cool with staying up?"

She said,

"As long as I'm with you I'm good."

I started to walk back to my car.

"Yeah I'm going to the house, you guys are too cute for me."

Kidd ran over to my car right before I got into the car.

"Ray, she fine, smart and funny. You know that's hard to find."

As I got into my car,

"Yeah, she's beautiful but remember beauty it's everything it's about the feeling she brings in your world."

He then smacked his lips,

"Whatever, I'm going to get with you in the morning or something."

I drove off to my house which was close to the view. As I drove home, I thought to myself, how weird is it that Kidd is now dating a girl with the same name of his true love? Maybe I was overthinking everything or maybe I should show him these letters? He will remember what true love is. I just can't see Kidd with this new Sherilyn. She's pretty and all that but the vibe she gave off didn't feel real. She was trying too hard to fit in, now that I think about it.

I got home and yelled, "Baby!" looked in the kitchen and she brought me dinner and some cheesecake. This is why Jasmine was going to be my wife, it was the little things she did that made the difference for me. After eating I went upstairs to the room and find her knocked out. I guess she had a great night with her friends tonight. She was sleeping so peacefully. I just climbed in bed and laid next to her.

The next morning Kidd calls me for what he liked to call his "good morning America run." It was a seven point four mile run he did before he got his day started. I got to the park where the halfway point was and waited for him to run pass, then I would start my run. I could see Kidd running with Honey, his dog. He runs passes me,

"Glad you decided to get up this morning, Ray."

He was laughing as he said that. I looked at him,

"Yeah, I guess so… if it was up to me I would still be sleeping. Dreaming and holding my beautiful fiancé."

Kidd just looked at me,

"Why sleep and dream when you can get up and live out that dream?"

He always found ways to be motivated and he always wanted the people around him to be just as motivated.

Our run was now coming to an end,

"So Kidd, you really like that girl Sherlyn?"

I asked. He still there for a little, thinking of what to say next.

"Ray she's super cool and beautiful beyond words."

I squinted my eyes as I looked at him,

"Weren't you the one who says don't for beauty?

He rolled his eyes and finished the sentence.

"Because beauty can get you killed. Yeah I'm the one who said that but I thought you would be happy for me."

I looked at him with a confused look.

"Kidd I want you to be happy but don't settle because you're lonely or anything like that."

We now walking to his house.

"Why do you say I'm settling?"

I was shaking my head,

"Kidd I know you and I just know you're trying to force something that's not there with her."

He brushed me off a little,

"Yeah whatever."

I smiled because he knew I was right.

As we walked in his house, I just remembered Kidd had to drive me back to my car. I told him he needed to drive me back. As were heading back to my car, *There Goes My Baby* comes on again. I looked at Kidd as he started to sing the song, he then looked at me,

"Damn this song bring back so many memories."

I smiled and said,

"Yeah, I know. Wasn't this you and Cherilyn's song in high school?"

Like I didn't already know the answer. Kidd smiled as he rubbed his head,

"Man, Cherilyn was my everything."

I responded,

"Yeah I know because until this day I haven't seen you any happier than you were when you were with her."

I was now getting into my car,

"Ray, that was a lifetime ago."

The way he said that sounded kinda sad.

"Kidd, you never know, you might run into her again or something."

Kidd shook his head,

"Nah, she probably don't even remember me."

I got out of the car,

"Kidd don't give up hope, it's not a good look on you."

Kidd got back into his car and rolled his window,

"Ray, I don't know where you getting all this hope shit from but you know how life works and she's probably out there keeping the world beautiful."

Kidd then drove off. It's funny how one little thing like a song can bring Kidd back to the days he had Cherilyn. After the good morning run, I didn't hear from Kidd the rest of the day. He probably was still thinking about Cherilyn and what he had with her. It was either that or he was with the other Sherilyn trying to make he something she's not. Since I didn't get a hold of him I just went to the shop to get a coffee and read these letters. As I took the jar out, I wondered if Kidd had ever tried to send her one of these letters. Knowing Kidd, he probably talked himself out of doing anything like that.

Chapter 5

Remember the night I asked you to be my girlfriend, yeah I know it look too long for me to ask. The way you looked that whole night was amazing, watching you cheer thinking to myself why can't she be cheering for me. Now knowing you would do that and more. When I asked you to be my girl, it was the best decision I could have ever made. Your smile is still the only think I look for when I'm goes through my day. I hope love still finds you, because happiness always looked so great on you...

Love.Kidd – xo

It was Friday night, by this time Kidd and Cherilyn had been talking all day every day and she was over at the house every night since they met. It was adorable, watching them be in love made me want to start having a girl. The thing was, they weren't even dating yet.

We didn't have a game Friday so we went to the Upper East Side school to watch their football game. Kidd really went to watch Cherilyn cheer, I knew he did. We got there when the game had already started. We were trying to find a seat. Being that everywhere we went someone knew Kidd, we had a couple of options to where we wanted to sit. Kidd was his older friend Money,

"Aye Kidd!"

Money got up to wave him over to sit with them,

"Come up here and sit with the fly guys."

Kidd was laughing, he told me,

"Don't pay that blind man no mind."

We got to where Money was sitting. Before Kidd could sit down, everyone was shaking Kidd's hand, girls were waving and coming over to hug him. If I wasn't with him or if I didn't know him, I would have thought he was famous or something.

We were about to sit when Kidd looked at Money,

"Oh so y'all the real fly ni**a huh?"

Money got up and said,

"Yeah we run this and ain't nobody got no heat no mo."

When Money said that he was referring to shoes. The more heat you had the better your shoe game was. After Money said that, Kidd put his foot up to show off his shoes. He always had some of the best shoes on that everyone wanted. He then said,

"I guess, it's a good thing that I'm the flyest guy known to man."

Money laughed,

"Damn why you always trying to come fuck someone's hood up?"

We were all laughing and then one of the guys sitting down said,

"You know Kidd always gotta make it one to remember."

We laughed again, Kidd just smiled,

"Sometimes it's hard being Kidd."

We sat down, Money asked,

"What you doing here?"

Kidd said,

"Just came to watch the game."

Money then gave him a sideways look,

"Kidd who the hell you trying to lie to?"

Kidd just smiled again looking at the field but his eyes were really on Cherilyn. He then asked Money,

"Yo who's that girl right there,"

As he pointed at Cherilyn. Even though they were together and talking all the time, they kept their private life private, before they got together officially. Money told him,

"Oh that's Cherilyn bro."

As he said that, I caught Cherilyn smiling and telling her teammate as she pointed at Kidd. Kidd was staring at her smiling so hard. Kidd then said,

"Man she is the prettiest thing in this world."

Kidd was talking about her like he just saw he for the first time. Money said,

"Yeah, I know and she cool as hell."

Kidd moved his head a little,

"Oh so you getting at her already?"

Money laughed,

"Nah she only mess with upper class-men."

Kidd asked,

"Does she be on dudes like that?"

Money was shaking his head saying no. Kidd was still smiling her way, it was like his eyes were falling in love with her. Kidd then asked,

"How does a girl like that no have a man?"

This guy sitting behind us said,

"Because some guy put her out over twitter, when she was a sophomore."

Kidd had this confused look on his face. I could tell this was news to him. Another guy that was sitting in front of us, looked back and said,

"Yeah Kidd I'm surprised you're just now hearing about her, it was everywhere."

Kidd was in total shock,

"Nah man I ain't never heard of her but that's in her past and the guy that did that doesn't deserve her anyways."

Money looked at him,

"Hold on is you trying to get at her?"

Money asked Kidd,

"I don't know, but she is a good look that's for sure."

Money smiled and said,

"Good luck bro."

The game was coming to an end and Upper East Side was blowing the other team out. Everyone was leaving and a couple people came up to Kidd and I,

"Kidd you gotta come to the party at Mindy's house."

Kidd looked at me,

"You trying to go to the party?"

I knew Kidd wanted to spend time with Cherilyn so I said,

"Yeah I'm trying to go."

Kidd then said,

"Text me the address and we in there."

The guy said,

"Okay we got you Kidd, you better be there too."

Kidd yelled out,

"When do I not keep my word? If I said I'm going to be there, then I'm going to be there, alright."

As he said that Cherilyn walked up and put her hands over Kidd's eyes,

"Guess who Mr. Kidd?"

He was smiling,

"Is it the beautiful, amazing, breathtaking Cherilyn?"

He then turned around.

"It is the girl I plan on spending the rest of my life with."

Her face lit up. He looked at her,

"Somehow I only see my heart beating for you."

Cherilyn just gazed into his eyes smiling from ear to ear. I looked at both of them and it was obvious to see they were in love with each other, they both had it written all over their face. She rubbed his arm,

"Kidd how did you make me feel this way?"

He looked her in the eyes,

"I told you, you wouldn't regret those five minutes with me."

She then asked,

"So where did you park?"

Until she said the, I had forgotten we didn't drive up here this time. We carpooled with some friends that were now gone. Kidd looked around,

"I thought maybe you could drop us off somewhere?"

She said,

"Of course I can."

We were walking to her car and even though they weren't touching, I could tell both of them wanted to make their relationship known and public. It is was easy to tell just by their body language. Cherilyn didn't know we were going to the same party. As we were drive Kidd told her,

"We're not going home, can you drop us off at this party?"

She was puzzled that the guy she liked would ask her to drop him off at a party but she said, "Yeah I got you. What party are you going to?"

The way that sentence came out of her mouth I could tell she didn't really want to take us but did anyway just to be with Kidd. Kidd turned around and looked at me, I give him a shrug. He then told her,

"We're going to Mandy's party."

She looked out the window,

"Oh I was going to go to the party but then I seen you."

She then asked him,

"So why did you come to my game?"

Kidd looked at her and smiled,

"Who said I came to see you?"

She gave him a mean mug look,

"Probably because you couldn't keep your eyes off of me.
Kidd I seen you staring at me the whole game."

I just sat in the back and started laughing, I said,

"Told Kidd, he was staring kinda hard."

Kidd turned around,

"Shut up, Ray. It's hard not to look at her."

She asked Kidd,

"Why is that Kidd?"

He placed his hand under his chin and said,

"Because every time our eyes lock, I can see my future."

As we were getting closer to the house for the party, Cherilyn
asked,

"So if you can see your future in my eyes then why are you
going to this party and not staying with me?"

She had him there, I had to hear what Kidd was going to say. He
took a breath and said,

"I'm a man of my word, I told them I would go, hoping you
were going as well but now I kinda gotta make an appearance."

She pulled up to the house. There were so many cars outside, people in the street and everything. I could tell this party was going to be the shit. Cherilyn put her head down kinda sad almost, it was over her face that she was feeling some type of way. I was out of the car waiting on Kidd to stop cupcaking with Cherilyn so we could get in this party. Before Kidd got out the car he asked her,

"What's wrong?"

She said,

"Nothing, I'm fine."

Kidd made a side face,

"Now I know something is wrong, so just tell me please."

She looked at him,

"I know, I shouldn't be mad or anything because we're nothing right now."

Kidd replied,

"What is there to be mad about?"

Cherilyn looked at him,

"I know girls are going to be all over you in there and I have no right to get mad about anything but I just want you to myself and that another reason I'm not going to the party."

Kidd's eyes got a little big,

"Awww sweetie are you getting jealous?"

She gave him that mean mug look again.

"Shut up and get in there. Just text me and I'll come back to pick you up."

Kidd told her,

"It's cool, it's going to be late when it's over."

She replied,

"I don't care, I just want to be back with you, dummy."

Kidd smiled and said,

"Okay I'll text you when we're ready."

As we started to walk to the party, Kidd stopped and said,

Ray, hold real quick."

I was looking at him wondering, what the hell he was about to do. I never knew what Kidd had up his sleeve. As Cherilyn was about to drive off Kidd ran in front of her car. She yelled,

"Kidd what the hell are you doing!?almost hit you!"

He told her,

"Get out the car real quick please."

She got out, he got closer to her and said,

"I don't want to walk in there a single man."

As he grabbed her hand he said,

"So will you go out with me?"

She was so lost for words.

"What does that mean Kidd?"

Kidd said,

"That means I want to be your man and I want you more than anything in this world. So will you make me the happiest man on earth and be my girlfriend?"

She jumped in his arms and they were kissing in the street in front of everyone. I guess they didn't care about anybody knowing now.

She left and we went into the party, girls were everywhere. I was dancing with several girls in that party. Kidd wasn't dancing with anyone. Girls were trying to dance with him but Kidd kept brushing them off one after another. I looked at him crazy,

"Kidd, what the hell you doing?"

Kidd looked at me,

"These girls don't do anything for me."

I couldn't believe what I just heard come out of Kidd's mouth. I then said,

"All these fine ass girls in here and they not doing nothing for you?"

He closed his eyes thinking about her. I told him,

"We can go whenever you're ready."

He texted Cherilyn so fast. She came back and got us real away.

Kidd was in love and it was obvious she felt the same way. After he asked her to be his girlfriend, they were now inseparable. It went from nobody knowing they even knew each other to being the relationship everyone dreamed of and prayed for. They were more than just a couple, they were best friends.

Chapter 6

Yesterday, Mia was watching <u>Tangled</u>, and I remember how you wanted to see that movie so bad when it was about to come out. I thought, how could it be that a guy like me could get so lucky as to fall in love with you? Just watching you smile was all I needed to ease the pain in my heart. You completed me in every way, plus you laughed at all my jokes. Wherever you're at, you deserve more than the best of than the best of the best. When I fall for you again in the next life, I'll make sure to keep you right by my heart where you need to be...

Love. Kidd - xo

They had been dating for about three months before they actually went on a real date. Mainly, they spent their days and nights at the house, getting pizza watching movies every other night, playing card games, just enjoying being with one another. The movie <u>Tangled</u> was being released and both of them were proud to be children at heart. Cherilyn wanted to see the movie, and every time she brought it up Kidd would try to talk her out of wanting to go. I asked Kidd,

"What are you doing this weekend?"

I wanted to see if you was going to this party with me. He told me what he had planned,

"Cherilyn really wants to see this movie so I got the whole day planned out to take her, but I'm going all out, flowers and everything."

I couldn't believe Kidd was going all out like this for her, I honestly didn't know he was that romantic. I don't know what Cherilyn did but she brought the lover boy out of Kidd. I looked at him then laughed,

"You about to watch that little girl movie?"

I then put my hand out and said,

"Give it here."

He stepped back and asked,

"Give you what?"

As I was shaking my head,

"Your player card, hand it over. You're no long in the game now Kidd."

93

He just smiled and laughed.

"Here Ray, you can have it."

He blew me away with what he said next. He put his head up and looked at the sky then said,

"I have something that's worth way more than the game Ray, so take because I won't be needing it."

I took a step back, this wasn't the same Kidd I had known.

"I don't know who this is, but bring Kidd back now, right now!"

Kidd laughed at me,

"I guess this is what happens when you find the one you're meant to be in love with."

Never seen Kidd get this way about any girl, so I guess he was right.

The weekend came and he was so excited to put everything he planned in play and to watch her smile light up the world. He got to her house and called her on the phone. She picked up and right away he said,

"Come outside."

She asked,

"for what?"

Kidd told her,

"You don't need to know everything, just trust me and come out side."

She told him,

"I just would like to know where I'm going that's all."

He then told her,

"Just open the door and you'll see why I need you to come with me."

She opened the door and saw rose petals on the floor that lead right to Kidd's car. He stood there with a smile on his face,

"See this is why I you needed you to come outside."

Kidd was now sitting on the hood of the car. He stood up again, she jumped in his arms,

"Babe what is all this for?"

Kidd made a confused look,

"I thought you knew?"

As he was putting his hands up.

"I just followed the rose and they led me right here to you."

She laughed and said,

"Babe, you must think you're a real romantic or something."

He said,

"No, I'll tell you what I think. I think you're cute, pretty, beautiful, gorgeous, and a goddess this list goes on baby."

He told her,

"But really I think we should follow the roses and get in the car to see where they take us."

She got in the car.

"So where are these roses taking us?"

Kidd told her,

"I don't know, you tell me,"

He reached in the backseat and gave her a rose with a note attached. It read: *Cherilyn, since I met you, my life has been the best and just to be tangled in your love makes the roses worth smelling."* She had the biggest smile on her face.

"Baby, you're the best boyfriend a girl could ask for."

Kidd then said,

"Oh, so you asked for me?"

He really knew how to be a smart ass when he wanted to. She pushed his head,

"I guess you think you're funny to don't you? But whatever, where are we going?"

Kidd responded,

"I don't know you tell me."

He then told her,

"Flip the note over and tell me where I'm going."

She flip it over and seen a map to the plaza, she told him,

"Go to the plaza, that's what the note says."

She then asked,

"Why are we going there?"

Kidd told her again,

"I don't know, just following what the card said."

They pulled up and where he parked there were more rose petals on the floor. He smiled looked at her and said,

"See I told you, I'm just following the roses."

As they followed the rose petals to the movie theater, she looked at him and he handed her another rose with another note attached. It read: *Once upon a time, this prince was lost and without luck. With no chance at love or happiness. This guy was lost on a path to find his meaning. He stumbled upon what look like to be a tree house, as he climbed the tree, he thought to himself that he should lock himself away. Only because happiness was a thing he had given up on. When he got in the tree house, he saw the prettiest rose he had ever seen in a glass. A voice said, "You can't have it." The guy looked at her and she was breathtaking the prettiest girl he has ever laid eyes on. He then told her, "I don't want it, I just want to be next to you." She didn't know this guy but asked, "why?" He told her when their eyes locked, he saw the happiness he was looking for his whole life."*

After she read the note, she looked at him,

"Am I the girl in the story?"

He smiled,

"I mean I do see happiness every time I look your away, I just hope you see the same."

She pulled him in close,

"I see everything I ever wanted when I look at you Kidd."

They began to kiss and then walked straight to the guy checking the tickets. She looked at Kidd sideways then stopped him,

"Babe, we didn't pay for any tickets."

Kidd laughed and said,

"I know, but the roses didn't tell us to pay for anything, did it?"

She was confused said,

"No it didn't say anything about paying."

He smiled,

"Okay then just trust me."

As they got to the guy, Kidd winked, the guy gave Cherilyn a rose with two tickets attached on. Kidd smiled,

"What movie do the roses want us to watch?"

She turn the rose around and jumped in his arms.

"Tangled! Babe, you didn't have to do all this."

Kidd said,

"I know I didn't, but looking at you every day, I knew you wanted this so I wanted it also. Making you happy is my only goal each day."

They went into the movie with popcorn and a drink. That was their first date and I haven't seen Kidd go all out for a girl since.

Chapter 7

Today, I was walking through campus and I saw this couple arguing over a sandwich. And I thought, that it was dumb, but two minutes later they were all over each other and it made me think of us when we use to argue over the dumbest things. How you would always make your mad face. Even when you were mad, it was the prettiest thing to look at, I always grabbed you and we kissed, hen somewhere all our problems were gone and we never remembered why we were arguing in the first place. It's crazy how I miss arguing with, I think it's because it let me know you cared about us. Even when you yelled at me, it just made me want to grab you and make you scream louder. Even though we fought like no other, I always wanted you to be happy. Even to this day I hope wherever you are, you're happy and enjoying life with that beautiful smile of yours…

Love. Kidd – xo

Their first argument was so cute, I remember how mad they were at each other over nothing really. We were in the middle of basketball season and she was the captain of her cheerleading team at the Upper East Side school. Kidd was the captain of our basketball team on the south east side. Since she didn't go to our school, she would rush over after school got out just to be in his arms.

One day after practice I asked Kidd to come with me and these girl to go get something to eat. Kidd was the best wingman, he always knew how to keep girls smiling and enjoying themselves. The girls ended up tweeting about how funny Kidd is and how they love going to school with him. It just happen that Kidd's phone had been dead since practice. Cherilyn had seen the tweet and didn't come by the house after she got out of class. Kidd was looking at the clock in the living room, he turned to me and asked,

"What time does Cherilyn get out?"

It was about 4:30 now and I said,

"I think she should have been out by now."

Kidd made a shocked face, "I wonder what she's doing." He then looked at the clock, "I hope she knows late practice starts in an hour."

I told him, "You should just text her or call her to see where she is."

Kidd looked at me eyes big and wide, "I called her twice no answer and texted her three times, she ain't talking to me Ray. Yo tell me did I do something wrong?"

I couldn't think of anything so I told him,

"She is probably busy or something, you know she can get busy pretty fast, so just relax, Kidd."

We on our way to practice when Kidd said he would just keep trying her after practice. As practice was going on, everyone kept asking me, "Yo what's up with Kidd?"

I told them, "I don't know, but I have never seen him play this bad."

Kidd was playing horribly. It was easy to see something was on his mind and I knew it was Cherilyn.

Coach even asked Aiden, "What the hell is going on with you, Kidd?" Coach was pissed off to watch the way his captain was performing. He even told him, "Keep this shit up and you can find yourself right next to me the whole game."

We were now scrimmaging and Kidd got the ball taken away and didn't even hustle back on defense and Kidd was known to block shots. Coach wasn't having that shit no more. We were fighting to be the best in the city and coach made sure we knew that. He stepped on the court and grabbed the ball, "Kidd get your shit and go seat down!"

Kidd stood there and looked at him, "So can't nobody have an off day?"

Coach looked at him, "Kidd you're done, sit yo ass on the sideline!"

Kidd started walking off the court and said, "This is some bullshit."

Coach shook his head, "If you playing like a sorry ass is some bullshit, then get to running until I get tired!" Kidd stood there with a dumb look on his face and got to running.

Kidd didn't get back on the court to play, he just ran the rest of practice. At the end of practice coach only made Kidd shoot free-throws to go home. When he made his first shoot coach said, "Since you think, you're above the team, you get to shoot everyone's shot and if you miss only you will run."

Kidd was known to step up to a challenge. He then made the next seven shots back to back. Coach looked at him and said, "Oh yeah and if you don't make the next two, you're not starting tomorrow." Kidd's mouth dropped, coach then said, "I don't give a fuck if you're our captain and leading scorer, your ass will be by me tomorrow."

He then stepped up to the line of the next two shots. He did his normal spin with the ball and shot the first one. It was nothing but net. The next shot was the last and he did the same spin with the ball and everything. This time when he shot the ball it hit every part of the rim before going in. I could tell Kidd thought he was going to miss that shot.

After Kidd's last free throw, coach let practice out and let us go home. And made Kidd stay there to workout. I could tell he was tired and exhausted from all the running. They were there for at least an hour after practice, doing drill after drill. He let Kidd leave but asked him, "Are you playing like this because of that little girl?"

Kidd didn't really want to tell him because the team rule was no girlfriends during the season. Kidd responded and told him, "I wasn't having a good day and I shouldn't have let it follow me into my place of peace." He went of to apologize and told him, "It won't happen again."

Kidd walked out, it was pretty late now and we were walking to his house for dinner. When we got there, Cherilyn's car was in the front. We walk in and Cherilyn is there with Mom and the family just hanging out like nothing was wrong. Kidd went straight to his room, he wasn't in the mood to talk to anyone. I mean after all that running and the way he played I wouldn't want to talk to anyone either. Mom looked around and asked me, "What's wrong with Aiden?"

I told her how practice went and how Aiden played like shit. Also how coach made him run, then workout after everyone left.

Cherilyn was in disbelief of how Kidd acted and performed at practice. She told me, "I'll go in and talk to him."

I told her, "I don't think that's a good idea."

She turned and looked at me, "Why not?"

I kinda rolled my eyes and said, "He's mad because he was looking forward to seeing you after school but you never showed and didn't call or text him back." I finished by telling her, "He thought you were done with him or something." She was smiling, I looked at her crazy and said, "Kidd is in there pissed off and you're over here smiling and shit like ain't nothing wrong. Cherilyn what the hell are you trying to do to my boy Kidd? Keep it real with me."

She stepped back and said, "What am I trying to do to Kidd? No, the better question is, what is Kidd trying to do with me?"

This is when I found out why she didn't come over or get back to Kidd. She looked at me and said, "I seen some girls tweeting about how being with Kidd was the best and all this other shit, so you tell me what he's trying to do."

After she said that I just looked at her and shook my head, "Kidd is madly in love with you." She rolled her eyes, I put my head down and said, "those girls ain't shit Kidd didn't even want go."

She quickly asked me, "So why did he then?"

I told her, "He came because of me, I told him to come because I wasn't trying to go alone."

She was in shock, the whole time she thought Kidd might be doing her wrong and messing with other girls. She walked in the room, Kidd was laying on the bed. "What do you want?" he asked.

She put her head down, "Can I sit down?" Kidd opened his hand indicating for her to sit down. She told him, "I'm sorry for not talking to you all day, I was just upset and hurt."

Kidd sat up, "Upset for what?"

She told him about the tweet and how she thought he was getting at of them trying to be a player. Kidd wasn't trying to hear none of that he just looked at her and laid back, "Yeah whatever."

She was getting frustrated and Kidd kept blowing her off. She got a little bit louder, "Now you're going to push me away?"

Kidd's voice raised, "I would never do you wrong so get that shit out your pretty little head."

She replied, "Don't get loud with me, I was just trying to tell you why I was mad earlier."

Kidd was hard headed, he still wasn't trying to hear that. "How about next time we handle this shit like we got some sense and not on some childish shit."

Her attitude came out, "Who the hell do you think you're talking to? I can leave Aiden!"

Kidd tried to show he was wearing the pants in the relationship. "Go ahead and leave, the door is right there."

She got up and went to take a step towards the door. Kidd pulled her back. She pulled away and Kidd grabbed her and was now hugging her. He asked, "So was that our first argument? She was still trying to get loose but Kidd held on tighter. "I'm not letting you leave here mad".

She looked up at him, "You're the one that was mad!"

Kidd lightly put his head on her cheek, "I could never be mad at you." He continued by saying, "Just a little frustrated at times because I'm really down for you." He picked her up, they looked into each other's eyes and kissed. After about an hour an half in that room they both came out smiling and laughing. Cherilyn's hair was a mess and Kidd looked like he was sweating. We all knew they were in there having sex, once we heard the music get louder.

Chapter 8

Now I was on to the next letter. I could really sit here in our coffee shop and smoke all day reading all of these letters. Just as I went to read the next one, Jasmine walked in. "Hey baby, what are you doing?"

I really didn't want to lie to her but I didn't want to tell her I was reading Kidd's personal love letters to Cherilyn, so I said, "Nothing just relaxing a little."

She made her I know you're lying face and then asked, "How long have you been here? I didn't even get to kiss my man this morning," as she put her hand on the table. She asked, "What's up Ray, that's not like you?" She made me feel like I was be interrogated or something.

I told her, "I went on the good morning America run with Kidd and Honey." I was trying to put the jar in my bag without her noticing, as I put it in my bag, she looked at me.

Her eyes went right to the jar, "So what's in the jar Ray?"

I was trying to think of something but I just said "It's just some old letters, that's all."

She looked at me sideways, "Ray you don't write letters. So what is that?"

I told her again, "Some old letters from high school and Jr college."

The thing about Jasmine was she knew me better than I knew my damn self. We originally met in high school. We really didn't know each other because she lived and grew up on the rich side of town and I stayed and went to school on the east side where it wasn't that nice. So during our freshman year of college, Kidd was getting at her roommate. Kidd told me one night, "Ray get out this dorm and come with me."

I remember asking him, "Where you going anyways?"

He told me, "Going over to Tiffany's house come with bro, her roommate is fine as hell."

I ended up going with him and years later we're still together and about to tie the knot soon. So she knew I was lying from the gecko, "Let me see the jar, Ray?" She put me in a position.

I said, "I can't do that babe." I guess that wasn't the answer she was looking for. She was highly upset that I didn't hand the jar over.

"So you're going to pick a jar over me?"

This wasn't a question I wanted to answer. The fire in her eyes, I could feel on my soul. She was now wiggling her ring off her finger. Didn't know what the right decision was, so I put Kidd's friendship on the line for my future wife. I then put my head down as I handed over the jar.

She pulled out a letter, "these aren't even yours." As she kept looking at them, "wait are these love letters from Kidd?" I told her that they were and explained how I got the jar.

She was still mad I didn't tell her right away when I first got it but it wasn't mine. I already felt bad for having the jar in the first place. Then on top of that, I'm reading his most heartfelt letters about his true love. I told her, "It wasn't my place to speak on his personal things. He obviously didn't want anyone to know he was still in love with Cherilyn."

She said, "You're right but dang they must be good if you're getting lost in them so easily." I could lie and say they weren't but each letter took me back to those moments when Kid was truly happy. As I sat there thinking about them being happy, Jasmine opened a letter, "Let's read it," she told me.

Hey Cherilyn so we had our first game and I still look up in the stands hoping you're up there watching. It makes me want to put on a show, so you can brag to all your friends like you did in the past. I loved playing in front of you. I also loved how you made every game even though you didn't even go to my school. I remember looking at you run in right before tip off and you were in your cheerleading uniform, I thought how could she be at my game when she has a game going on at the same time. Then you looked at me and blew me that kiss, I knew as long as you were watching I would do find and ball out. Every win didn't mean anything to me unless I got to touch and kiss you right after the game. I still can see you blowing me that kiss before each game and that's why I leave it all out there just hoping you're watching, like, "Yeah that's my man." because no matter what my heart belongs to you...

Love. Kidd – xo

Jasmine looked at me, eyes big and surprised at what Kidd had wrote. "Did Aiden really write this? "She asked me.

"Yeah, he was really in love with her." I responded

She looked at me, "this is so beautiful, why don't you write something beautiful like this for me?" She had her hand in the air waiting for me to say something. She was always putting me on the spot, didn't know what to say.

I just told her, "I didn't lose you, so there was no need for me to write anything besides my vows." I could tell she wasn't expecting me to say that.

She gave me a kiss and asked about the letter she just read, "So did Cherilyn really go to every game?"

Even though she knew Cherilyn, she wasn't able to see how special she was to Kidd. I told her, "Yeah she didn't miss a game, even when she had to be at the own game." I went saying, "She made it her duty to support Kidd no matter what."

Jasmine couldn't believe what I was telling her about Aiden. For all she knew, Kidd was a mystery, he really knew how to be social but kept to himself a lot. Even though he was a people person, he always isolated himself from the world. I told the story of Cherilyn when she left her game to get to ours. Then I told another story that revealed a lot about the Kidd and she had no idea existed.

We had our first game of the season and Kidd wasn't playing like he should. Kept looking in the crowd for Cherilyn and she was nowhere to be found. Our coach called time out and pulled Kidd out the game. "When you're ready to stop playing soft let me know." Kidd sat down and when he did, Cherilyn ran in with her red cheerleading uniform on.

Kidd locked his eyes on her and told coach, "I'm ready, put me in."

Coach U looked at him, "If you're still out there bullshitting, I got a seat right next to me."

Kidd went to check into the game, wiping his shoes looking right at Cherilyn as she stared at him. She winked and she blew him a kiss. Kidd came in and within five minutes we were up by double digits. Kidd was everywhere on the floor it was like there were five of him out there. Rebounding, blocking shots and scoring at will. It was amazing just watching him go off the way he did. After each shot he looked right at Cherilyn, she loved watching Kidd play.

After the game, she waited for him to come out of the locker room. She saw me first. "Ray, good game but where's my man at?"

I told her, "He should be coming out anytime now."

Kidd came out, headphones on, right when Cherilyn saw Aiden, she ran over jumped I'm his arms kissing him. He asked, "Did you like how I played?"

She looked at me, "Ray, is your boy serious right now?"

I raised my eyebrows and shrugged, "I guess so."

She looked back at him, "I love watching you play the game you love it makes me happy seeing you doing the your passionate about."

Kidd smiled and picked her right back up and kissed her. As he had her in the air, he looked her in the eyes, "You know what Cherilyn I lov…"

Right before he could finish, she out her finger over his lips, "Don't say anything you don't mean, Aiden."

He put her down. "I wouldn't say anything I didn't mean and I know how I feel about you." He then pulled her closer. "I love you and it's because you give me a feeling I never felt before."

They ended up getting in her car and going to Aiden's house where they watched a movie and had dinner.

Jasmine was again in disbelief. "Kidd was really in love once upon a time?" she asked.

I told her, "Yeah, Cherilyn is the only girl I seen Aiden really in love with."

Jasmine said, "I bet those were the best times for Kidd."

I replied, "No that was when I seen Kidd the happiest, haven't seen him like that in almost ten plus years now."

Jasmine always knew how to make light of any situation. "Kidd is a great guy, I'm sure he'll find true love again." As much as I wanted to believe that I knew his heart still belonged to Cherilyn.

Chapter 9

The weekend was upon us, Money and Kidd were going to be opening their nightclub this Saturday. Kidd wasn't big on going to parties or clubs, he suffered from Post-Traumatic Stress Disorder. This was a big deal because Kidd and Money were childhood friends and had always planned on opening a club together. I was there, waiting for Kidd to show up. Money walked up, "Ray, you know where Kidd is?"

I told him, "Nah, I have no idea, thought you knew where he was." I decided to walk outside to see if his car was in the lot.

As I'm walking, Sherilyn bumped into me, "Hey Ray."

I looked her up and down asked, "You seen Kidd anywhere?"

She shrugged her shoulders, "I thought he was going to be here with you."

I told her, "I'm about to go find him."

She said, "If I hear anything from him for see him I'll let you know Ray."

I put my hand up and told her, "Okay."

As I was making my way outside, Money waved me back over. I start to walk towards him, I turn my head and see a group of girls walking in the club but really didn't pay that much attention to them. When I get over to Money, he put his hand around me saying, "Where is Kidd? Look at this…"

I told him, "Your guess is just as good as mine."

Money said, "The last time I talk to him he was getting ready to come here."

I put my head down and said, "You know Kidd, always gotta be late and out shine everyone else."

Money pointed at the group of girls that had just walked in, "Yo, you know them girls that just came in Ray?"

Now I was looking a little harder I asked him, "Aye do one of those girls look like Cherilyn?"

Money leaned over to take a better look, "If it is she's still fine as hell! Ray go over and make sure that's her."

I looked at him and laughed, "Ni**a if you don't go over there and see if that's Cherilyn. This is your club isn't it?"

We both wanted to be sure but at the same time neither one of us wanted to go over there. She still had this beauty that made it almost impossible to speak to her. We sat there arguing who would go over there, to make sure that was her.

The whole time I was waiting for Kidd to walk in, but he didn't show. After about five minutes, I decided to make my way over to the group of girl. My eyes stayed on Cherilyn just to make sure she didn't disappear. Sherilyn walked up to me. I could smell the liquor on her breath. She grabbed me, "Have you seen Kidd!"

I pulled away from her, "Nah I haven't, I was about to go over his house to make sure he was still living."

She was drunk and starting to get a little loud. "When you see Kidd, tell him I want him right now." She was still trying to hang on me.

I pulled away again, "Okay, when I see him I got you but stop leaning on me."

She stepped back and looked at me, "What's your problem?" Just when I opened my mouth she cut me off and said, "Don't you know I'm the future Mrs. Brewing!" I was in disbelief she even said anything like that.

Giving her a sideways look, I responded, "You must think, you're hot shit or something." She was just about to say something when I put my hand up and finished by saying, "Kidd would never give his last name to a shallow pretty face woman like you." I turned and walked away before she could respond.

Forgetting why I even walked over here, I made my way to the door. Then a voice yelled out, "Ray!" Looking around I saw Cherilyn waving and calling me over to her table.

I walked over to her table. "Hey pretty lady, how you been?" as I learned in to give her a hug.

She said, "Everything is beyond great. How's life for you?" I was in disbelief the woman who has Aiden's heart is standing right in front of me.

All I could think about was Kidd walking in here and seeing her one more time. It was the perfect timing, the perfect setting, everything. She tapped me as she yelled my name. "Ray!"

I looked at her, "Yeah my bad."

She asked me, "So how is ya boy Kidd?" as she scanned the club looking for him.

"He's doing big things, has a lot of things going his way." I continued saying, "He just moved into his new house, it's breathtaking."

She then asked, "So where is he then?"

I looked around to see if I could see him. I told her, "Your guess is just as good as mine."

She was now introducing me to her friends when Money walked up putting his arm around me and said, "Ray, I wish someone as pretty as this could introducing me also."

She turned and looked at him, "Marc!" they hugged.

He smiled and said, "Nobody has called me by my first name since high school."

Cherilyn rolled her eyes, "Whatever you say Money." She smiled at him, "How you been?"

He looked around and put his hands up, "I guess you can say life is good. What brought you out?"

She looked around. "My friend said this new club was opening and I was going to know the owner."

Money smiled and said, "You do know the owner, you're kinda standing right in front of him." He laughed.

Cherilyn looked around the club once more. "I know I do but I don't see Aiden anywhere."

Money laughed and stepped back, "You know I'm part owner also right?"

She looked at him, "You are?"

"Yeah, me and Kidd went in on it together."

She smiled, "Oh, okay I didn't know that

Money looked at me and asked, "Where is Kidd? He was supposed to be here an hour ago."

I looked around the club once again to see if Kidd snook in but still no sign of Aiden anywhere. I told Money, "I'm going to run to his house and make sure everything is cool and he's alright."

Money told me, "Hurry up before Cherilyn leaves." Looked at her as she was laughing with her friend, "I'll try and keep her here as long as possible."

Cherilyn asked me, "Ray, where you going?"

I told her, "Just wait here and you'll see soon enough."

As I start making my way out, Sherilyn came out of nowhere. Still smelling like liquor asking, "Who was that girl you and Money were with at that table?"

Walking to my car, I replied, "Don't worry about it, you can't compete."

She was beyond upset that I said that and it was noticeable. She stood there looking lost, she then followed me to my car, "Ray, why don't you like me?"

Getting in my car I said, "I know women like you Sherilyn that's why I don't like you."

She looked at me sideways and asked, "What is that supposed to mean?"

In my car I answered her question, "That you only see Aiden for the dollar signs." She was blown away that I said that to her. I started the car and rolled the window down. "At least you don't have to know how to swim, when you as shallow as you are."

I was now on my way to Kidd's house to see what the hell was taking him so long. Still thinking about what I said to Sherilyn, maybe I went too far. I didn't really know her, but the vibes she gave off was all types of wrong. I knew she was just using Kidd for what he had. Honestly didn't really care, I was just excited for Kidd to see his true love and that's the real Cherilyn.

I get to his, and see his car is parked right in front. I get to the door, it was unlocked and that was odd because Kidd always kept his doors locked. It was, he like was paranoid. I walked through the house yelling out "Kidd!" but didn't get a response. Then I walked to the back, I saw Aiden sitting on his poolside bar looking at the view smoking a joint and there was a bottle of Hennessy beside him. I walked up to him and saw a paper and pen, "Kidd, what the hell you doing?"

Kidd turned and looked at me, "Ray, have I ever told you my biggest fear?"

Where is this coming from I thought, I just came to get him for the club opening not for a life talk. I told him, "Nah I don't think so, why?"

He slowly put his head up, his eyes closed as he brought his eyes back down to look at me. His voice cutting in and out, "Because I'm living it right now, Ray!"

Confused I asked, "Living what? You got everything…" He then opened his hand.

I was trying to look at what he had but wasn't able to see it. He just said, "I'm living my biggest fear and this shit hurts." He put his hands on his head, the picture fell to the floor. It was an old photo of him and Cherilyn.

I reached down to pick it up, as I grabbed it I said, "Dang, I still remember this night."

Kidd opened his eyes, looking at me now, "Yeah I do too." He went on telling me the story of that night, I could tell it was taking him back to a place he loved. "We were high, I loved that she only smokes when I rolled up. We went bowling and she was just like me talking shit, thinking she was going to win. The way she walked up to the lane and let the bowling ball leave her precious soft touch was breathtaking and then bomb strike. She started running her mouth, it was so sexy."

As he was telling me the story, I could tell he was still in love with her. He ended the story after I asked, "How did y'all take the picture bowling?"

He looked at me, "Damn, Ray let me finish and you'll know." He had the picture in his hand looking at it, living that night. "She wanted to go to the arcade room after losing in bowling, pushing me saying "I'm a better shooter than you, babe," over and over so we went to play and got carried away with both of us being so competitive, we ended up playing damn near every game in there. We walked past the photo both like five times and she asked me like three times to take a picture but I told her, 'I don't do those little couple pictures, it's so cliché. 'So as we're walking out an older couple stopped us and told us, 'You two remind us of us when we were that young'. I then asked them, How long have you two been married?' He said, 'fifty-eight years.' I remember looking at him like how does that even work, so I asked him when Cherilyn and his wife started talking, 'How did you do it?' He told me, 'She's my best friend and still to this day, when I look at her she freezes time for me and nothing matters but being with her.' I remember looking at Cherilyn after he that and wishing that moment would never end. That's when I told her, "Hop in this photo booth with me and let's take a picture."

She turned to me with this sexy sassy look, "I thought you don't do couple pictures, it's cliché remember?" I remember laughing as I told her, "I know but were not a couple, we're soulmates." he pushed me, "You're so corny." I grabbed her and pulled her close, then we took the pictures."

He looked up at me, "That's how she became the first girlfriend to have a picture with me." He had the picture in his hand, holding it tight. "My biggest fear was to be successful and get to the top and have no one to share it with."

I told him, "It's okay Aiden, come to the club and get some good vibes around you."

He lit a joint and said, "I don't know if I feel like killing everyone's vibe right now."

I told him, "Believe me, you're not going to kill nobody's vibe. We might want to be at the like now. You'll smile and have a good time once we get in there, don't worry." We walked to the car. He was walking so slow, I was trying to get him to hurry, so he could see Cherilyn.

We got into the car headed to the club. Kidd said, "Ray, you know I love being on top and everything but I would trade all this bullshit in, in a heartbeat to be in love one more time." I didn't know how he wanted me to respond to that.

As we pulled in the parking lot I said, "Wouldn't it be crazy if you ran into Cherilyn in here." Which is exactly what I was hoping was going to happen. Hopefully she is still there and could make Kidd's time freeze one more time. Walking in the club Kidd put his happy-to-be-here face, speaking to everyone being funny and what not. I was probably the only one who could tell he wasn't happy on the inside. It always amazed me how easy it was for him to hide his pain. Nobody ever knew what Kidd was feeling or thinking because he always wears his joyful mask.

Money ran over to me, "Yo, you missed it!" Kidd got caught up giving everyone hugs and handshakes but when he seen Money run over to me so quick, he made his way to us.

Before Kidd could get to us, I asked Money, "What I miss, what happened?" Moving my hands around signing him to hurry up with the story.

He said, "Long story short, Cherilyn and the other Sherilyn got into it." I then put my hand on my head in disbelief, running my fingers across my face.

Kidd walked, put his hand around Money's shoulder, "Yo boy we really did it, look at this shit, this is something you see in the movies."

Money looking at the club, "I know man, I still can't believe it and to think we still have so much more to do."

Money gave me a head nod, I could tell he wanted to tell me what actually went down. Money waited for Kidd to walk off and talk to others, before he told me what really happened. Pushing him, "What the fuck happened?"

Money always had his head to the side, so this time he put his head straight. "Man, so me and Cherilyn was just kicking it, I sparked a joint and got the best bottle we had…"

I cut him off, "Man, I ain't trying to hear y'all kicking it. Get to the good shit."

He rolled his eyes, "Man, if you don't shut yo ass up and wait," taking a sip of his drink "I'm getting there." He went on telling the story, "So we kicking it and the other Sherilyn came up to me. She walked over and I could smell liquor all over her. Shaking his head, "She asked me 'Where is Kidd?' as Cherilyn was taking a drink she asked, 'yeah, where is Kidd? Haven't seen him in forever.'

Money pulled me in a little closer. "Ray, this is when shit got crazy," he kept going. "So then Sherilyn turned around and looked Cherilyn up and down, looked at me and asked, 'who is this bitch?' Ray you know how Cherilyn can get."

I smiled and said, "Yeah, I remember how she can get."

Money looked at me, "Bro, Cherilyn stopped smiling and said, 'first off, don't come over here in my section, talking reckless and acting like you're hot shit or something.' Ray Before I knew it they were in each other's face. Sherilyn then stepped closer to her and said, 'Bitch you must not know who you're talk to.' Cherilyn stood straight up. 'I don't give a fuck who I'm talking to but you better slow your roll'. I stepped in saying 'come on ladies let's not fuck the vibe up in here'. He shook his head, "Man this is where drinks started to fly and I wish you and Kidd were here. Sherilyn had her drink in her hand and said, 'You must not know, but I'm the future Mrs. Brewing. Which means this something like my club too' Cherilyn made this confused face, 'Mrs. Brewing?' then went, 'Oh, you must be Aiden's new girl or something.' Sherilyn said, 'Bitch I'm his future wife.' Cherilyn laughed and said, 'I don't see a ring on that finger.' Then asked her, 'Can you leave my section so me and my friend Money could finish catching up.' Right as she finished, she looked at me with Sherilyn still there and asked, 'So this is who Kidd is going to marry?' Putting her hand up looking at Sherilyn, I then told her, 'I never know with Kidd.' Sherilyn didn't leave but instead looked at me and asked, 'Is this bitch for real right now? And who is this bitch anyways?' I told her she can't keep calling her that but this is… Cherilyn stopped me before I could finish, 'This bitch doesn't need to know who I am.' Looking her up and down. All she needs to know is I'm someone she could never be'. She looked at her friends told them, 'Let's go ladies.' She said to me, 'Tell Kidd, I wish I could have seen him but he still can't keep his girls in line'. I laughed and said, 'You're saying that like you were ever in line.'

Looking at Money with my head to the side now, "Why would you say that right in front of them?"

Money put his hand on his chest. "Yeah, that's on me." He finished the story saying, "Sherilyn put her head back a little after Cherilyn said that. Then threw her drink at Cherilyn. She ducked that drink like the matrix and it had to be the fastest smack I saw in my life because Cherilyn threw that hand like a lighting strike. So you know I broke it up before they could fuck up my shit and I had to kick both of them out."

I was in shock and lost for words, couldn't believe all that happen while I was gone to get Kidd. Before Kidd got back to us I asked, "Why did you kick Cherilyn out, stupid?"

Money looked around to make sure Kidd wasn't close to us and said, "Because I didn't know which one to pick and plus Cherilyn was on her way out anyways."

Kidd walked back to us, "Who was on their way out?"

Damn I know Money didn't want to tell him so I said, "Oh Money was telling me about these girls that got into it and had to go."

Kidd looked at Money then back to me, "Ray, last time I checked your name wasn't Money unless you changed it on me." Looking back at Money, "So what happened at our club?"

Money put his head down, "These girls just got into it and I had to get them out of here." He then said, "Come on Kidd, let's have a good time and live like we should."

Still mad Kidd wasn't able to see the girl he fell in love with. If he knew she was here he would definitely be mad or feel some type of way. Right then Dre walked up and said, Yo Kidd guess what?" I was trying to get his attention so he wouldn't tell Kidd but he went on, "Bro Cherilyn was here."

Kidd didn't seem to surprised or happy, "Yeah, she told me she was coming." Me,
Money and Dre looked at him confused.

I then asked, "When did you see Cherilyn?"

He made this confused looked and replied, "Ni**a I'm dating her."

Dre then cut in, "No, no not Sherilyn that fake ass girl but Cherilyn, like high school Cherilyn, you know first love."

Kidd's eyes immediately searched the building. He then asked looking back and forth for her, "Where is she at?"

Dre looked at Money. Money said, "Yeah about that, remember those girls I had to kick out, well they just happen to be both of your girls."

Kidd looked at him, "Why?"

Money told him the story of what happened and how Sherilyn, his so called future wife acted. Kidd was pissed I could tell he wanted to see Cherilyn. Once he found out about everything, it just killed his vibe even more and he walked off to the bar, "I need some time to think shit out." He ended up going to the box room which happened to be empty or maybe Kidd had it emptied out, one or the other.I walked in with a joint in my hand.

I sat down, "So Kidd, what's going on up there in that head of yours?"

Kidd, scratching his head said, "I didn't think it was possible Ray."

Here he goes again confusing me and shit. I didn't know what he was talking about. I asked, "Didn't think what was possible?"

He kinda smiled at me, "That all those feelings would come running back so fast." As he was holding himself thinking of Cherilyn.

I asked, "You really miss that girl, don't you?"

His smile was even bigger now, "It's not every day someone comes along and makes an impression worth cherishing, Ray."

There goes my great plan down the drain. Who was I trying to fool maybe it's not meant for Kidd to see her again, maybe that's why he holds the memory of her so tight.

Chapter 10

It's the next morning, still upset my boy wasn't able to see his girl. I decided to go back to the shop to get my nose back in those letters of his, one of a kind love.

Today was kinda weird, this boy came up to me and asked if I was scared of anything, I told him no, but that question sat in my mind all day. All I could seem to think about was the way I lost you and how that was my biggest fear. Then I thought about how I lied to that boy, about not being scared of anything. Cause, the truth is I wake up each morning in a panic and almost in tears, from the fear of never seeing you again. You, know even dying has never been a fear of mine, but dying without you in my life is the only thing that gives me chills. Can't believe that the girl who wanted to stay by my side when a gun was pulled, is now a distance memory. Just know I still hold all our memories close to me heart. Hope you're still smiling somewhere out there, reminding the world to love…

Love. Kidd – xo

I could only think of one night where a gun was pulled and Cherilyn was there. I almost forgot that night even happened. When we were at the skating rink. Kidd, Cherilyn, Pop and I went to the rink with Mia and Little Jay who are Kidd's brother and sister. We were all in having a good time skating and enjoying each other's company. Kidd skated over to check on Mia to make sure she was doing fine on the skates. This guy rolled over to Cherilyn and grabbed her arm to skate, she pulled away. Pop most have seen it because he skated over and pushed the boy, "Yo, don't put your hands on my brother's girl."

The boy stood there. "I don't give a fuck who girl she is but you gon' get yours."

Pop went off, "Fuck all this talking shit, let's get this shit popping then."

Kidd skated over pulling Pop back, telling him, "Yo chill, this ain't the spot Paul, we got the fam with us."

That was my first time hearing Pop's real name, never would have thought it would be Paul. Pop looked at Kidd, "But this little ni**a thinks he can just put his hands on Cherilyn any kinda way."

Kidd was getting mad. But he knew we had Cherilyn and the kids were with us. So Kidd tried to let it go and said, "It's cool, just a misunderstanding that all." Then looked at the boy, "Yo man we just having a good time, we don't want no problems."

The boy wasn't trying to hear none of that shit "Nah fuck that, we got a problem, yo boy gon' get his don't trip."

The boy skated over to get his older brother who was older than both of us. We watched them point over to us. Kidd didn't want anything to happen to Cherilyn and the kids, so he told everyone to pack it up. The boy's brother stepped in front of Kidd and Pop, "So which one of y'all got a problem with my brother?"

Kidd looked at Cherilyn, "Take Mia and Jay to the car and y'all get out of here." As he gave her the keys. Kidd then said, "Ain't nobody got a problem with nobody,"

The boy stepped up and pointed at Pop, "It was his ass."

Kidd stepped up, "Y'all ain't gonna jump my boy." He told the boy's brother, "Your brother thinks he's big and bad let him handle his own then."

Pop stepped up and was ready, but the boy's brother said, "Fuck that, we gon' kick this ni**a's ass" and then they both stepped up.

Kidd looked at Pop out the side of his eye, stepped up, "Y'all ain't going to do shit, but we can throw them hands what's good?"

When Kidd did that a van pulled up and another guy hopped out. He looked a little bit older, come to find out it was their eldest brother. Cherilyn put Mia and Jay in the car and ran back over to us, Kidd looked at her, "I told you to get them out of here, take the car and go." Kidd then looked back at the older brother, "So what's good?"

Right after that the oldest one pulled a gun and pointed it at Aiden. Me and Pop were stuck, I couldn't move never been this close to death. Kidd stepped closer, "Don't talk about it be be about it."

Everyone's face including mine was lost and in shock the guy said, "I'll blow yo shit right off, don't you know that."

Kidd bit his lip, "You ain't never kill nobody in yo life, I can see it in your eyes."

The guy put the gun back in his plants. "Imma catch you don't trip!" Then they drove off.

Me and Pop pushed Kidd and I said, "You crazy! NO NO you stupid!"

Pop looked at him, "Ni**a he could have killed you!"

Kidd didn't even seem scared when everything was going on. I thought to myself what is this Kidd made up of?"

Cherilyn was the only one he wanted to see or even talk to after. She came back up to us, "Kidd,you're fucking crazy!" Pushing him, "Are you trying to die?"

Kidd then grabbed her arm and pulled her in, "I guess that just means I would have to find you in my next life."

I don't know if she was mad, sad or happy but tears were in her eyes and she jumped in his arms kissing him. "Don't ever do that to me again, I'm not ready to live my life without you."

I remember the way Kidd looked at her, as if nothing else mattered. He smiled at her with his eyes starting to get watery, "I will always be here with you, you're my happiness, my everything and that's why I love you." When she said that he kissed her.

I looked at Pop, "Does this fool know we almost got shot?"

Pop walked towards the car, "It don't matter what just happen, what really matters is Kidd got what he always wanted."

As I turned and started to walk to the car, I looked back and said, "Yeah you right, that's all that matters, I guess."

Kidd really did find the girl he was meant for and I thought they would be together to the end of time.

Just as I put the letter down and went to reach for another one. Sherilyn walks in. I was hoping she didn't see me but she did. She was ordering a drink, then turned her head to the right where I was sitting.

Chapter 11

Her eyes hit me like a windy storm, "Ray!" she yelled as she made her way to me. Putting the letters back in the jar and the jar in my bag I said, "Sherilyn, long time no see." It came out kinda sarcastic. She was now standing where I was sitting, smiling at her, "So I heard you got kicked out of The Spot last night." I laughed.

With a surprising soft voice she responded, "Yeah I know, I got out of hand."

Looking at her, "Yeah I know, I heard what happened. Kidd couldn't believe what happened."

She was shaking her head in disappointment, "Do you know where he is?" she asked.

Looking at her confused, "He's not at home?"

She said, "No, and I've been blowing up his phone."

Shaking my head now, "That's crazy, I haven't heard from him since we left the club."

I could tell she really wanted to apologize for what happened at the club but she ended up asking me, "Do you know who that girl was?"

She put me in a position that I didn't want to be in. I wanted to lie but reading these letters, how could someone lie about love? "Yeah I know her," came out my mouth.

Once they brought her drink out, she sat down at the table I was at. "So what's her name?" She asked me.

Looking at my bag I said, "Her name is Cherilyn."

She leaned back, "That girl has the same name as me?"

Before she could keep going I said, "Not quite, her name is spelled with a C and your is with a S, so calm down."

She rolled her eyes, "You say it the same so it doesn't matter."

Leaning back putting my foot on the chair beside me I asked, "Why are you asking all these questions about a girl you don't even knew?"

She squinted her eyes, "Ray, I don't know if you seen that girl, but she is beautiful."

To hear her say that was surprising she kept going, "I'm not jealous, just want to know if I have anything to worry about."

I asked, "Do you want me to be honest?"

She put her head down because she knew it wasn't good if I asked that but she said, "Yeah."

I then told her, "I don't know if you should be worried but she was Kidd's first love, his first everything."

Sherilyn passed. "Wait that was the Cherilyn?" She said that like she knew her or something.

I looked at her puzzled, "You know her?"

She shook her head no then said, "I heard someone say something about her one time and how Aiden was a different person with her."

I started to smile because it was true. He was a different person with her. I told her I was going to get some work done, so that I could get back to reading the letters. I told her, "If I hear anything from Kidd, I'll let you know."

She got up and walked out with no goodbye. Then I got up to order another drink and joint, it was back to reading.

Cherilyn, as you know my family is in love with you. My aunt asked about you today. I wanted to know how you were doing. I told her we haven't spoken for some time now but if I ever speak to you I would tell you she asked about you. It always blows my mind the way you came into my life. Suddenly, everything was ten times better. You didn't only make everything around you better but you made me better. My aunt told me you brought out the best in me and let me show my soft side, whatever that means. I guess in a way you did bring out the sensitive side in me, it must just be because I was scared to lose you and what we had. I just hope when we meet in the next lifetime and you allow me to fall in love with you again. Hopefully I don't show you my tears like I did before even though I knew you were there to catch them. Still wish you could hold me on days when I felt alone. Knowing God made someone like you gives me the best reason to smile. Miss you a little more each day…

Love. Kidd - xo

Cherilyn was the first girl to see Kidd cry and really break down. It was on Thanksgiving, Kidd's family had a trip planned to go to Arizona. Me and Kidd played on one of the traveling teams. Which meant we only had one day off during Thanksgiving break. Kidd knew if he went he wouldn't start in the tournament coming up. He ended up staying at his house by himself. I ended up staying with him so he wouldn't be alone. Cherilyn felt so bad that Kidd didn't have his family so she ended up staying the whole week. It was like watching their future. They would cook, order pizza, watch movies and clown around all the time and it was beautiful to watch. It was the morning of Thanksgiving, Kidd was up early that morning and made breakfast for me and Cherilyn. She walked out of his room, with one of his shirts on barefoot, Kidd stared at her as if she as if she was making his life freeze. I remember looking at him and seeing nothing but happiness on his face.

Kidd walked up behind me, "Ray, how crazy is it that, I wake up next to the girl of my dreams?"

Looking at him as she hugged him, "Some call it crazy, others would say you're a lucky man."

She looked at me then right back to Kidd, "Babe, who's lucky?"

Kidd smiled, "Nobody, Ray just said I'm lucky for having you and he has never been more right in his life."

I rolled my eyes, "Here he goes with this shit again."

She pulled him in, "I love it babe but I'm the lucky one." She looked at the food, "Who's boyfriend would do all this for their girl? No one that I know."

Kidd bit his lip, "I wish I could gift wrap the globe and hand you the world babe."

She stood right underneath him looking up, "Babe, I don't need the world, just you beside me in it."

I got up and threw my hands in the air, "I can't deal with you two and y'all always being cute and shit around me."

After I said that Kidd laughed and said, "Ray, one day you're going to meet that girl that makes you feel unstoppable.

I looked at him and said, "Yeah, I doubt that but thanks anyways."

They ate and went back to the room to lay down.

It was now afternoon, Cherilyn went to her house to get ready for her family brunch. Her mother invited Aiden and I to the brunch. She was in love with Kidd, always calling him son and wanted Cherilyn to marry him asap.

We got there, her family and all Aiden thought he was the best fit for Cherilyn. They thought Aiden and Cherilyn were made for each other , really. Everybody thought that.

After brunch with her family, we went to Aiden's aunt's house. It's not really his aunt but blood couldn't make them any closer. That is really how it was with all his family, other than his mother, nobody was really blood related. We got there and it was mirror image with Cherilyn, everyone loved her. She interacted with everyone, played games with the kids, talked to his aunt and cousin like they were hers. It was great being able to watch them both bring happiness to each other's life like that. Watching her laugh and be a part of everything, I knew she was meant to be in Aiden's life. I turned and looked around but I didn't see Aiden. After Cherilyn got done talking to everyone she walked up to me, "Have you seen Kidd?"

I looked around once again. "I thought he was with you."

She looked around, "No, he's not I thought he was with you." She spotted him sitting outside on the phone. She went outside to make sure he was okay and everything was good. When she walked over to him, he put his head up then right back down.

Kidd had his head down and said, "Stop, I just need a minute." Kidd never wanted anyone to see him when he was sad or anything like that. He wanted people to know he was strong and could handle anything. This is why I loved Cherilyn for Aiden because she seen through all the bullshit he put up with. And forced him to show the side that he tried so hard to hide. With his hands on his face and arms holding his head.

Cherilyn bent over in front of him, "Babe, tell me what's wrong."

Aiden wiped his eyes responding, "Nothing's wrong, I'm good let's get back in there." as he tried to get up.

She pushed him back down, "Don't give me that shit about you being good or cool, I know something is hurting you." She then asked again, "Tell me what's wrong?"

Kidd looked at her, eyes red and watery. "That was my grandpa and he said he was in Hawaii when he told me that I was happy. But I could hear in his voice that even though he was there, he was feeling broken." Cherilyn put her hands on his lap, Kidd then said, "So I asked my grandpa what's wrong? He told me this was the last place my grandma wanted to go before she left, it was where they met." Tears started coming out of Aiden's eyes. "I miss her so much babe, all I wanted was to tell her goodbye." Cherilyn pulled him as he was saying, "Why didn't I tell her goodbye?"

Cherilyn was wiping his face, "It's okay babe, I'm here."

Kidd balled up his fist and said, "That's just it,I know how life works and it tends to take the people I love away and I don't know if I can live without you."

She held his head in her arms, "Babe you're not going to live without me."

They kissed, Kidd wiped his eyes got up shoot it off and smiled. He looked at her, "I'm glad, I have you."

They came back inside, Kidd had piece of cheesecake and we said goodbye to everyone. We headed back to his house. On the drive back Kidd pulled up to the stop light looked at Cherilyn then said, "I never really had a family growing up but y'all my family and I love you guys forever." Then he pulled off. When we got back to the house, I sat there and thought about what Kidd said about us being his family. He really was my brother and Cherilyn completed him in every way, so she was family also. They went into his room, this time no music just them two quietly making love to each other passionately. At least that's what I remember Kidd telling me. That was the first time Aiden showed his tears to a woman and it was because he felt safe with his heart in her hands.

Chapter 12

I was never a real big Christmas fan, I usually try to not have a girl during the holidays but being with you the only place I wanted to be. Even though I had to be out of town and couldn't be with you it was still the best Christmas to date. You ended up giving me the Cool Grey elevens. There still one of my favorite shoes, not for the hype or them being limited, But because they came from you. I can't even explain what I was feeling when I seen your smile light up after giving me the shoes. To see you so happy that you got me what I wanted was more than magical. I know you thought I was happy about the shoes but I was more happy knowing I had you. I just wish these days I was still the reason for your smile to shine bright and your eyes are still the only light worth watching during the holidays but until we meet again…

Love. Kidd - xo

We were in Utah for this big high school tournament. Since we were playing in the championship game, we had to stay an extra night. Kidd stayed on the phone with Cherilyn all night, as we were in the hotel room. When they got off the phone Kidd hopped in the shower. My phone rang, it was Cherilyn. I answered it, "Hello."

She quickly responded, "Ray is Kidd in the shower?"

Told her, "Yeah, why what's up?"

She then asked me, "What does Kidd want for Christmas?"

Thinking of all the things Kidd would like so I just said, "It doesn't matter what you get him, he's happy with just having you."

She kinda got a little loud with me, "I know that Ray but that's my baby and I want him to have what he wants."

I told her, "He's been talking about the Cool Grey elevens for a minute, I would assume he would love those to add to his collection." Kidd was a big time sneaker head and having the best shoes was something he had. So I told her, "The only problem is they drop at midnight and they might sell out, so I would head the way now if you want a pair."

Her reaction rang through the phone, What the hell Ray?! Why are you just now telling me about this?"

I was guessing she never been in the sneaker game. I replied, "You never asked me, so how would I know what to tell you?"

She laughed a little, "Ray, you're just supposed to know these things, like just me a hint or something."

I was looking at the phone in disbelief, "What the fuck, do I look like a fortune teller?"

She wasn't trying to hear anything I had to say, all she cared about was getting these shoes. She asked me, "Ray how do I get these shoes?"

I reached over and grabbed Kidd's phone, then gave her our homeboy's number. I told her, "This is our boy Jamal he works at Footlocker, tell him your Kidd's girl and he's gonna hook you up with a pair." Then told her, "Give me a minute, let me call him and I'll tell you where to go and get them at."

When I called Jamal he told me that Kidd already gave him money to put a pair in his size away but I couldn't tell Cherilyn he was already getting the shoes. So I told him to still hook her up and not to mention anything about Kidd already having them. She went down to the mall where the FootLocker was and met with Jamal. I remember Kidd calling her when she was down there and they FaceTimed, Kidd was amazed that she was willing to stand in the long line for him. After they were done talking, Kidd looked at me, "Ray, I love that girl so much." He laid back on the bed.

Looking at him, "I know you do bro and you better not mess it up."

He looked at his hands, "I pray every day I don't."

When we got back to town, Cherilyn was waiting for us at our school. As soon as Kidd walked off the bus she ran over jumped in his arms and started kissing him. Kidd pulled a little box out of his bag. I had been with him the whole time and I still don't know what was inside of the little box. Her eyes dropped to the little light blue box, "Babe, what is this? I told you not to get me anything," giving him a little punch to the chest.

He said, "I know, but I need you and everyone to know how much you mean to me." He opened the box and pulled out a beautiful yellow gold necklace with two hearts twisted together in white gold.

Her mouth opened and her eyes got big looking into his. "Babe, you're the best boyfriend in the world!"

Kidd turned her around and put the necklace on her, "Everyone sees this necklace I wear and they know why I wear it, I just want people to see yours and know you have my heart." He pulled her in and kissed her.

When Cherilyn gave him his shoes, he was overly happy. I pulled him to the side, "Why you acting like you don't already have them?"

Kidd smiled at me, "Ray, it's not about the shoes, it's the fact that she's was willing to do anything to get them and that means more to me than some damn shoes."

Even then Kidd knew that being in love was a special thing.

Chapter 13

New Year's is coming closer each day and I still can't believe you're the only girl to touch my lips on that special night. Parts of me want to relive that night, just to have you in my arms one more time. The other parts still take me back to the yelling and fighting we also did that night. It's funny because you were the one who said love is bipolar because one minute you would love me like no other, and the next second you were more than upset with me. Just know each year that comes I wish, I had you in my arms. So we could watch the fireworks one more time. We're lucky because we have a whole new year to find each other…

Love. Kidd - xo

That New Years was a night I will never forget. I remember Kidd and Cherilyn going at, it over something dumb and petty. She was mad because some girls after out New Years tournament ran up to Kidd and jumped on him as they kissed him on the cheek. They were just some of our friends, nothing else. Kidd never cheated on Cherilyn, at least that I knew of. It was New Years Eve and they weren't talking to each other, so I asked Kidd, "You kicking it with Cherilyn tonight or what we doing?"

He was so mad, "I don't know what we doing but I ain't saying shit to that girl."

I asked, "Who, Cherilyn?"

He looked at me with a mean look, "Yeah, fuck her, she always trying to be mad over some bullshit."

I didn't know they were beefing like that so I walked away and said, "Let me know what you want to do, I'm down for whatever."

Kidd was on his phone looking for something for us to do tonight. He ended up texting Samantha and she called him. They were on the phone for a little, then Kidd looked at me. "Ray get dressed."

The way he said that sounded like he meant business tonight, so I asked, "How fly are we getting?" I wanted to know if I had to be kinda fly or super fresh.

He shook his head slowly. "I'm about to kill the game tonight."

I knew what that meant. He was about to bring out some heat and make sure all eyes turn his way.

I put on a nice fit and was feeling good about what I had on until Kidd hit the door. "You ready?" I asked. My mouth drooped. "Damn, you about to kill everyone's hopes tonight."

Kidd had no some limited edition Jordan six's with a white and red polo shirt and a his gold chain hanging down. He was rubbing his hands together, "That's that point, it's about making a statement."

There he goes again, confusing me and shit. "What statement are you trying to make?" I asked.

He replied, "That there's nobody better than me in this city."

I turned my head to the side and said, "You doing this because of Cherilyn aren't you?"

Kidd said, "Hell no, ain't nobody thinking of her."

I smacked my lips, "Shut that shit up, you know you want to be with her right now and that's why you mad."

Kidd was in denial and wasn't trying to hear anything I had to say to him. Grabbing his keys he said, "Yeah whatever Ray, what are you like the love expert or something?"

I was walking to the car, "Nah, I just know you and I never seen you look at anyone the way you look at her."

He started the car, "Yeah well you ain't gotta worry about her no more."

Shaking my head I asked, "Where are we going then if we no going to see her?"

Kidd told me, "We going to Sam's party, I haven't seen her in a while."

Looking at him at as we drove to Sam's house. I had to make sure Kidd thought this all the way through. "You sure you want to throw away everything with Cher…"

He cut me off, "Ray, why the hell you worried about my love life, let's worry about getting you a girl!"

Looking at him in disbelief that he snapped at me like that, I told him, "I'm just making sure you don't lose the best thing that ever happened to you, that's all."

We were now pulling up to Sam's house. "Ray, don't worry about me I handle my own."

The party was crazy packed and Kidd was dancing like he was a free man or something. Dancing with every girl. Kidd and Sam were hanging on each other since Kidd got there. After an hour or two, the countdown to midnight started and I couldn't see Kidd or Sam. I put my hand on my head saying to myself, no Kidd don't do it.

Ten minutes into the New Year, I saw Kidd outside with Sam, hugging and laughing. He looked back and seen me, "Ray you going to stay or come back to my house with me?"

I made a side face, "I riding with you."

I walked down to the car, gave Sam a hug goodbye. When I hugged her she whispered in my ear, "Don't let Kidd fuck it up with Cherilyn."

Now I was lost because I just knew Kidd and Sam had to have done something. The way they were on each other that night.

In the car Aiden was on the phone, I heard him tell the person on the phone, "I'm sorry, can you just come to the house please."

When I got in the car I asked, "That was Cherilyn, right?"

He smiled as we drove off back to his house. "Yeah, I was tripping."

I smiled at him, "Yeah you were bro, just glad you know what's best for you."

We pulled up to the house and Cherilyn was waiting outside with her friend Taylor. Cherilyn always had fine ass friends but never tried to hook me up with any of them. Right when we got out the car, Cherilyn asked with an attitude, "So where y'all coming from, Ray?"

I looked at Kidd, as he put his eyes and head down. "We was just chilling." He told her. She looked back at me, "I didn't know you changed your name, R ay."

Before I could say anything Kidd walked over to her, "Come on babe, let's not fight no more, please. He then brought her hands to his lips and kissed them. "You know you're my everything."

We were still standing outside. Taylor and I looked at each other and I told her, "They do this all the time."

She laughed and said, "Yeah I know, Cherilyn always calls me when they start fighting."

We ended up going into the house and Taylor and I stayed in the living room as Kidd and Cherilyn made their way to his room.

After about an hour or so we heard Kidd and Cherilyn going at it again. We both got up to get closer to the door, all we heard was Cherilyn say, "Tell me who your New Year's kiss was!"

We then hear Kidd get loud, "I told your ass already that I didn't kiss nobody."

Cherilyn yelled, "Don't give me that shit, I know you went to Sam's party."

When she said that, Taylor looked at me, "You ni**as ain't worth shit." I turned and looked at her, she then asked, "So did Kidd kiss Sam?"

I hope she didn't think that I knew. I looked at her and told her the truth, "I was in the house when Kidd and Sam were outside or wherever they were at midnight so I have no idea." I put my hands up. She rolled her eyes as if I was lying or something. We both just put our ear back up to the door.

We heard Kidd say, "I would never cheat on you, so stop thinking that bullshit."

Cherilyn yelled back, "Whatever Kidd!"

Taylor and I were going back to the living room before we heard Cherilyn tell Kidd, "If you tell me who your New Year's kiss was, I'll tell you who mine was."

My mouth dropped and then I turned to Taylor, "Who did Cherilyn kiss?"

Taylor's eyes got big, "I didn't know she kissed anyone!"

Smacking my lips I said, "Yeah whatever."

She said, "No really, she didn't kiss anyone, I was with her all night."

I put my hand on my head, "Yeah, I bet."

After Cherilyn said that, we heard Aiden's voice get loud and clear. He was pissed, "BOUNCE!" Is all we heard come out of his mouth. He then opened the door yelling, "Bounce, get the fuck out!" Taylor and I tried to move before the door opened but he saw us, "What the fuck y'all doing?" Before either of us could say anything he said, "Nah fuck that, both of y'all get the fuck out!"

Kidd ended up kicking everyone out, including me. Cherilyn was getting her things while saying, "Kidd I didn't kiss nobody, I just said that to see if you kissed anyone." He was so mad, he paid her no attention and closed the door in her face.

It was the longest walk to the car. I could see tears forming in Cherilyn's eyes. "Cherilyn, Aiden is just mad, let him cool off, don't worry, he still loves you." I tried saying anything to keep her from crying.

Cherilyn let out, "No he doesn't!" as tears ran down her face she said, "I shouldn't have said that."

We were in the car now and she was saying all the things she wish she could redo. I couldn't sit in this car the whole time and not say anything so I let out, "Cherilyn, I never seen Kidd looked at anyone the way he looks at you." I finished saying, "I don't know what it is about you two but you guys are meant for each other and don't forget that."

She said to me, "Promise me one thing, Ray." I turned and looked into her eyes which were now red from all the crying she was doing.

As I looked at her I asked, "What would you like me to do?"

As her voice cracked she said, "Make sure we always stay together." She then put her pinky up to me.

Looking at her I said "Watching you two be in love is the best thing." I then put my pinky with hers and I promised her I would make sure they stayed together.

Now that I sit here reading these letters, I know I should have tried a little harder to make them stay together.

Chapter 14

Days started to add up and nobody heard anything from Kidd since the night at the club. We all tried calling him, but no answer. I knew how to find where he was. I called Mom and asked her is she heard anything from Aiden. Even Mom hadn't hear anything from him but I knew if she called more than two times he would pick up, so I asked her to find out for me.

Maybe five minutes went past and she called me back, and told me, "Aiden doesn't want anyone to know, so that means don't say anything Ray."

I knew everyone would continue to ask me but I wanted to know, so I told her, "Don't worry I won't say anything to anyone."

She then told me, "Aiden went to Oregon, he said, he needed some time to himself and think about some stuff. When I asked him what stuff he was thinking about, he didn't tell me anything, Ray. What's going on with my son?" She asked me.

I told Mom, "He's probably saying that because Cherilyn was at the grand opening and he didn't get to see her."

Mom asked with a shocked sound in her voice, "Cherilyn? Like Daughter-in-law Cherilyn from high school?"

I smiled at the phone, "Yeah she was there and still beautiful but Kidd was at home, when he got there she was nowhere to be found." I ended up telling Mom just to call me if she heard any new word from Kidd.

She told me, "Just give him some space, he'll be okay."

We got off the phone, now that I knew Kidd was safe and what not, I went to the shop because I could not stay away from his letters. When I got there the worker said, "Hey, Ray I see you can't stay away."

I said, "Yeah, I'm reading this book, turns out it's really good and I can't stay away from the pages."

She smiled then asked, "What's the book called?"

Thinking out loud I said, "Damn what's a good book I can say?"

She laughed, "It's okay, if you're not reading a book Ray."

I put my head down in shame that she heard me say that. I tell her, "It's not a book, but my best friend's letters and I like going back to the good time when he was in love."

"If you don't mind me asking, but isn't Mr. Brewing your best friend?" She asked then said, "Because everyone knows you guys own this place and your rags to riches story."

I look at her in shock, I had no idea that she knew all this about us. I couldn't tell her yes, it was bad enough I had the letters so I tell her no as I smiled and go to my seat in the back.

Finally, my drink and joint come out. A young lady puts it on my table I said, "Thank you", as I have my head down grabbing the jar out my bag, I suddenly look and Jasmine is standing right in front of me.

"Hey baby I can see you're still reading Kidd's letters." She said to me as she put her hand on my shoulder.

I know she doesn't want me to keep reading them. "Baby, I'm going to give them back, but these letters just draw me in. I don't know how to explain it."

She sits down next to me, "Yeah I know they do, it's like your watching the "Kidd" that Aiden doesn't show the world." I look and smile at her. She asks me to read one.

So I hand her one, "Babe you can't tell no one about these letters." I tell her.

She grabs it out my hand, "Yeah I know," She opens the letter.

Days like today get hard, when it's raining and I'm lying on the couch I wish you were here on my chest. I miss how we would do dumb things but just being with each other was where we needed to be. Staying up until five in the morning and watching you lay so peacefully. I would give anything to have you in my arms again. Until this day, I can't go to Target without laughing, and thinking about all the crazy things we did. Like that one time we went in there and acted like we worked there, priceless moments I can't have back. Hope one day I get the chance to look into your eyes and see everything I hoped and dreamed of again...

Love. Kidd – xo

Jasmine looked at me in shock once again, I say, "I already know, you can't believe Aiden would write something as beautiful as this."

She looked at me, "No, I knew Kidd was sweet and good with his words but I never seen or heard him be so vulnerable and especially over a female."

I tell her, "Yeah, I know, it's because he hasn't found no one like her since her."

She asks me, "Were you with them at Target?"

Laughing, "No, I wasn't but he told me everything that happened."

I begin to tell her the story of Target and what happened. "So Cherilyn and Kidd were waiting on me and my date to meet up with them so we could go to dinner and the movies, it was a double date thing we had set up. My date was taking forever to get ready so we kept pushing the time back. I ended up calling Kidd, "Yo man we gotta catch the next movie time or the last one, she is taking forever to get ready."

Kidd told me, "Ni**a, I don't think you know who my girlfriend is, Cherilyn is just like me and we hate waiting, you know this."

I then told him, "Come on bro, look out for me one time."

He laughed, "I got you, don't trip but hurry up." He then told her, "Babe so Ray and whatever her name are going to be a little later than we expected."

She had a attitude, "Ray always taking forever and shit!"

Kidd shook his head as they drove to the place we were going to eat at. Kidd told me he was looking for something to do, to kill time. He seen a Target and said, "Babe, don't get mad that just means we have some time to kill and I know just the thing." He then told me he didn't know if it was a coincidence but they both had red on so he told, "Babe, we should go into Target and act like we work there."

She looked at him crazy and said, "Babe, why would we do that?"

Kidd told her, "Because we could be the total opposite of what a salesperson is."

She laughed, "Okay, but let's make it fun with a bet."

Kidd smiled, "Okay, what's the bet?"

She said, "Whoever gets fired or caught first, has to do whatever the others wants tonight."

Kidd parked the car in the lot and said, "Bring in on babe."

They went into the store and Kidd pulled his pants up tucked in his shirt in and went to the hair products section. He then said a guy came up to him and said, "Aye man can you tell me where the movies are?"

Kidd said, "Bro, does it look like I know where that shit is, if you would look up and start reading these signs then maybe you could find it."

The guy looked at Kidd in shock, "What kind of bullshit customer service is this?" Then walked off.

Cherilyn was up next, she went to the food department. Kidd said he watched her act like she was putting things away and he knew he was falling for her more each time he looked at her. He said this lady came up to Cherilyn and asked her, "Hello sweetie, do you know where the toothbrushes are?"

She looked at her, "No, I don't madam but I'm pretty sure you need to find it fast because I smell why you need to get."

The lady was in disbelief and walked away with a mean look on her face.

Kidd moved to the movie section. This man with his wife came up to Kidd and asked him, "Excuse me sir, but could you show us where the kitchen appliances are?"

Kidd looked at both of them, "Yo first off, don't just walk up on me like that, and I don't get paid enough to be showing people around."

The guy looked at his wife and looked back at Kidd, "I'm going to get your manager."

Kidd put both of his hands up, "Get him! I ain't scared of no damn manager."

Five minutes later Kidd was kicked out. Cherilyn then came out and said, "Okay, you won babe."

Kidd told me that was one of his best moments with her because she was with him and he was with her, they were so in love."

Jasmine looked at me and said, "I wish I was there to witness his happiness."

I tell her, "It was something worth watching." She now wanted to read more, so I thought to myself, why not, this way we're spending time together and she gets to see some of my best-friend's love story.

Chapter 15

Jasmine grabs the next letter looks at me as I nod my head. She began to read the note,

Funny thing is, until this day, I drink with two straws. People asks me all the time what's up with the two straws, Kidd? I laugh and tell them because when we dated, you always made me grab more than one straw and it was because you always had your lips on my drink. Oh how I miss the days when you used to take my things and say babe it's not yours, it's ours. I guess the real reason I still drink with two straws is because I hope one day, you'll grab my drink and say it's not mine but ours. Having this world means nothing, if I don't have you to share the stars with. Watching the sun shine bright give me hope that you're still showing off that beautiful smile. Miss you every day, but it gets a little harder when the sun is shining bright and I'm having a good drink and I think about how much you would love the drink…

Love. Kidd – xo

I could feel Jasmine's eyes on me again, "Babe, is that really why Aiden drinks out of two straws?"

I laughed and answered, "Yeah that's why."

"I've always wanted to ask him but was nervous." She said.

I can't help but laugh again, "Yeah, she's the reason for a lot of things Kidd does. I don't know if he would have told you even if you asked. At least not the true."

That made her laugh, "I know, that's why I never asked him."

I tell her how Cherilyn always made Aiden get more than one straw, and if he didn't, that was a fight waiting to happen. They shared everything, he made sure if he had something she had it too and the same went for her.

I found myself getting caught in the moment talking about them. "I remember when they got into it over one straw and she made him go back through the drive-thru to get another straw. He give her the drink, she turned and looked at him when he started driving off, "Where the hell is the other straw, Aiden?" When she called him by his first name, that meant she was upset. Kidd looked around and "I thought they gave us more than one." With attitude in her voice she said, "No, so go back through and get the straws, Kidd!" I believe it was after one of our game because I remember we went back through because he wasn't trying to fight with her all night."

Jasmine stopped me, "Aiden really went through all that to make her happy?"

I looked at her and said, "Yeah." I then continued with the story. "She was already mad that they were back waiting again and that Kidd didn't get more than one straw in the first place. As he was waiting, his phone rang .The only reason why he answered was because she told him to. He knew it was this old girl we used to kick it with like two years ago. He told her, "Babe, I don't feel like talking to no one, I'm tired and want to go to the house." She looked at his phone, "Is it because that's a girl's name that popped up?" Kidd put his head down, "Fuck it okay, you want me to answer well here it goes." He picked the phone up and had it on speaker. The girl on the other end said, "Hey Kidd, what are you doing?" He said, "I'm getting something to eat with my girlfriend," looking, at Cherilyn as he said it. The girl on the line said, "Oh yeah, I seen her at the game, you two are like the cutest couple I ever seen." Cherilyn turned her head and looked out the window.

"Kidd said could tell she was pissed off. He told the girl, 'I gotta talk to you late, my girl is getting mad.' The girl said, Please tell her not to be mad, we're nothing and that I just wanted to tell you good game," and then hung up the phone.

"Kidd got the straws and drove off when Cherilyn snatched the straws out of his hand. He stopped the car. What the fuck is you deal?" She snapped at him, "So I guess you don't see a problem with girls calling your phone, trying to hit you with that soft voice shit!" Kidd put his phone down, 'You heard me tell her I was with my girlfriend.' His eyes got big, "Keyword, GIRLFRIEND!" She looked at him with fire in her eyes, "Aiden, you really must think I'm stupid of something. Know these girls are all over you and shit!"

On the way to his house, Kidd stopped the car in the middle of the street. "Fuck that, I ain't dealing with this shit. I'm just going to walk home." He got out of the car, got his backpack and began to walk. She hopped in the driver seat driving next to him as he walked. "Come on, stop this and get back in the car." Kidd said, "Nah just meet me at the house." Still driving slow, "Kidd, I'm not going nowhere without you." Kidd kept walking, he told her, "I'm not getting in the car if you gonna keep going off on me for no reason." They continued to argue as he walked home. She told, "There is a reason why I'm mad." Kidd said, "That's a dumbass reason, I can't control the girls that hit me up." That response made her mad all over again. 'Yes you can control these hoes!' He stopped walking and said, "See that's that bullshit." She stopped the car, "That's what bullshit? Tell them you have a girl and to leave you the fuck alone." Kidd was so frustrated. "Everyone already knows you're my girlfriend!" He continued to storm towards his house and she sat there in shock that Aiden got that loud with her.

She beat him to his house. He got there and surprisingly no one was home, it was just him and Cherilyn. She said, "What were you trying to prove, Kidd?" He didn't say anything and just walked to his room. She got up and stepped in front of him. "So now you're not going to answer me?" He moved her to the side a little roughly. He told her, "Watch out, ain't nobody got time for this shit." She didn't like being moved to the side like that, so she punched him two times, right in the mouth. Kidd was in shock. "I know you didn't fucking hit me." Walking over to her she tried to swing again and Aiden grabbed both of her hands slamming her to the wall. She looked at him, "Go ahead, hit me." By this time Kidd had her up in the air on the wall. He told me he was pissed and wanted to punch her but the way he had her up kinda turned him on at the same time.

It's funny how love could be bipolar, one minute he wanted to go off on her and the next they were on each other like nothing ever happen. They locked eyes and she wrapped her legs around his waist, pulled him closer started to kiss and before you know it they were having make up sex.

When he told me that story I told him, "Y'all just argue for the make up sex." Jasmine looked at me and laughed. "Well damn, I guess we need to start fighting so we can have some of that make up sex."

After she said that I turned my head to the side and said, "As much as I would love to throw you around the room and get it on, we have nothing to fight over and if you hit me I might knock yo ass out. So let's not try anything foolish." She knew I was just joking about knocking her out. I just wanted her to know that we have no need to fight. If we wanted to spark our relationship up we could get into role playing or something.

I'm guessing that story of Kidd and Cherilyn turned her on because licking and biting her lip she told me, "I'll be waiting at home for you, babe."

I knew what that meant so I put the jar of letters in my bag fast and headed straight to the house.

Chapter 16

The next morning feeling good, I came right back to the shop and continued to read. It was really something about these letters that just kept me reading. I knew if Kidd found out he would be beyond pissed off. For some reason, even knowing that, I still read the letters. I guess it was the thrill that kept my eyes on each note.

Today I was trying to write a paper for class and all I had was you on my mind and every letter, every word decided our love and how I miss you like the night sky missing the star that sparkles. Probably because it was getting close to Valentines and it made me think of our first Valentine's how I went all out to see you smile in front of your whole school. But the gift you gave me was the best and the fact that we stayed up all night playing it made it everything I needed in life. I knew you never liked me getting you anything but how you matched my fly so perfect and every time I seen something I couldn't help but see you wearing it. Until this day, you're the reason I'm a sucker for a girl with a beautiful smile and a nice style. Honestly, just miss having my best friend, a person I could do any and everything with, but I'm sure somehow life will bring us together for a chance for me to see your beautiful smile one more time...

Love. Kidd – xo

That Valentine's was one to remember, that's for sure. I still remember when Kidd walked up to me, almost in a panic, "Yo Ray, what should I do for Cherilyn?" Looking at me as we walked to our next class.

I asked, "I thought you and Cherilyn agreed to no gifts?"

Kidd looked at me with the biggest smile, "Yeah we did, but I just agreed because I didn't want her to get me anything."

We got to class and I was still thinking of what Kidd should get her. I had no idea about this kind of stuff. Kidd was always the romantic one and I didn't know where to start. So I asked him, "What does she like?"

Kidd told me, "I already got her everything she likes."

It was early in the morning so we had time to brainstorm. We got out of school before Cherilyn ended her last class. Kidd called Mom and within five minutes he got the keys and said, "Come on Ray, I got an idea."

We ended up going to the party store. "Kidd, what the hell are we doing here" I asked.

He looked at me and said, "hurry, grab all the heart and love balloons."

Looking around I started to get any love balloon that I could get my hand on. Kidd went and got a life size teddy bear.

When we were in the car I noticed we weren't going to his house, nor were we headed to Cherilyn's house. So I asked Kidd," Yo, where the hell are we going, you know we still have practice right?"

He smiled and said, "I'm trying to get to Cherilyn's school before they get out of class."

It was starting to make sense now. We ended up getting to her school right before they got out. Kidd was on a mission. He jumped out of the car put all the balloons in her car. Watching him do all this for the girl he loved, made me want to be in love and have a girl also.

He told me, "Ray call her, freak out and tell her you were driving by and couldn't stop but it looked like someone broke into her car." I then called her and told her what Kidd wanted me to say. I really went all out yelling and just in a panic over her car. She was freaking out on the phone and I could tell she was scared and wanted to cry. We had practice and couldn't really stay the whole time but Aiden wanted to see her expression, so we made time. Cherilyn and her friend came running out in a panic. Also school had just got out for them so everyone was on their way out. Kidd got out his phone, made a phone call and people were coming with cameras and everything. I even heard him tell people to make sure this goes viral, he wanted everyone to know that Cherilyn had the best boyfriend. When she came out and saw her car, tears started to come down her face. Aiden looked at me and smiled, "See with she did there? That's all I need in this life, is for her to show off that beautiful smile."

We now had to go before we were late to practice, as we drove away Kidd was honking playing, *There Goes My Baby* real loud in his car. He had two huge speakers so everyone heard the song. As we drove off, I could see all her friends envious telling her "I wish, I had a boyfriend like that." I then checked social media, pictures were everywhere, everyone was talking about it. Kidd really made sure, everyone knew how much he loved Cherilyn.

We got to practice and our teammates were talking about it also, "Dang Kidd, you really love that girl I seen how you went to her school and did the whole I love you thing." Kidd was so happy that she had that big smile on her face. This was probably the happiest I have ever seen him. After practice we went to his house and Cherilyn was waiting like usual. We got in the house and she was kicking it on the couch with Mia and Mom.

Cherilyn looked at Kidd, "Kidd, didn't I tell you, I didn't want you to do anything for me?"

Kidd smiled, "Yeah I know, but you deserve the world and I plan on giving it to you."

She got up, hugged and kissed him. Mom said, "Hey, take that in the room."

He told me to wait in the living room. When he got in the room, all I heard was Kidd say, "Babe you're the best!" I got up to see what she did. His door was open, there were balloons everywhere, candy on the bed, a little teddy bear holding the new *Call of Duty*. Picking her up and kissing her, he told me, "Yeah man I don't think I'm going anywhere anytime soon.

Smiling I shook my head, "Yeah I figured that."

He laughed, "already then Ray, I'll just get with you tomorrow."

The next day he told me that they didn't do anything but play the game all night. They even go to level forty on zombies. I remember him telling me, "Ray, I didn't think it was possible for a guy like me to find love."

I laughed, "Now all you need to do is not fuck it up."

He told me, "I won't, don't worry."

Thinking about it now, I'm mad he met her at such a young age. If he had met her even a year later, he might still be with her today but life make mistakes.

Chapter 17

The craziest thing happen today. I was asked by my coach, what I wanted most in life. I told him with no hesitation, all I wanted was to be truly happy. He looked at me, surprised at what I had said. I knew he was expecting me to say the NBA or something. I mean that was my dream for so long, and then you walked in and everything changed. It wasn't until I got to my house that I really thought about the question that was asked of me. Mia walked in with your old cheerleading hoodie on. I asked her where she got it from. She told me her best friend Cherilyn gave it to her and I can't have it. Seeing your hoodie after that question was enough for me. Ever since I met you on that night, in front of my house. I saw the happiness I was looking for my whole life. It was like your eyes were my crystal ball and every time I looked into them I saw our future. Never knew I would have to live my life without you. I've been through a lot, but living without you has to be the hardest thing. I'm just glad I was able to meet someone as special as you…

Love. Kidd - xo

Reading this note made me laugh. I thought about Cherilyn's hoodie and how Aiden got in trouble when he wore it to one of our tournaments and Coach U was beyond pissed off. He walked up to Kidd when he saw him put the hoodie on after our game. He asked Kidd, Who do you play for, Aiden?"

Kidd looked at coach and said, "I play for the East Side Devils best in the city!"

Coach looked Aiden up and down. "So why the fuck you got a upper East Side Wildcat hoodie on?"

Kidd laughed. "Nah coach, it's my girl's hoodie."

It was like clockwork, Cherilyn then walked up. Coach looked at her as they hugged. "I'm glad you're here Cherilyn because if I see Aiden in some shit like this again, you won't see him on the court but next to you in the stands."

After coach said that, he walked off. Kidd looked at Cherilyn. "He just be tripping babe, don't even worry about what he got to say."

She then said, "I know, but I just want to see you play baby, so you gotta follow the rules babe."

Kidd smiled. "You right babe." She was wanting him to be better and do better. The next day I saw him at school and he had her hoodie on again.

"Yo Kidd, what the hell you doing?" I asked, as I ran over to him.

He turned to me, "What are you talking about?"

I grabbed the hoodie, "This! You know coach is going to trip if he sees you in this."

He looked down at her name, it was stitched on the patch, real big "Cherilyn." Then looked back at me, "Yeah I know, but I can't help it," he said while he was gripped the hoodie. "It just makes me feel closer to her."

Until this day, I haven't seen him head over hills for any girl but her. It's hard to believe Cherilyn had Aiden ready to give up everything and how he always willing to show the world how much he loved her.

Now that I think about it, a few years ago Mia found the hoodie when they were moving. I remember Aiden snatching it from her and hugging it like he had Cherilyn in his arms again. I knew he could feel her touch when he did that, the smile on his face said the whole thing.

Kidd has been gone for some time now, I imagined him running into Cherilyn and them just trying things out one more time. Wherever he was I hope he finds the peace he is looking for, as for me I'm picking up the next letter.

Chapter 18

After every championship game we won, I found myself sad and in no mood to celebrate. I guess it's because I still think of the night we lost regionals. I broke down crying on the court. I still have the newspaper picture of you holding my head as my jersey is over my face. My mom told me you were scared to drive me home because you knew I was upset over the loss. She even told me you wanted to take all the pain and sadness away. I guess you told her it hurt you to watch tears come down my eyes. The way you made me smile and laugh again on the kitchen floor that night. Made me forget about the game and anything in the outside world. That's the thing I miss the most, how everything disappears when I'm with you. Yeah, I always wanted to be the star and all that, but if I knew it meant giving you up, I would have never chosen this life. You were my reason to breathe each day, waking up with you made me smile because I knew the girl of my dreams was the one right next to me...

Love. Kidd - xo

Kidd still talks about that game. It was one for the books, that's for sure. He said that was the day that he didn't just lose a game, but his happiness. I remember the game like it was yesterday. Aiden had the ball on top of the key, made his move and blew right past the defender. Down the middle of the lane and dunked the ball hard, you could hear the rim rattle. We were all hyped up now. The momentum was on our side and Kidd had just caught fire. The next play we came down and I tried to go right back to Kidd, and when the ball left my hand, Kidd yelled out, "No, Ray!" It was too late, the ball was out of my hands. Tom, who was the best player on the Central North team, stole the ball. Kidd tried to run him down for the block. Tom was moving fast with the ball. By time Kidd got to the three point line, he was in the air and it was show time. He brought it back and threw it down hard then stood there and looked at the crowd. Coach called timeout and any life we had before that was gone. Being that me and Aiden went to Central North our freshmen year we weren't going down that easy.

We ended, us losing by four. As we were shaking hands after the game. Aiden sat on the bench, jersey over his head to hide the tears that were coming down his face. Everyone was coming up to him rubbing his head telling him it was good game. That's when Cherilyn came over grabbed his head and pulled him closer to her and told him "Win or lose, you're still my favorite player, and I will love you forever no matter the score."

He ended up coming in the locker room, eyes bloodshot red. We all knew how bad Aiden wanted to win, it would have put him as the top player in the city. We would have finally beat our old team. He wanted them to know he was the best and that they should have moved him up when they had the chance.

Mom told Cherilyn to get him and bring him to the house, because she knew if anyone could put a smile back on Aiden's face it was her. The whole drive home he didn't say a word. She was scared that if she said anything he could flip so she stayed quiet the whole drive. When they got to the house, Aiden still didn't say anything and just went to the kitchen. Cherilyn came in a little after him and Mom asked her, "What happened? How did it go?

Cherilyn had tears in her eyes, "He didn't say anything and I didn't want him to get mad if I said the wrong thing."

Mom said, "Aiden, there's no need to shut everyone out, you played your ass off." Kidd was not trying to hear anything about the game. He didn't say anything back, Mom then said, "I know it hurts but that's a part of the game and you know that."

Kidd punched the refrigerator. "It's not supposed to be like that!" He then turned with his back to the fridge, "I played my fucking heart out!" Sliding down to the floor, tears coming out of his eyes.

Cherilyn came in, his head went up, looked her in her eyes and head went down in between his legs. She then sat right next to him, "I'm not going anywhere anytime soon." Then she put both hands around him putting his head on her shoulder. It only took ten minutes and they were laughing. She made Aiden forget all about the game. The next day in the newspaper, there was a picture of Tom looking at the crowd and the other half was Aiden sitting with his head down and in Cherilyn's arms. The article read, "Aiden Brewing had game high scoring twenty-seven, but it wasn't enough to overcome the Cav's rise to victory." Aiden read the article and took each word to heart. He started going to the gym every chance he got.

This was when Aiden slowly started to push Cherilyn further and further away. Reading these letters now I understand why that game means a lot to him. I remember him telling me nothing in this world could bring him down as long as he had her by his side he would be fine. I just hope he's doing okay without her now, I know that's why he left and hasn't spoken to anyone.

Chapter 19

As you know, I have a lot of tattoos now and I know you have some too. Everyone always asks me about my first one, it's my favorite one for the whole lot of reasons. Being that you were there for it makes it even more special to me. It was crazy how everything went down that day, I never wanted to put you in harm's way. I didn't think a tattoo could cause so much commotion and violence among people. I remember Mom and Jay even trying to ground me, taking my phone away so I couldn't text or talk to you. Guess they didn't think I knew your number by heart. Sometimes I catch myself about to dial your number but then I talk myself out of it every time. Maybe the next time, I'll hit send and that angel-like voice will hit my ear. That might just be the only thing that would make me believe in happiness again. All I know is that every memory with you in it brings a smile to my face. You were the best part of me, and that's why I fell in love with you...

Love. Kidd – xo

Aiden's first tattoo caused so much trouble. Kidd had been talking about getting a tattoo the whole week. Cherilyn got a tattoo about two days before Kidd got his. He told her, "If you get one, I'll go ahead and get one too." So now that she had one, he had to be a man of his word and get one. The rule was as long as he was living under Mom's and Jay's house there would be no ink on the body. Kidd came to me the day of and asked, "Ray, you coming with me to watch me get tatted?"

I looked at him puzzled because I was there when they told him no tattoos while he lives there. He asked me with a straight face. I gave him a confused look as we walked down the hall. "You know you can't get a tattoo Kidd."

He stopped and looked at me, "It's better to ask for forgiveness, than for permission," he smiled, "Ray make sure you don't forget that."

As we got to class, I asked him, "What does that mean?"

He told me, "You should do whatever you feel in your heart," he continued saying, "the ones who love you, will forgive you for the wrong they see in their eyes."

Looking at him and taking everything he said in, "Yeah, I guess that makes sense," I said.

He had this grin on his face, "Ray, we sin every day, but the one above doesn't hold that against us, he still blesses us each day with a new chance to make things right."

I couldn't believe what he was saying, he was always so ahead of his time. I remember thinking to myself, like this guy cannot just be sixteen with all this knowledge. After school, we went to his house. Cherilyn made her way over and asked Aiden, "So you're really going to get a tattoo?"

Kidd looked her in the eyes, "You know me, I'm a man of my word."

She looked right back at him, "But you know you don't have to get one if you don't want to."

He looked at me sideways then went right back to her. "I can't have my girl getting all the ink, plus I've been wanting a tattoo. You just gave me the perfect opportunity to get one."

Shaking her head, "Whatever, but I'm not taking you because I don't want your mom mad at me."

Kidd laughed, "Babe, you were never taking me, my big cousin is coming to pick me up and take me."

Kidd's big cousin Harp was big and built, guess he was locked up for a while. He got to the house to pick up Kidd, I asked him, "Can I come with?"

Kidd looked at me and said, "Yeah, come one get in."

We ended up driving to what looked to be run down apartments. We got inside and it was nice, clean. Kidd knew the guy from where I don't know, but they were talking like they knew each other. Nick was his name and he did almost everybody's tats in the city. Well him and the two other guys that worked in there with him, Mat and Jamal. Kidd still only goes to our three boys to get tatted.

Kidd and Nick were finishing the sketch that was going on Kidd's arm. Cherilyn ended up coming to the Nick's spot to watch Kidd get his first tattoo. Me and her sat there as Aiden was getting ready to feel that needle. He put on "Ink my whole body" by Wiz Khalifa and played it the whole time he was getting tatted. He hardly even moved I asked him, "Does it hurt?"

He looked, "Not really, it just a little hot that's all."

The tattoo probably took twenty minutes total. When he was done she said, "Babe it's nice, do you like it?"

As he looked at his arm in the mirror, "Yeah, I love it but not as much as I love you."

We were now on our way back to Kidd's house. Harp said, "You going to tell your mom about it right?"

As we pulled up to his house Aiden told him, "Yeah, I don't like keeping secrets from my mom."

She was at home when we got there, she was getting ready to go to a old school concert. We got inside and she was in the kitchen. We sat down in the living room. Kidd called her to come sit with us, when she walked in the living room, "Oh hey Harp, how you been?" Seeing Harp there took her by surprise.

He said, "Not too much just enjoying life to the fullest,"

Mom replied, "As you should, Harp."

He then said, "Aiden got something to tell you."

Heads turned quickly to Aiden. I could tell he was nervous, "Sooooo I got something to tell you."

Mom looked at Aiden, "Am I going to be mad?"

He smiled a little, "I mean yeah, but not at the same time."

Mom now looked at all of us, "You got Cherilyn pregnant?" she asked.

Kidd put his head back, "No!" They both yelled out. Then Kidd's smile got a little bigger, "Okay see things could be worse."

Mom then said, "Cut the shit and tell me."

Kidd said, "I got a tattoo."

She looked at him in disbelief. "No you didn't, let me see."

He rolled his right sleeve up and showed her the tattoo. It was a basketball with the same necklace Kidd wears around his neck on the ball with a halo on top of the basketball. This tattoo was for his older brother who passed. He said, "It's because he's my angel and he came in the form of a ball."

When mom seen it she shook her head. "You know you're going to have to tell Big Jay right?"

Big Jay is Kidd's step father but he's been in Kidd's life so long blood couldn't make them any closer.

Kidd said, "Yeah I know, I'll tell him."

Mom didn't seem that mad. We were all sitting there talking until Big Jay came home. Right before he walked in the house. Mom told Aiden, "Tell him before he gets inside."

Kidd stopped him at the door, "Hey Jay, I got something to tell you."

He asked, "What up Kidd, what you got on your mind?"

Kidd rubbing his, "I got a tattoo." It came out of his mouth low.

Jay said, "Boy, what the hell did you just say?"

Kidd said it a little louder, "I got a tattoo."

Jay said, "Ni**a I heard you say, you got a tattoo, let me see that shit."

Kidd then rolled up his sleeve and showed him the tat. Jay shook his head, walked in and went straight to the back room.

Mom then went back there to see if Jay was okay, two minutes later they called Aiden's name to come back there. He got up and walked back there, I was sitting with Harp and Cherilyn. We all said Kidd is definitely in trouble for life, Harp said, "If I knew he wasn't supposed to get a tattoo, I wouldn't have took down there to get it."

Cherilyn said, "You know Kidd, even if you wouldn't have took him, he would have found a way to get what he wanted." We sat there shaking our heads in agreement because we knew she was right

I guess Jay asked Kidd who took him to get a tattoo and Kidd told him his cousin took him. Jay never met Harp and this was not a good way for them to meet. Jay came from the back room and he had been drinking before he got to the house. All I heard next was, "Who the fuck you think you are taking that boy down there to mark up his body?" Jay asked Harp.

Harp then said, "I'm Harp Aiden's big cousin, ni**a who are you?"

Jay looked at him, "It don't matter who I am, you in my house and you had no right taking that boy down there to get a tattoo."

Harp came back with, "That's my little cousin and whatever he need I got him."

Jay got louder, "Not while he lives under my roof."

Harp then told Jay, "I got a five bedroom house, he could come live with me whenever he is ready."

They just kept going back and forth then Jay went back to the room. "You can show yourself out!" he yelled as he walked back there.

Harp went to his car and told Kidd, "I'm going to run back in and tell your mom bye."

Kidd looked at him. "Okay cool."

As he went to hug mom Jay came back to the living room and yelled, "You a bitch, fuck you get out my house."

Harp had enough of the going back and forth words. Harp was outside in the front yard, "Bring yo ass outside and stop running your mouth!"

Jay got in the doorway and Harp pulled out his gun cocked it back and pointed it at him. "You talking real hard." Harp said as he cocked the gun back. Mom was not trying to hold Jay back. Kidd was standing in the middle of both of them. Me and Cherilyn were in the living room scared as shit.

Jay said, "Ni**a what's that going to do besides make me mad?"

Kidd's face had fear written all over it. "Just go home Harp!" Kidd said.

He looked at Kidd's face and said, "Okay, love you Aiden." That right there put Kidd in a position where he felt like he was choosing a side.

Kidd looked at him, "Alright love you."

Harp got in his car and drove off. Mom looked at Cherilyn. "Go home and can you take Ray with you?"

She said, "Yes, I can and for the record I told Kidd it was a bad idea with the tattoo."

We then got up to leave. Jay stopped Cherilyn from trying to give Aiden a kiss.

The next day at school, I came up to Kidd, "Yo what happened? You good?"

Kidd had his head down, "Yeah, I'm straight, they just took my phone away and told me I can't talk to or see anyone."

All I could say was, "Better you than me," As I laughed a little.

Kidd laughed a little as well, "Let me see your phone?" he asked me.

I took my phone out of my pocket and gave it to him. I knew he wanted to talk to Cherilyn, so I asked, "Who you texting on my phone?"

He had this big smile on his face, "Who else would I be taking to Ray?"

I then said, "Yeah you right, tell Cherilyn I said 'what up'".

After school, Cherilyn was right there waiting for Kidd. She ran into his arms and kissed him. You would have thought that they hadn't seen each other in years. She then smacked him, "I told you not to get that tattoo, now look at you I don't even get to spend time with my baby."

Kidd laughed, "Yeah I know, but sometimes you just gotta do what you gotta do."

Cherilyn said, "Yeah, but you could have waited."

I was still trying to figure out how she was at our school when her school hadn't even gotten out yet. So I asked, "Aren't you supposed to be in school?"

She laughed, "Yeah, but I'm ahead in my class and I told my teacher I had to go to do some cheer stuff."

I said, "Okay." Then I asked Kidd, "What happened after we left?"

He took a deep breath, "Man shit was crazy."

Cherilyn looked at him. "Tell us what happened!"

Both of us were dying to know what went down after we left. Kidd told us his father ended up calling, when Jay was going off on him and Aiden picked up the phone. Aiden Jr, Kidd's dad heard Jay in the background yelling at Aiden and asked to speak with Jay. They went at it for a good amount of time. Kidd finished the story saying. "Yeah then my father called me when Jay left and told me to tell him to tell his children goodbye because he was coming out here." Aiden then looked at both of us. "I don't want no one to die over this shit."

Cherilyn said, "Yo stupid ass should have never got it, you wouldn't be in this position."

He then said, "Yeah I know but I got this shit now and there's nothing I can do about it."

We kicked it for a little then Cherilyn had to go back to school. Kidd went home, he wasn't allowed to have anyone over. Even with him being grounded and all he still found ways to talk to and be with Cherilyn.

Chapter 20

You're still the only girl who has ever met my father. I remember telling you we were going to meet him because he was in town. You were so scared and wanted to impress him because you wanted everyone to fall for you like I did. I told you, you shouldn't worry about impressing him, he should be the one trying to impress you. I came to pick you up so we could go to dinner with him and his girl. You stepped out of your house with that black dress, the one that dropped my mouth right to the floor. Watching you walk to me was more than anything I could have ever asked for in this life. I knew you were the one I wanted to see walked down the aisle. If I wasn't so dumb I would have just married you right then when I had the chance. Hopefully the next time I see you, that finger will still be empty and we can start where we left off...

Love. Kidd - xo

Kidd really didn't have a relationship with his father. Being that Kidd could count on his hands how many times he seen his dad. It was a big deal for a girl to meet him. When Kidd told stories of his dad, it kinda sounded like myths or old camp stories. So when I heard his dad was coming in town, in my head I was telling myself I need to meet this guy. Aiden asked Cherilyn first if she wanted to meet him, she was so blown away that Kidd asked her. She told him she would and Kidd told her, "Go get ready and I'll pick up for dinner." She left his house and went to get dressed. Kidd then asked me, "You ready?"

I looked at him confused, "Ready for what?"

He smiled and told me, "It's time for you to meet this ni**a Aiden Jr."

I laughed and said, "Ni**a I already know yo ass."

He laughed, "No, fool I'm the third, my so called father is Jr."

I said, "Oh yeah I'm always ready."

We got in the car and left to meet his dad. We ended up meeting him at this Italian restaurant, real beautiful and elegant. Right when we walked in, a guy stood up and I grabbed Kidd, "Yo that guy looks just like you but just bigger and a little darker."

Kidd smiled, "That's my father,Ray."

Looking at both of them, there was no denying that, that was his father. He stood up when he saw Kidd. "Boy get over and show yo pop some love." We walked over there, Big Aiden pulled Kidd in closer. "Man, I missed you so much."

Kidd then said, "Yeah, I bet."

Big Aiden said, "No real talk, I miss you every day."

Kidd with a quick reply said, "You really have a funny way of showing it."

I couldn't sit here and watch them go at and not say anything. So I introduced myself. "Hey, what's up I'm Ray." Big Aiden then shook my hand, he wasn't just big but strong also. I noticed the strength when he grabbed my hand the way he did.

After those first couple of minutes, they were almost like best friends. Watching both of them trade stories was like watching two Aiden's bond, it was crazy to watch. Big Aiden asked Kidd, "So where's this true love of yours?"

He told him, "She's coming to dinner with us tonight."

Big Aiden said, "Okay for sure, don't let her be no duck or anything."

They both laughed Kidd then said, "She's the prettiest girl on the face of earth and I can tell you that right now."

Big Aiden said, "Okay just meet me and my girl at Harp's house around nine."

Kidd told him, "Okay we'll be there and make sure your girl don't look like the back of my shoe." We laughed as we got in the car.

As we were leaving Big Aiden saw this beautiful tall blond walk pass and he stopped her. Within the next five minutes she was giving him her number. We drove off and I told Kidd, "So I'm guessing you got that smooth criminal shit from yo pops."

Kidd looked me in my eyes, "I didn't get shit from him remember that Ray." He continued saying, "Everything I have and everything I am is because of me." I didn't know my comment was going to upset Kidd so much.

As we got to his house I asked, "Don't you think some stuff should stay in the past?" He made a weird look like I said something wrong.

Putting his down and both hands on his head, "Ray, that's all it is. I leave his ass in the past. The same way he left me." Kidd really took not growing up with his father hard.

We got in his house and Kidd started to get ready for dinner. Mom walked in, "Where are you going?"

As he looked for a pair of shoes to wear, "I'm going to see, your so called baby daddy."

Mom looked at him, "Jay is in the living room Aiden!"

Kidd said, "No not him. We going to dinner with that ni**a Aiden."

Mom's eyes got big, "Oh big Aiden is in town?" she asked Kidd.

Still looking for a pair of shoes to wear, "Yeah he out here and we having dinner with him and Harp, it's a Brewing's night."

Mom then asked, "Is Cherilyn going with you guys?"

When she asked him that, the doorbell rang. I looked at the door confused because I thought we were picking her up but I guess she couldn't wait and decided to come over.

Kidd smiled at Mom, "Yeah that should be her at the door."

Little Jay opened the door, "Kidd! Your so-called girlfriend is here."

Kidd yelled out, "Babe come to my room!"

As she started walking to his room Little Jay told her in a light voice, "If you keep going straight, you can just go to my room."

Mia then came over, "Shut up Jay, don't nobody want to go in that dirty-ass room."

Cherilyn laughed a little, "You're so cute Jay."

Little Jay then asked, "Cute enough to steal you away from Aiden?"

Mia cut in and told him, "Jay nobody wants you."

He quickly came back with, "Girl stop lying, everybody wants me." They started to argue and Cherilyn came to the room.

She told Kidd, "Your brother is just the cutest!"

He was pulling down a pair of shoes now as he said, "Babe you can think he's cute and all, as long as you love me."

He had his back to her, when she came in so he didn't see the black dress she had on. My eyes couldn't believe what I was looking at, the whole time she came in the door. Thinking out loud I said, "Damn Kidd better marry this girl!"

He turned around, looking her up and down. He had the I'm in love look in his eyes. "Fuck going to dinner, Ray is right let's go get married."

She laughed, "Babe, we'll get the chance in due time."

Kidd made her pinky promise they would get married in the future. I wonder now if Kidd still remembers that promise. I know if he did he would hold Cherilyn to it and they would be married now.

We ended up going to Harp's house for dinner, I guess they ended up grilling some steaks and chicken. As we walked to the door, Kidd told her, "Don't fall for none of his bullshit."

She looked at him, "What bullshit?"

Kidd said, "The bullshit he says out his mouth."

We were now walking into the house, Kidd was introducing Cherilyn to Big Aiden. They were holding hands when we walked up to him, Big Aiden said, "Hey beautiful, you must be the one who has my son's heart."

Cherilyn said, "No, it's more like he has my heart." as she grabbed Kidd's hand.

Big Aiden then said, "If your mom is anything like you, Kidd might just have to be your step brother."

Kidd looked at him crazy and said, "Yeah knowing you, you'll probably find some way to fuck it up." That statement ended all conversations.

Cherilyn looked at Kidd, "Babe I get the pain your feeling but let's have a goodnight. Give him a chance, who knows you might like him."

We decided to eat and sit out on the deck in the backyard. It was beautiful outside that night, the moon was full and shining bright. Ever-time I looked at Kidd, his eyes were on Cherilyn and a smile remained on his face. He got up and started to walk to the back of the yard until he got to the end of the gate. I then got up and walked that way also, just wanted to make sure Kidd was okay. He was leaning on the gate when I got to him, "Kidd, you good bro?" I asked him. He turned towards me and now we were both looking at the moon and everybody talking on the deck.

He told me, "Yeah, I'm good, just can't believe that God really put one person on this earth to take all my pain away."

I was speechless because I wasn't ready for Kidd to say something like that. The only response I had for him was, "Every chance you get, you let her know how much she means to you."

Kidd smiled and looked at Cherilyn. "She's something I will forever cherish close to my heart."

The look he had on his face was magical. We walked back over, sat and talked for a little longer until it was time for us to head out. Kidd took me home, he wanted to have some alone time with his girl. They went to their favorite place in the city on top of the hill overlooking the view.

Chapter 21

I think you're still the only girl I get jealous over. Never really been a jealous type of guy but thinking of you being with someone else scared me the whole time. That's why when I held your hand, I held it tight because letting go meant not being with you. Living without you would be living in a world with no sunny days. Ever since you left I can't see anything but the rain drops. It's okay because each drop feels more and more like your touch and each splash sounds a lot like you voice. Even though I didn't like the jealousy, I miss it the most. It let me know how much you loved me and didn't want me to go. You always said death would be easier than to watch me be with someone other than you. Even when death came for me, all I wanted to do was to be close to you. It still breaks my heart that we lost the best reason to be alive, and that's to find and cherish love. I know saying sorry doesn't take the pain away but I want you to know that I will forever cherish the love we once had…

Love. Kidd - xo

Both of them were jealous of the other. They hated the thought of the other being with someone else. I believe this is why their relationship was so great.

I sure hated when they fought over little petty shit. There was this one time after one of our spring game that we won. Kidd and Cherilyn were holding hands walking out of the gym. Kidd liked to take his shirt off after games and walk out to the car. Cherilyn wasn't a fan of Kidd doing that but he still did it and she learned to accept it. As they walked out to the car, two cheerleaders ran up to Kidd and gave him a hug, "Good game Kidd, we love watching you play."

Kidd being nice said, "Thank you and make sure y'all at the next game."

When she heard that, Cherilyn threw his hand out of hers, "How about you go walk with them hoes then."

Kidd turned as I walked up, "Ray, see this is that bullshit I can't deal with."

I just walked up so, I asked, "What shit are you talking about?" He told me about the cheerleaders coming up to him. I couldn't help but laugh only because they were always arguing. "You better figure something out," is all I could really time.

He ran over to her to talk. Just like all the other times they were back on each kissing and forgetting what they were mad about.

The crazy thing is, when Kidd is jealous, he takes it all little too far and when it came to Cherilyn he was ready to kill.

This was one of the craziest things I had seen happen with them. We had just gotten to Kidd's house from practice. Cherilyn was on her way over, Kidd couldn't wait to see her. "Ray, I don't know what it is but having her body touch mine is the best feeling I have felt," is what he told me.

Laughing as I usually do I said, "yeah, I know, shit I need to feel her touch too."

Still laughing, Kidd grabbed me and push me on the way. "Aye don't talk about her like she just some girl."

Looking at him crazy as he still had his hands on me, "Talk about her like what?" I asked pushing him off me.

"You talking about her like she's not my girl or something and that shit ain't funny."

Shaking my head, "Come on Kidd, now you tripping, don't get mad over that, you really…"

He cut me off, "If it was any other girl alright cool but this ain't just another girl, this is my future wife."

In shock and once again lost for words all I could say was, "Wow, you really feel that deeply about her?"

She was just about to walk in when Kidd said, "Yeah she's my world Ray."

She walked in as he finished, she asked, "Who's world are you talking about?"

He got up and picked her up, "You baby, I was telling this fool how you were my world and nothing is better than having you in my arms." They kissed as he put her down.

She asked about practice, Kidd told her, "It was the same old, same old."

She said, "Oh babe, let me tell you about your so called friend Rob." Robert was one of our teammates and Kidd hung out with him from time to time. They were pretty cool with each-other but not close. Kidd stopped laughing and smiling.

"Tell me what?" he asked as he folded his arms. She looked at him eyes big, she could tell he was getting upset.

She reached in her bag, taking out her phone. "Promise me you're not going to get mad, Aiden."

Kidd looked at her sideways raising his eyebrow. "Why? Am I going to get mad if I read this?"

She then said, "Just promise me, you won't get mad." Kidd was getting impatient and started to reach for the phone. But Cherilyn would not give it to him unless he promised her.

So finally Kidd said, "Okay, I promise. She then handed him her phone, it was already on her and Rob's conversation, it read:

Rob: Hey pretty girl what you doing?

Cherilyn: Nothing just waiting for Kidd to get out of practice.

Rob: Oh you should come over my house and wait.

Cherilyn: No thanks, you know Kidd wouldn't like that.

Rob: I don't even know why you're with Kidd he don't love you.

Cherilyn: Why you say that?

Rob: He's always talking to girls at school you need a guy like me.

Cherilyn: You're going out with my friend though.

Rob: You know I always had my eyes on you,I don't ever really like Amy like that.

Cherilyn: What if Kidd finds out?

Rob :Kidd ain't gonna find out, Cherilyn I've been in love with you since day one.

Cherilyn: Yeah me coming over ain't going to happen and you can stop texting me now.

Rob: Don't act like that,Kidd can't love you like I can.

Cherilyn: Stop texting me before I tell Kidd.

Rob: Yeah whatever ain't nobody scared.

As Kidd was read each text, I could see fire building in his eyes. Kidd couldn't hold back anymore. "Fuck that put the word out, I 'm looking for his ass."

Cherilyn got up, "Babe, you promised me you were not going to get mad."

Kidd looked at me, "Find where that ni**a is!"

I got on the phone started calling everyone on the team to see if anybody knew where Rob was. Kidd called Rob's phone about two times and each time you could see his anger rising. Cherilyn was trying to calm Kidd down but nothing seemed to be working. Kidd was ready to fight and all friendships went out the window. The phone was ringing, it was Rob. Kidd picked up and put it on speaker. Rob said, "What up bro?"

Quick and fast Kidd respond, "Fuck that bro shit, when I see you it's on site, I'm knocking yo ass out."

Rob said, "You tripping Kidd, and plus you don't even know where I am."

Cherilyn asked Kidd to look at her Kidd looked to the left making no eye contact. He was pissed and it was showing. I looked down at my phone as I got a text from his girl. She said they were at the track meet. When I saw that, I put my phone on Kidd's lap. His eyes hit my phone and the fire in his eyes seemed to grow. He then said, "Yo bitch ass is at the track meet, don't worry I'm on the way!"

Cherilyn looked at me upset that I showed Kidd where Rob was at. "Ray, do something."

Looking at her in confusion I responded, "I am doing something, helping Kidd find this snake ass ni**a."

Cherilyn stood there and shook her head. She then asked, "Aiden, you love me?"

He looked up at her. "More than anything in this world."

She then said, "Then don't do this, he ain't worth shit."

Kidd looked at the phone. With Rob still on the phone he told him, "Ni**a if we ain't on the court don't say shit to me."

Rob said, "If we going to be boys then it's all the way…"

Before he could finish Kidd said, "Okay fuck it don't say shit to me at all. Don't look at me, and if you say anything to my girl I'm going to break your fucking jaw. Think I'm playing and it's over for your ass believe that." He then hung up the phone. Kidd was still mad. "Get up Ray let's go, he at the track field right?" I shook my head yeah.

Kidd was getting his keys off his head board, Cherilyn started to push him until he fell on the bed. She then jumped on him, "Kidd you promised!"

Pushing her off, "Yeah I know, but that was before I seen that shit." He was getting up from the bed.

"Babe just know you're going to hurt me way more than you can hurt him if you walk on that door."

Kidd looked at me, "That ni**a is nothing to us!"

He then texted Rob and said, "If you think of talking to me or my girl ever again, I'm going to beat the shit out you and you better not lay an eye on Cherilyn. Think this a game and I'll show you."

Rob text back and saying, "okay".

Cherilyn was still a little mad after everything was over. "Babe, you can't fight everyone."

Kidd said, "It wasn't because of you, it's the fact that, that ni**a is a snake."

Cherilyn pulled his head up, so he was looking at her. Kidd looked her in the eyes. "Okay maybe you're a park of it a little."

We all started to laugh, she looked at him and said, "See babe nothing should ever get you to that point because you got me and that's forever." She grabbed his hand and put it on her chest so he could feel her heartbeat. Kidd then put his head on her chest. She pulled him closer he was holding her tight.

"I hope, I never have to live without your heartbeat." He said as his head laid on her chest.

She pulled his face up and kissed him, "Don't worry babe, you won't have to."

After watching that, I had to get up and leave the room. Couldn't handle all that lovely-dove shit they had going on.

Thinking about it now, I know Kidd's life would be set if he had her heartbeat once more. To this day, Kidd doesn't talk to Rob. I remember the day after those text messages Kidd was still upset no matter how hard he tried to hide it. We had Rob for student council and Kidd walked right up to his desk fists balled up ready to punch him if he looked up. Rob kept his head and eyes down until Kidd went to sit down.

Class was starting and I asked, "What was that for?"

Kidd looked at me, anger still in his eyes, "I wanted to see if he thought I was playing when I said don't fucking look at me."

Putting my head down on the desk, "Kidd you need some help or something."

He laughed, "Nah, it comes with being in love."

As I put this letter back in the jar, I thought how crazy life is. And why is that we have to lose something before we realize just how special it is to us.

Chapter 22

I knew Kidd said he needed some time to think but it's been three weeks and still nobody has heard from him. Not only that but he hasn't been on any social media. I was starting to get worried, hoping wherever he was, he was safe.

I called him multiple times to check up on him but he didn't answer. After Kidd's life was put on pause and he was in a coma, he made sure he kept in touch with the people close to him. This is why I couldn't figure out why he wasn't talking to anyone. Knowing Cherilyn was in the club must have been a big deal for him. The fact that he didn't get a chance to speak to her, I know that must be pulling his heart strings. I heard my phone ring looked over and Jasmine's name popped up I pick up.

She said, "Babe, what you doing?"

I looked at the phone kinda weird and said, "Just at the shop, having a joint and clearing my head." Then I ask, "Why what's up?"

She asked me, "Have you talked to Kidd?"

I told her no and asked, "Why, what up?"

Her voice got low, "Because I think he needs you no more than ever."

I pulled my phone away from my face and looked at it, "What the hell are you talking about, baby?"

She told me, "Go look on his page."

I made a confused face, "On which page?"

She told me, "He's putting stuff on all of them."

I told her, "Thanks babe I'll go look at them when we get off the phone."

Right when I got off the phone I saw what she was talking about. Kidd was definitely in his feelings and letting the world know how he felt. The first post I read was on Insta. *Do you ever feel like your heart is too small for the things you love the most, and that's why we let them go.* I put my head down, because I knew Kidd was feeling alone and broken again. I looked on twitter and saw he tweeted. *I love the moon but I can never really have it, maybe that's why I fell in love with the girl I can never call mine.* I rubbed my head and smiled at the same time, I knew he was thinking about Cherilyn. He never told anyone but she's the real reason he started writing poetry and displaying his feelings more. I saw that he also wrote a poem on Facebook it read: *Knowing someone like you lives one this planet, brings a smile to my face every time. I sometimes whisper your name when the wind is blowing and hope you can hear my voice, I even carved our names in trees hoping you will see it and think about us one more time, I know somewhere hidden far away a couple will stumble across our one of kind love and it will be enough... - Love. Kidd - xo.*

He signed it like he did with all the letters. After reading all those different posts, I tried blowing his phone up texting and calling. He still didn't answer or respond back.

Sherilyn came to the shop out of nowhere yet again, tears in her eyes and everything. She had her sunshades on trying to hide the tears running down her cheek. So I got up and went over to her. "Hey Sherilyn, you okay?"

She turned to me, "Does it look like I'm okay Ray, this was probably your idea or something."

Putting my head back, "I just came over to see if you were okay but since you're feeling some type of way I'll leave you alone."

She grabbed me and pulled me back. "First, tell me if you know?"

Looking at her with so much confusion I said, "Nah I don't, that's why I came over here."

She stood up straight, trying to act like she wasn't just crying. Looking at her I asked, "Are you going to tell me what happened?"

She put her head up, "Aiden broke up with me."

My eyes got big and I put my hand over my mouth in disbelief, "What!? When did he do this?" I may be asked her too many question all at once. Before she could answer, she started crying again. She put her head on my shoulder, being nice I put my hand on her back and said, "Don't worry you'll be fine."

She looked at me, "Ray, do you really mean that?"

We were now looking each other in the eyes and I said, "Yeah, you're a beautiful girl."

Right when I said that smack is all I heard and my ear started to ring. I turned around and behind me stood my fiancé Jasmine. She started going off on me, "Oh so this is why you're always at the fucking shop, it ain't because of those fucking letters, it's to see this bitch? As she pointed at Sherilyn.

I was trying to tell her, it wasn't what she thought she saw but before I could say anything, Sherilyn and Jasmine were now getting into it.

"Who the fuck you calling a bitch?" Sherilyn asked Jasmine as she stood straight.

Jasmine looked her dead in her eyes, "The only bitch I'm looking at."

I got between both of them. "Yo chill!" I then tried to grab jasmine but she started to make her way for the door. So I went after her, pulling her back. "Babe, it wasn't like that?"

She pulled away from me. "Yeah, whatever Ray and I guess her head on your shoulder didn't mean shit either."

I put my hands up, "She was crying and all alone when I got up to see if she was okay."

She turned back and looked at me. "Why the fuck do you care if she's okay or not?!"

I looked at her side ways, "Because I'm a nice guy babe, that's why. Kidd broke up with her that's why she was crying and all emotional."

She stepped toward me, "Kidd really broke up with her?"

I said, "Yeah."

She put her hand over her mouth, "So why did he post all that stuff on social media and not call you?"

I couldn't really answer that because I still didn't know. Just shrugged my shoulders looking at her lost, "I wish I could tell you babe."

She then said, "Ray, you're his best friend why isn't he talking to you?"

I put my hands up, "I don't know babe, when it came to Cherilyn, he never let anyone know exactly how he felt about her. But we all knew that losing her hurt him to his heart."

She then came in closer to hug me, "I'm sorry, I overreacted in there."

I looked at her, "Overreacted? Babe you went of the deep end, smacking me and shit!"

We both started to laugh and she said, "I know, it's just with the wedding at the end of the year and you always being gone or here running the shop, I just let my mind get the best of me."

Picking her up, "Babe, ever since I looked in yours eyes, I saw my future and that will never change. You're my reason to see the next day." I looked into her beautiful eyes and we kissed.

I put her down and she said, "Oh, I see all Kidd's letters got my baby feeling like Romeo or something."

Laughing as she said that, "Nah babe, just want you to know how much you mean to me."

She was getting in the car, "Okay babe, sorry again and tell Sherilyn I'm sorry also but I still don't like her. I love you and will see you tonight."

I walked back towards the shop and yelled over my shoulder, "Where you about to go?"

She told me, "Going over to Kim's house to look at different themes for the wedding."

I shrugged my shoulders, "Okay babe, I'll see you tonight and don't let that woman pick everything, it's out wedding not hers."

She blew me a kiss as she drove off. I went back into the shop, to make sure Sherilyn was cool and to apologize for what happened. Right when I walked in the door, I saw her reading one of the letters, I ran over. I passed as a tear ran down her cheek and hit the paper. She looked up at me and said, "Kidd never loved me, his heart has been with someone else this whole time." I put my head down and looked at the letter she had in her hand.

`It read: *"My love is forever yours, I sometimes find myself listening to my heart and I hear your voice again…"* I had both of my hands on my head. It was now only a matter of time before Kidd knew I had his letters.

Chapter 23

The next morning instead of going to the shop, I went on a hike with Jasmine. We needed some time to talk and enjoy each other like we did in the past. When we got to the top of the hike trail. We found a good place to sit and looked at all the beauty the world had to offer us. As we sat down she asked me, "So what happened to Sherilyn?"

I told her, "She told me Kidd broke up with her because he feels like they're both searching for different things when it comes to love or something like that."

Jasmine looked in shock, "What made him say that and hurt that woman like that?"

I told her, "I don't know, we didn't get that far. When I got back to the table she had Kidd's letter in her hand and was reading it." I continued saying, "Before I could grab the letter, she had already read too much."

Before I could say anymore Jasmine told me, "Kidd never loved her, he's only been in love with one person and his heart knows who it's meant to beat for." The way Jasmine looked at me after was priceless. I imagine Kidd once looked at Cherilyn the same way. She then asked, "So what all did the letter say?"

Smiling at her I said, "Babe, that shouldn't matter, let's listen to some music and enjoy this beautiful view."

She then said, "We're still going to enjoy the view and music but it's like you're adding a love story alone with it." She smiled back and added, "Plus, I love hearing that Kidd was in love and all that because he doesn't show it that much these days." She was right, even though Kidd was smooth and a flirt he really didn't let anyone get as close as Cherilyn did with his heart. She then asked me, "So what did the letter she read say?"

Smiling a little bigger I told her, "It was the letter of their prom night."

Jasmine then asked, "So are you going to tell me about that night?"

I laughed, "Didn't know you wanted to know so bad babe." She smiled as I brought out the letter from my backpack.

Our prom night was everything I could have ever asked for, watching you glow so gracefully was breathtaking in every way. That yellow dress did something to me, made me feel like I was in a fairytale. It was the way your eyes sparked, every time you looked at me and your smile white as the heavens. You were everything I ever prayed for and even better than my dreams. I knew that corsage was more than lucky to be on a woman's wrist as beautiful as yours. Diamonds last forever was the theme and I knew this prom was made just for us because our love was made to live forever. That night was better than perfect, full moon out just to see you beauty. Heads turned when we walked through the door and I loved how you didn't care who was looking, as long as I had my eye on you. Close my eyes and still see you scared to put the rose on my tux because you thought you would stab me. Being without you, stabs at me each day and it feel like I'm slowly losing sunshine. That's why I relive the great moments we had it's my way of seeing the sunshine one more time. Just like diamonds lasting forever, I know our love is still going to be here forever. Someone, somewhere will stumble upon our love where we hide it and will cherish it like I should have, close to the heart...

P.S. My love is forever your, I sometimes find myself

listening to my heart beat and can hear your voice again...

Love. Kidd - xo

After reading it to Jasmine, she asked, "Was their night really that special?"

Smiling as I closed my eyes and answered, "It was more than special, it was perfect in every way imaginable."

I then began to tell her about the night. Kidd was coming up with so many ways of asking her. He kept asking me for ideas. So I ended up asking Cherilyn, "How would you want someone to ask you to prom?"

Smiled and said, "Why because I already told Aiden I wasn't going to no dance." I looked down real quick and she put a eyebrow up and said, "Is Kidd planning on asking me?"

I put my head down because Kidd told me not to say anything to her about prom. I told her, "Nah, Kidd hasn't told me anything, I'm just trying to come up with a way to ask this girl and not be totally lame."

She made this side look at me, she knew I was lying. Then asked, "So who's this special girl, Ray?" She was putting me on the spot with question after question. "What's her name? How did you meet her? Why haven't I never met this girl?"

Then I told her, "Yeah never mind, I'll figure something out."

She smiled and said, "Make sure Kidd knows not to ask me, because I don't want to have to tell him no."

I laughed as I walked out, "Okay, I'll make sure to let him know."

Jasmine was so into the story, she kept cutting me off asking, "What happened next?" If she wasn't my soon to be wife, it probably would have gotten on my nerves.

I continued telling her the story. Kidd was still trying to put together the perfect way to ask her. When I seen him, I told him, "You know Cherilyn doesn't even want to go to prom or any dance, right?"

He smiled at me, "Yeah I know, she would rather go to the movies or something else but it's more than prom. It's about creating timeless moments." I could tell he had thought about every way he wanted to ask her and somehow he put them all together.

It was amazing how fast Kidd made everything possible, it was call after call. With some help, Kidd put together one of the best scavenger hunts of all time. Everything he did was over the top. We drove over to Cherilyn's house, he put the hazard lights on and ran to her door and came back. He started with a note, it read: *Love is a crazy ride and I'm glad you stayed for the scary parts.*" She looked down and there was a little train track leading to her car. She followed it to her car and balloons were all around. She saw the next clue on one of the balloons. The note attached read: "*I tried to catch butterflies, so you could see the beauty you create inside my heart*" When she opened the door, the balloons went straight into the sky and there was a jar in the driver seat. Butterflies filled the jar. She started to tear up when she opened the jar and all the butterflies flew into the sky as if they were catching the balloons. She pulled out the note in the jar it read: *When it's hard to sleep or I feel alone again, I think of you and there's only one place I can go where I know I can still stare into those eyes that captured me at first sight.*"

She sat in the car for a while calling her friends, asking for help. She called me. "Ray, I know you're in on this."

I tried to act like I had no clue what she was talking about. I answered back, "In on what?"

She giggled a little, "Ray you can't lie for shit but are you in on this cute-ass scavenger hunt or whatever Kidd is making me do."

I said, "Oh that's what Kidd had planned. Well I don't know what he wants you to do or where he wants you to go."

She said, "Okay then help me, where would this place be?" She then read the note to me.

I told her, "I don't know, you're supposed to know Kidd better than anyone." Right before she could say anything I said, "I guess you're going to have to find out or give up on Kidd. I mean the scavenger hunt."

She laughed after I said that and said, "Ray, I will never give up on Kidd and I'm not starting now," then hung up on me.

I remember looking at Kidd right after she hung up and told him, "I don't think she's going to get it, bro."

Kidd smiled at me, "Ray you're always worrying about the wrong things, she hung up on you because she realized which spot I was hinting at."

Kidd always had hope when it came to her. It turns out Kidd was right, she ended up at the view overlooking the city, this was the spot Kidd was talking about. She looked around for a note or a sign. What she thought to be trash, was actually chocolate kisses leading her to another note that read: *You are more than my queen, you're my reason to live and I would kiss the ground you walk on so that you never forget it.*" She then flipped the note around looking for what was next. There was one kiss that was bigger than the rest, she spun it and on the inside wrapper read: *When we can't decide on what to eat, this is always the best resort.*" Thinking about what the note said, she sat on the hood of her car and thought about it for a little then headed to the next spot.

She knew exactly where to go. She pulled up to the pizza place where they go all the time when they fight over what to eat. She walked in and the pizza guy asked, "Pick up?"

She looked around, "Yeah, I guess so."

He asked, "Name?"

She told him, "Cherilyn or it might be under Aiden Brewing."

He then said, "Oh yeah, your order had been waiting," he pulled out a box of pizza. He told her, "Make sure it's the right pizza."

She opened the pizza. It was pepperoni pizza in a shape of a heart, on the inside of the box read, "*I know sometimes you think I'm cheesy, but that's just because I love you more than Mikey loves pizza.*" She laughed after reading that, she knew Aiden loved the Ninja Turtles. The pizza guy then gave her a little bag and said, "He told me if you laughed or smiled to give you this."

She then asked, "What if I didn't laugh or smile?"

He told her, "I guess we will never know," as he laughed.

She then opened the little bag he gave her. It was some banana pudding and a lock attached to the note. She didn't want to pull the lock because it would rip the note. The only way was to find the key. So she's there looking around for what look like a key. The pizza guy then asked, "What are you looking for?"

She told him, "A key to open this lock."

He then said, "Maybe all the clues come together or something."

She started to look at all the other things she had gotten. As she was going over everything from the hunt. She got the jar from the first note and beneath the lid of the jar was a key tapped inside. She unlocked the lock and read the note, "*Even when those butterflies left, you still knew how to get the lock off my heart, and love is never in a rush but always right on time, so you can find me in the same place I called you mine at.*"

After reading the note she was lost for words. The only place she could think of was Kidd's house. That was the first time he laid his eyes on her and that was when he told her, "I'm going to make you mine, I promise you that." She remembered that night and headed straight to Aiden's house. When she got there Mom and the family were excited to see her. She asked, "Where's Aiden at?"

Mia told her, "He's in his room, I think he's waiting for you." Cherilyn dashed into his room. When she opened the door and turned on the light. There was blue paper hanging down and gift cards to Victoria Secret attached to them. On one of the gift cards, there was a note attached that read: *"I hope showering you with gifts made up for me not being here and I pray that masterpiece of a smile stays on that beautiful soul I fell in love with. There's this place I go when being around you is all I want to do."* She sat there with Mia thinking of places where Kidd could be. After a couple minutes Little Jay comes in the room and asked her, "Did you check your room?"

Cherilyn and Mia looked at each other then said, "Why would I look there when I started there?"

Mia turned her head to the side and said, "Probably because if I would have set it up. I would know that's the last place you would look and the first place you would go if you go frustrated and gave up." His brother and sister knew he was at her house. She headed to her house with Mia riding in the passenger seat. Those two really got close since Cherilyn was always at the house waiting for Kidd. Plus Mia always wanted a big sister to bond with, which she found in Cherilyn. They got to her house and Cherilyn's mom walks out hands behind her back.

Cherilyn asked her mom, "What do you have behind your back?"

Her mom slowly turned her hands around with a note in one hand and a rose in the other. Her mom then told her, "You can only pick one but you cannot have both."

Cherilyn stood there complaining on which one to choose. She ended up picking the rose, her mother then read a note out of her pocket and read: *"If she takes the rose tell her, just as the rose blossomed and became beautiful god made her and each time another rose blossoms it's to reminded the world that there is still beauty and a reason to smile, each petal tells the story of how I fell for you."* She open the door and seen rose petals leading up the stairs into her room. Opening the door she seen rose petals in a shape of a heart on the bed, with pictures from each moment they had on the scavenger hunt she went on. Looking for Kidd she turn around and he was on one knee with a promise ring. He said, "I know this ain't a glass slipper but hopefully you'll still be my Cinderella and go to prom with me?" Tears coming down her eyes, she tackle Kidd on the ground kissing him and saying yes at the same time.

Jasmine was so into the story, wanting to know what happened next. We started to make out way back to the car. She asked, "I thought Cherilyn didn't want to go to prom?"

Laughing as I said, "Yeah she didn't. But Kidd convinced her to go." I began to tell her how Kidd persuaded her to go to prom. He said "I want to experience everything life has to offer us, so let's have a night we will never forget."

She pulled him in and said, "Baby I will never forget you or us."

Kidd then told her, "Promise me in every lifetime, you will find me and convince me that we are meant to be."

She looked into his eyes, "In every lifetime I will search the world for your heart beat."

Kidd picked her up and they kissed he said, "Good because there's only two times I need you in this lifetime and that's now and forever."

Jasmine eyes were getting watery. She then asked me, "So that made her agree to go to prom?"

Shaking my head yes. On the path back down, we see a trail that broke off and lead to this beautiful view of the city. We got there and I thought Jasmine was done with Kidd and Cherilyn's past but she wanted to know more about the prom night and everything else. She then asked me, "So what happen on their prom night?"

As we got to the car we decided to sit on the hood and watch the clouds. I told her, "Their night was simple but amazing at the same time if that makes sense."

She looked at me sideways, squinting her eyes, "How could that be when Aiden went all out like that?" She then asked me, "Are you going to tell me about the night or what?"

Smiling as I put my head down, "Yeah babe, don't rush me."

She smiled then said, "Babe you know how I get, when I want to know something."

Looking at her, "Yeah I know." I proceed to tell her about their night at prom.

Kidd went all out to make sure the night was perfect. He had a fly rental car to pick her up in. He also got a table at one of the best romantic places in the city to have dinner. How he got a table there still amazes me. Kidd had everything set and planned for the night, it was time for him to get ready. I thought it was so crazy that, they both didn't know what the other one was wearing. Kidd had a black tux, white dress shirt underneath, a yellow vest and yellow bowtie around the neck. Kidd was waiting to show me what shoes he had for the night, I couldn't wait to see what he was going to put on. He starts to pull down this black box, trying to read the label on the box but couldn't make it out. Opened the box and my mouth dropped, he had one of the hardest shoes you could get your hands on. They were black with a icy button, just a beauty to look at if you were a sneakerhead.

Getting caught up talking about the shoes, Jasmine said, "Ray, I don't care about no fucking shoes."

I looked at her, "Oh, yeah back to the story." I responded.

Nobody was ready to see Cherilyn walk through the door looking the way she did. Kidd wanted to pick her up but her mom just brought her to the house, so both families could see them together. The doorbell rang and Mia sprinted to answer the door. She opened the door Cherilyn's mother and little brother walked in and then turned back. Mom screamed out, "Girl if you don't bring yo ass in here!" She walked through the door. Right then, I knew what Kidd meant when he said she can freeze time. Her right her leg hit the door first, then her beautiful body followed. It was as if she floated into the room with angel's wings or something. We were all blown away, we knew she was beautiful but she was way more than that, that night. Silent for a minute Cherilyn then said, "Do I really look that bad? Somebody say something."

Me thinking out loud, I said, "Beautiful would be a understatement to what you are."

Mia turned and looked up at me with a crazy look and Mom said, "Ray you ain't never lie."

I then yelled out, "Kidd, you better come out and see this beauty you get to call your date!"

Kidd walked out of his room, eyes locked on her and he was speechless. It was obvious that he was lost for words, I then said to Mom, "I guess she does more than just freeze time but she can freeze him too." She laughed.

Kidd then said, "No, Ray that's not it."

Looking at him I asked, "Then what is it?"

Kidd paused and looked at her, "Something this beautiful, deserves the whole world to freeze and look this way."

Cherilyn smiled and said, "So does that mean your going to come over here and kiss me?"

Kidd looked at me, then right back to her, "I'm going to do more than kiss you but love you until my heart no longer beats." He then grabbed her and they kissed, he stepped back, "Damn, I'm going to have to do more than just kiss you now." He then laughed.

Mom looked at Cherilyn's mom and said, "Hey, we don't need to know everything!"

Kidd smiled, kissed Cherilyn once more, "My bad, I thought we were keeping it real." Laughing as he tapped me on the chest. Before I could say anything, cameras came out and it was picture time for the cutest couple I've ever seen. These two could not make a serious face for the pictures. They kept putting tongues out, making all these different funny faces. Even though both mother's wanted a good picture, knowing them two it wasn't going to happen because it was their night. Watching them enjoying each other, was the best because I could see how they brought nothing but happiness into each other's heart. Right before they left, Kidd pulled me to the side and said, "Who would have known that, the happiness I was looking for would be her two arms and that beautiful smile."

Looking at him as he stared at her I responded, "Yeah, I know."

He then said, "She the closest thing to perfect in this world."

I told him, "Aiden, I'm more than happy for you bro, just don't find a way to fuck it up."

He laughed and said, "When the game is on the line, who do you want to have the ball?" Before I could answer he said, "Kidd that's who!" as he tapped his chest.

I laughed and said, "Yeah, whatever, just make sure you have a great night man."

Walking towards her, he looked back at me and said, "Look at her, the night is already great!" That was his first time looking away from Cherilyn since she walked in the house. They walked out the door and to the car.

I remember Mom looking at me and saying, "This is the happiest I've seen Aiden."

I looked at him, smiling as he got in the car, I said, "I know, that's what love does to you."

We got back to the car and Jasmine wanted to know the rest of the story. She looked at me right before I put the car in start, "So that's it? What happen at prom?"

Making this funny look at her I said, "Babe I didn't go to prom with them."

She pushed my head and said, "Yeah, I know that dummy and I also know Kidd is your best friend, which means I know he told you about the night."

Smiling and shaking my head I said, "Yeah, you right." Before I told her what happen I asked, "Why is it that you want to know all this about Kidd?"

She made her upset face at me and answered with, "You know I love that mushy stuff and to know Aiden was doing all that intrigues me. It's a side no one gets to see." Then with an attitude she said, "You know jealousy doesn't look good on you right?"

I took a deep breath, "Okay, babe whatever and ain't nobody jealous." Still sitting in the car I began telling her about the night at prom.

So they went out to eat first and Cherilyn was in shock that Kidd took her to this top rated restaurant. The candle lighting was perfect and he told me her dress, the light jazz music in the background made him want to propose to her right there. They tried all the desserts, or just the ones they thought they would like. After that they went to the dance. When they hit the door heads turned from every side, it was like Will and Jada walked in or Bee and Jay. Everyone was blown away to see them so flawless. Her black and gold complexion, matched him the best way imaginable. People at prom told me, when they walked in, it was easy to see they were made for each other. Crazy thing about their prom was they didn't even stay the whole time. They took pictures and had one slow dance then left.

Jasmine looked at me, "So,what did they do after, they left?" with her hands out, waiting for me to answer.

I then told her, "I would tell you, if you would stop cutting me off."

She smacked her lips and said, "Whatever, Ray just finish the story!"

So I went on telling her what happen next. Cherilyn didn't really want to do anything big. The New Fast and Furious movie was premiering at the square, which is this pretty wealthy part of town. Kidd had the hook up and had it set up, where they came in and had first pick of sits.

When they got to the Square, Cherilyn asked, "What are we doing here?"

Kidd told her, "Don't worry baby, just trust me." They went to the movies. It was good he did that for her because she loved when it was just them two. Even though it was just the movies.

She told him, "I know you went all out for this night to be special but you know every time I'm in your arms is special enough for me."

He smiled so big, her saying that to him was everything he needed to hear. They sat there and watched the premier of the new Fast movie. He told me the movie was so dope and had him feeling like he was it the movie afterwards. When they were on their way home, Kidd pulled up to this guy who had his window down. They looked at each other, Kidd throw his hands up and when the light turned green took off. Cherilyn was laying back in the passenger seat, sleeping. When she woke up, she almost lost it because Kidd was now pushing 120 mph on the freeway. She screamed and smacked him, he yelled out, "What the hell are you doing?"

She yelled back, "What am I doing? No, what the fuck are you doing trying to kill us?"

They were getting off the freeway Kidd said, "You right baby, I was tripping thinking I'm in the movie or some shit."

She then said, "Yeah, yo ass is going to kill one of us if you keep playing so much."

Kidd laughed, "I'll make sure just to kill my side."

Cherilyn looked at him and rolled her eyes, "Me without you, is death already."

They then came to a red light. Kidd told me he looked at her, the red light hit her cheek and everything he ever wanted was right next to him.

Chapter 24

We pulled up to the house, "Babe, is that how the night ended for them?"

Looking at her I reposed, "No, babe that's not all that happen." I then told her, "I know you want to know so relax and I'll tell you all the good parts." Continued to tell her the night. After Kidd told me how the red light made him feel.

He told her, "Babe let's go to the view, I don't want this night to end just yet."

She looked at him, "Aiden as long as I'm with you, we can go anywhere."

They made their way up to the view. Drove up there and parked in the dirt, the view of the city lights was magical in every way. They sat up there staring at the city, telling each other stories they never told anyone else. Music played in the background, Kidd grabbed her hand, "Baby no matter what happens in this life, my heart and soul will always have your name engraved in it."

She looked him in the eyes, "Aiden your my everything and I know we'll be together to the end, I feel it in my soul."

Kidd pulled her in closer and they began to kiss but this wasn't just a regular kiss, but more like their hearts were doing all the kissing. Soon after that, they got in the back seat of the car.

Jasmine was all ears and full attention to each word that came out about that damn night. She grabbed me, eyes big and wide then asked, "So did they get it on, in the back seat?"

I put my head down, "Babe, that's Kidd's business, it's not my place to talk about it."

She paused then said, "Business? Ray, really your reading all his love letters that he wrote to a woman who has his heart and you're going to give me that business bullshit."

She was right, I was already in all Kidd's personal business with reading the letters and what not. So I told her, "Yeah, they got it on in the backseat of the car, Kidd had some blankets he left in the back for their picnic he was planning." When they were done, they stayed in the car looking out the foggy windows at the moon holding one another.

Kidd told me, "When she laid on my chest and I looked up at the stars, it was like our love story was being told to the Gods." The crazy thing is I could see him speaking those words to me today.

After the story Jasmine was in their emotions, I told her, "Kidd was so in love and he thought everything out when he did anything for her."

We started walking into the house, Jasmine stopped, grabbed me then asked, "So, what happen to Aiden and Cherilyn?" Putting her eyebrow up.

Shaking my head I reasoned, "Babe, I don't think you want to know that."

She squinted her eyes, "Why, you say that Ray?"

Putting my head down once more I said, "Because it's sad and I remember how depressed he was not being with her no more."

Right before Jasmine could say anything back, my phone rang. I looked down at my phone and Kidd's name popped up. Showing her the phone I said, "Speaking of Mr. Romantic himself."

Chapter 25

When I answered he said, "Boy, what the hell are you doing?"

I replied, "Just getting to the house to spend a day with my wife to be. What you doing?"

He told me, "don't worry about what I'm doing Ray, only worry about what you're doing." he then laughed.

Jasmine looked at me and said, "ask him where he is?"

So I did, "Kidd where the hell are you?"

He then responded, "I'm outside, you should let me in because it's hot as shit out here."

Jasmine then ran to the door to let him in. Kidd stood there, "So, I'm guessing you guys missed me?" as he smiled.

Jasmine gave him a big hug, I then came over and we shook hands and he pulled me in close. It felt like I hadn't seen him in forever. We sat down in the living room, lit a joint and started talking about what happen and why he left. Looking at him taking a puff I asked, "So, where did you go?"

He blow a smoke ring out, "I went away, needed to clear my head and be alone." He then apologized for leaving without a word. "That's my bad Ray, I just needed to find me again."

I thought it was interesting he said again. In shock of what he just said Jasmine asked, "Why did you say again? Is it because of Cherilyn?" I turned and looked at her because I couldn't believe she asked him that. I should have known she would ask about her when she saw him. Especially, after all the stories of them two together and how their love story was amazing.

Kidd put his head down, with a big smile on his face. He then answered. "Yeah, I never thought she would appear in my life ever again." He put his head up and looked at us, "It's crazy because my body feels so great and my heart beats even harder hearing him name."

I told him, "Both of you guys were young, when you met."

Jasmine then said, "Yeah, maybe you two just needed, to grow and the older versions of you guys are better for each other."

Looking at him thinking of her, it was easy to see she still had his heart. The feeling her name brings to Kidd's emotions is incredible. He never could stop smiling when she was on his mind and it was a great thing to watch. He wasn't saying anything back to us, either he was stoned or in deep thought. I then yelled out, "Kidd!"

He looked at me, "What's up Ray?"

I then asked, "Did you hear anything we said?"

Kidd said, "Yeah I heard you .But you know some dreams don't come true."

Jasmine looked at him with one of her eyebrow raised and said, "What does that mean?"

Kidd turned his head to look her in the eyes, "Cherilyn doesn't want me, she never did." Before I could say anything, he went on to say, "It's okay I just pray I was special part of her memories."

We both sat there, looking at him in lost for words and it total shock us. I told him, "Bro y'all were just young." The crazy part of all, was he still had a smile on his face. So I asked him, "If you not going to have hope, what's with the smile?"

He giggled, shaking his head and looked at me, "I'm smiling because I remember what it's like to feels like to never want to let her leave my arms, and at least now I know she's okay and not hurt or anything like that."

Jasmine started tearing up and getting all dramatic, "Kidd you really loved her, didn't you?"

Kidd smiled, a tear forming in his eye, "Yeah, with everything in my body and I feel like she's the last one I will ever love."

Shaking my head as that sentence left his mouth, I pulled Jasmine in close to me and whispered, "I wonder if you'll be the last one I love."

Kidd got up, "This is why I can't come over here." Laughing a little as he pulled his hair back.

After I finished kissing Jasmine, I asked, "What the hell are you talking about?"

Kidd made this smirk, "I love y'all being in love and all that but it reminds me of what I should of had."

Before he could walk out the door, I ran over and grabbed him, "Bro love is forever and I know somewhere hidden, behind the darkness, is where you and Cherilyn left that one of kind love."

He turned the doorknob, "Yeah yeah Ray, I thought I was the hopeless romantic?" He shook my hand and walked out the door.

I stood there watching him walk to the car with his head in the sky. Jasmine pushed me, "Go after him, he needs you right now." She paused, "Was that something he wrote in one of those notes?" She then waved her hand, "Never mind that, go make sure Kidd is okay."

I turned put my head down and went outside. Before he could get into his car, I yelled out, "Kidd, what's the real reason you came by the house?"

He turned and looked at me. As he was putting his foot in the car door, he said, "I just wanted to remember what true love looked like and I see it in your eyes, every time you look at Jasmine."

Running my hands across my face, I asked, "Why do you say that?"

He was now sitting in the car, rolling the window down. I leaned onto the window, waiting for a response. He put the car in drive, looked at me and said, "That's how I use to look at Cherilyn, with no worries of tomorrow, I knew nothing could hurt with her by my side and that's what I see when I watch you and Jasmine." He bit his lip put, his dead down and rolled up the window, then drove off. He left and even though he didn't say much, I feel like he said everything he needed to say. Came into the house, Jasmine looking at me waiting for me to say something to her.

She asked, "What happen?" I told her what Kidd said and how he left right after. She was confused, "Why does Kidd do shit like that?"

Putting my head down, "It's too painful for him and then feels alone all over again."

She looked at me confused all over again and asked, "What is too painful for him?"

Sat down and told her, "He hurts when he watches couples in love."

She was in total shock and after that brief second of silence, she said, "How the hell does Kidd not like the meaning of love? When he was the one who wrote a book on why we need love as humans." She rubbed her hand then continued saying, "Kidd does everything and puts love dead in the middle of what he does. So what the hell do you mean he doesn't like love?"

Putting both of my hands over my eyes, I responded saying, "No,it hurts him to watch others being in love because it reminds him of what he lost or could have had."

She sat down next to me before she could ask me, I said, "Kidd told me when we were in college, that every time he saw a couple in love, it reminded him of what he had with Cherilyn and nothing about the outside world mattered."

Jasmine laid her head on my shoulder, "I hope Kidd finds love, his to good of a guy not to have anyone."

I smiled, kissed her on the forehead, "You're right babe, Aiden is too good of a guy not to have a lover by his side."

Chapter 26

After a couple of days or so, I decided to take Jasmine to the shop so we could smoke and relax. I was thinking about Kidd and hoping he was okay. I texted him, "What up bro?" Ten minutes went by and no response. I was guessing he was out doing something and was to busy.

Jasmine watched me check my phone more than once, before she said, "Babe, Kidd is okay just relax."

Looking at her, "You're probably right, I'm just overthinking."

We're at the shop sitting in our usual table, in the back. Jasmine asked, "So I know how perfect Kidd and Cherilyn relationship was but I don't know why it came to an end?"

Putting my head on the table, I looked at my bag. Her eyes went to my bag also, "You, still have his letters don't you?"

I put my head up and looked at the door, then put my eyes on her, and answered. "Yeah, I still have them." I then reached in my bag to grab the jar.

She seen all the letters and asked, "How many did he write to her?"

As I pulled one of the letters out I said, "I don't know exactly how many but I know each letter he wrote, he put his heart on the page."

I opened the letter and started to read it to Jasmine.

Today, I saw a shooting star and thought of you. Then remembered that today marks the day I made the biggest mistake of my life. You were always the reason the sun came up the next morning. Putting my future ahead of the life we wanted to build, was the dumbest thing I could have done in this life. You were always the one I wanted to build this life with, not having you makes all this success pointless. After everything that has happen to me, from watching people die to seeing death in the face, losing you is still the hardest thing to live with. Still can't believe I put my ego and image before the woman who gave me the reason to love. I close my eyes and can see you smiling, sometimes when I'm having a drink I can hear your voice. Cherilyn, I love you more than anything in this world our souls become one. It hurts knowing I will never have that part of me again, didn't know what I said and meant losing you...

Love. Kidd - xo

I began to tell her the story behind the letter we just read. The day that define everything and what made Kidd and Cherilyn no more. The summer was about to start, so that meant school was coming to an end. Kidd and Cherilyn were fighting more than often, over every little thing. Our coach was almost forcing Kidd to break up with Cherilyn and dedicated each minute in the gym. It was coming up on our senior year and Kidd was now raked in the top twenty-five on the west coast. Being that he was always in the gym, his time was limited with Cherilyn. They still seen each other but it was only for a couple of minutes at a time and when they seen each other Kidd was tired and wanted to sleep. Not being able to be with him was making her depressed and insecure, she felt like it was her and that's why Kidd didn't want to be around her. They went from seeing and hanging out with each other every day to seeing one another for a couple minutes at a time. I remember the night they broke up I called Kidd and asked. "What are you doing when you get home from the gym?"

Kidd told me, "Going to change then head back out to the gym on the south side, gotta put this work in."

Looking at the phone I asked, "Aren't you supposed to be going to the movies with Cherilyn tonight?"

I could tell by his voice he felt like he was making a hard decision. He looked at the phone and said, "I forgot I told her we could go out tonight."

I asked, "So what are you going to do? Go to the movies or go to the gym?"

Kidd paused for a minute, "Man she's going to understand this is my life, you feel me Ray?"

Didn't really know what to say back to that. This was the dream, to be the best but she was the best for him in every way. I had to tell him the truth, so I said. "Kidd, I watch you with her and all I see is happiness in your eyes and I say that because you need to understand you're pushing her away."

Kidd didn't really like to hear when he was doing something wrong. He just told me, "Ray, don't worry about it she'll be alright." Took a step then said, "This is my life, shit we can go to the movies tomorrow if she really wants to see a damn movie." After getting off the phone he grabbed his backpack and headed to the door.

She just pulled up to his house, as he was walking out the door. Getting out of her car she asked him, "Where are you going? And why aren't you dressed?"

Kidd told her, "Going to the gym to put this work in." As he was walking to his car.

She got an attitude and could hear it in her voice, "You're always at the fucking gym Aiden!"

Kidd was putting his bag in the back of the car, "why you tripping?"

She then went off on him! Everything she was holding in came out that night. She started with, "I'm tripping but I can't get no fucking time with my boyfriend, the only time I get to see you is when I bring you food to the gym and even then you barely talk to me, sometimes I can't even get a kiss. But you say you love me? Yeah right, save that shit for your groupies hoes Kidd!"

That set Kidd off and sometimes Kidd doesn't know when far is too far he says "What the fuck are you talking about? I told you from day one there was only one thing I love and that's playing ball. This is going to get me and my mom's a better life." Her eyes quickly filled up with tears, that ran down her face to the floor. Kidd continued to let his words do all the abuse, "You're a fucking bug, always trying to be up under me and shit. Don't you understand I have a life, you know what, it's time for us to take a break."

Tears coming down her face one after another she asked, "So you're breaking up with me?"

He stepped back, "No, not breaking up. Just taking a break."

She tried to pull him in but he moved her hands to the side. She was not looking at him eyes red and watery, "You're really just going to let me go like this?"

Kidd put his hands together, "I'm not letting you go, we just need to see where we're going without each other." Kidd turned and got in the car, pulled off headed to the gym.

That night she went over her best friend's house and cried for hours. Angel was her best friend's name. She called mad at me, asking why Kidd said all this stuff to Cherilyn. I wasn't with him so I didn't know what was said or anything. "What are you talking about? What happen?" is what I asked.

She told me what happen between Kidd and Cherilyn that night. Couldn't believe what was being told to me. Couldn't think of any reason why Kidd would ever act like that. Especially when it came to Cherilyn. I told them, "I'll talk to Kidd when I see him and see where his head is." It was the best thing I could think of after I heard what Kidd said to her.

The next day I seen Kidd at school, "Yo, what the fuck is wrong with you!" I asked as I pushed him into the wall.

He turned fixed his backpack and shirt, "Nothing what the fuck is wrong with you, running up on me like you trying to get yo ass whooped or something." He popped his knuckles, "I should have just knocked yo ass out, for putting your hands on me."

Right when he said I knew he was upset. Even if he tried to put on that fake ass smile bullshit he does. Looking at him sideways I said, "What's up with you breaking up with Cherilyn like you don't have nothing beneath your chest for her?"

He started to walk to class, "It doesn't matter what I got beneath my chest or who it beats for. Why you always in my business and shit."

Putting my head down as I went to pull him back, "It matters because all night I had to hear, how you went off on Cherilyn and she's been crying ever since. Bro you just broke that girl's heart and you act like she doesn't matter." I was looking at him with so much disappointed.

Kidd put his hands on his head, "Yeah, I know but so what if I took it a little too far." He tried to justify why he did and said what he did, "Ray, she knows this is my life, you know I only love ball and that's it."

Even if he was right, which he wasn't I knew Kidd was in love with Cherilyn. I watched him try to act like it was bothering him. I ended up telling him, "I know you love ball and everything but do you not see what Cherilyn does to you?"

He quickly responded, "Yeah, she gives me a fucking headache twenty-four seven."

Shaking my head, "Bro I never seen you as happy as you are when your with Cherilyn. Kidd rather you like it or not I'm going to keep it real with you and you know your wrong for pushing that perfect girl way."

We were now walking into class and Kidd grinned, "Ray, don't worry about what the fuck I'm doing okay."

Still shaking my head, "Whatever you say, Kidd."

Until this day I knew, I could have tried a little harder. Kidd was so hard headed and thought he knew what was best.

Chapter 27

They could have still gotten back together after their break was over. But Kidd's ego and pride got in the way once again. After a couple of days without seeing her, Kidd was now feeling empty without her. Each day not being with her was now driving him crazy, he always told me, "I wonder what Cherilyn is doing?"

I gave him the same answer. "Call her and find out."

He would say, "Nah, she probably not worried about me or if she is, I know she's still pissed off at me." Couldn't believe Kidd talked himself out of talking to her every day. The weekend was among us and Kidd told me, "Yo, I think I'm going to get back with Cherilyn."

This was the best thing Kidd could have told me. We hung out with her so much I was starting to miss her ass my damn self but I never told that to Kidd. I smiled and asked, "When do you plan on doing this?"

Kidd told me, "After the festival."

We were going to this big Italian festival that night. It was the biggest festival to come through the city. We were going up to the festival with all out boys which was Kidd, Money, Pop, Tay and I .We knew for sure we would know a lot of people there, especially Kidd. People knew he wasn't with Cherilyn no more. When we got there, girls were just throwing themselves at Kidd. Each girl that came up to him made us turn our heads and looked them up and down.

I then said, "Yo, we gotta be doing something wrong."

They laughed and Tay said,"I don't know, what it is but this ni**a Kidd is getting all the girls."

Pop joined in, "I know shit, let me get one to."

We laughed again, Kidd smiled and said, "Y'all better start talking to these pretty ass girls here."

Pop said, "We would but we don't know which one to pick, you got all of them already."

Kidd laughed again, "Nah, I don't. Cherilyn is the only one I need."

Everyone stopped walking for a second and looked at each other Tay asked us, "Did this ni**a just say he only needs Cherilyn?"

I answered, "Yeah, that's what I heard."

We were all laughing. Money stopped laughing and said, "Oh Kidd, I forgot to tell you."

Kidd turned back and looked at him, "Forgot to tell me what?"

We all sat down at the food spot they had set up at the festival. Money said, "I forgot to tell you how Cherilyn came into class after you broke up with her." Kidd wasn't sitting yet and when he sat down, Money stood up acting out what happen. He said, "So you know I have her for home period in the morning right?"

We all wanted to know what happen so together we said, "Yeah we know get to the good shit."

Kidd didn't say anything stayed silent until the story was over. Money went on saying. "Okay, so me and Michael were chilling in class and we were talking about y'all breaking up."

Kidd made this confused face and asked, "How did y'all even know, we broke up?"

Money looked at him sideways, "Really Kidd, everyone knew y'all broke up that night."

Kidd shook his head, "Yeah, you right."

I said, "Continue with the story."

Money laughed, "Okay, so we're talking about the breakup. What he heard and what I heard, trying to figure out if it was true or not because I refused to believe y'all two broke up. The door opened and Cherilyn comes walking in and it was like she got hit by a damn truck or something."

Kidd cut him off, "Aye, don't be talking bout my girl like that."

Money looked at him eyes big, "Nah, you didn't see her Kidd, she was beat. Her hair was all messed up, she had your red hoodie and grey sweatpants on. I never seen her look like that and I don't ever want to see her like that again."

Kidd asked "What else happened besides how she looked?"

Money finished, "Oh yeah, so when I seen her I said out loud got damn what happen to you?' she put her head up tears came down her face and she said, "Aiden broke up with me." I had to put my head down because I didn't want to laugh or anything."

I shook my head as I looked at Kidd, "Told you, you fucked up."

He put his head down in shame, "Yeah, I know but I'm going to make it right don't trip."

We all told him, "Yeah, you better."

Pop grabbed Kidd and told him, "She's the best thing to happen to you for real for real don't fuck it up if you get her back."

Kidd gives him and head nod and told us, "Y'all my boys if I even think of doing some dumb shit like this again, I give all you guys' permission to whip my ass."

We paused looked at each other and said, "Hell yeah."

It's crazy how life works out, right before we started to walk out. Kidd stopped to say goodbye to this girl and her friends from school. We counted to walk out. Pop stopped us and pointed, "Yo, I know I ain't tripping but is that Cherilyn over there?"

We all stopped turned and looked, "Yeah, I think that is." I answered back.

Tay asked, "Yo, who is she with?"

Money said, "It looks like her girls from school but I don't know who them ni**as talking to them is."

Pop turned and looked at us, "Make sure Aiden don't see this shit."

We all looked back as Kidd, was walking up to us. When he got to us we all had our eyes big, he asked, "Okay, one of you better tell me what the fuck is going on?"

Tay looked to the right where Cherilyn was, Kidd turned to look. His face dropped, the smile ran off his face faster than it could appear. I asked, "Kidd, you good?"

He turned to us straight face, "Don't trip I'm fine but let's get this shit poppin."

I put my hands on my face because the way he said that, I knew it wasn't going to be anything good. He turned around and got his phone out. We just followed, Money asked "Kidd, I don't like that look you got in your eyes, what's on your mind? Come on talk to me."

He looked back then looked at Cherilyn once again, "Don't trip two can play this game."

Every pretty girl that we walked passed Kidd had to talk to her and get her number, it was like he had something to prove. I pulled Tay and Pop to the side, "Yo, we better get Kidd before he throws the best thing that happen to him away."

Tay laughed at me, "Look at how happy Kidd is, he'll be alright just cool it Ray and come help us with all these girls."

Pop added, "Yeah, Kidd is fine plus he knows what's best him."

We walked back over to where Kidd was and he was talking to another girl, who just happens to have four other friends with her. Jasmine, smiled big when I said that she cut me off. "Was that the night we first met?"

I looked at her, "Yes, it was." Who would have known that a couple years later we would meet again in her best friends Tiffany's room. I continued to tell her the story. "Later, that night it seemed like everyone knew we were all with you girls. It wasn't a good look for Kidd because Cherilyn found out and she was pissed off. They decide not to talk to each other and soon that break turned into a break up. I still kick myself in the ass every day knowing that I'm happy with you, my baby and the person that got me her, lost his true love the same night."

Jasmine mouth dropped, "The night we first met in high school, is the same night Kidd lost Cherilyn?" It was just not hitting her how everything worked out.

Smiling as I put my head down and said, "Yup, the same night I fell for you, is the same night Kidd gave up on love." I got up and told her, "I'll meet you at the house tonight." Then kissed her on the forehead and headed for the door.

She yelled out, "How am I going to get home?"

Stopped and looked at her, "Oh yeah, I forgot we drover together." I asked her if she could call her sister or her best friend to come pick her up.

As I was walking out the shop she asked, "Where are you going?"

Told her, "I need to make a run real quick." I got into my car and head to Aiden's house. I had this really weird feeling and needed to make sure he was okay, since he doesn't text or call back.

Chapter 28

Pulling into his house, I saw his car in the driveway so I knew he had to be home. Ringing the doorbell, no answer. After about five minutes or so I opened the door it was unlocked again. I wondered what the hell Kidd was thinking keeping his door unlocked. Anybody could come in the house. Kidd wasn't in the living room nor was he in the kitchen. Yelling his name, "Kidd!" as I walked to the back yard. Walking out to the back I stopped and looked at the view. I always forgot how beautiful the view was up at his house. Went into the stoner's room, where I found Kidd sitting down under a cloud of smoke. I asked, "You, good bro?"

He looked up at me and replied, "The funny thing is I knew she was going to be the one to hurt me but she spoke my language and that made everything okay because we were both lost."

I sat down next to him as he handed me the joint from his hand. I said, "I know, she was crazy just like you and that's why she will always have a hold on your heart."

As I handed the joint back to him. He said, "You know my life would be way different right now if I still had her."

Watching him blow smoke in the air, I asked. "Do you think, you would like the life with her?"

He looked at me sideways, "Ray, I would love any life with her in it." Putting his fingers together, he continued saying. "I know if I had her, my life would be more of a struggle but at least I would be truly happy and that's all I ever wanted."

After he said that I asked, "Why do you think you would struggle if you and her were together?"

He pulled his shirt to the side and showed me the footprints he had tattooed on his should going to his heart. Putting my head in my hands, I said. "Damn bro that happen so long ago, I would have thought you would be over that by now."

He turned his head to look at me and I could see the pain in his eyes, he told me. "Ray, I look at these footprints every day and think about when she laid her head right here. And then my memories stab at my heart when I think of the child we should of had laying here." His eyes started to get watery, "She always told me, this was here favorite spot to lay on."

Looking at him like this, I couldn't sit here and let him beat himself down like this. I said, "Kidd, life comes at us all kinds away and you should know that better than anyone and sometimes there's nothing we can do about it."

He let a teardrop go before saying, "I know and that's the problem it was always my fault." Before I could say anything he finished with, "I will always be the reason shit didn't work out, why she gave up that child, why I'm lonely as fuck each night in this big ass house and that's not on nobody but me."

Grabbing my hair as I put my head down, telling him. "I know it hurts bro…"

Before I could let anything else out he turned looking me dead into my soul. His eyes bloodshot red and said, "Ray, you don't know what hurt is, until you know what it feels like to have everything you ever dreamed of in a heart as special as hers, and you be the reason it's broke. Don't ever tell me you know what pain is, you will never know what I'm feeling." He paused squinted his eyes, "You got Jasmine! So don't ever say you know it hurts, I hope you never have to feel this pain in your heart."

Just sitting here in total shock, I said, "Kidd, now I get it she broke your heart and shit but don't take that hurt out on me. He turned his head the other derision, I said, "Aiden, I'm your best friend been with you through everything but I'm not your fucking punching bag and don't forget that shit."

He turned back to me to, "Ray, I love that shit about you."

I smiled. "What the hell are you talking about?"

He had a grin on his face, "That you never back down when it came to me. Ever since the first day I met you in that park. You never back down or let me push you around and I like that shit about you Ray."

Laughing as I responded, "I love how, you always change the subject real quick when it comes to your girl."

He leaned back, blowing smoke in the air once again. He pass the joint to me and said, "I just hope she's somewhere out there living her crazies dreams and showing off that beautiful smile in the meantime."

I took a puff of the joint and said, "Yeah, yeah, whatever, I know you Kidd and you wish you could have her in your arms every moment of the way."

He gave a small smile and said, "Damn, Ray I would love to see that girl one more time before it's all said and done for me here."

Watching him smile each time he thought about her. I could see her come back to him and that was always a reminder that love is real. I smiled and told him, "Kidd life is going to bring you guys together just wait for it, you can't rush greatness."

He smiled as he rubbed his hands together, "Ray, I don't think she would even talk to me if we ran into each other."

Squinted my eyes, "Why, do you say that?"

He looked at me and said, "For one she probably wouldn't even recognize me and it's been so long she probably wouldn't even remember who I am."

Shaking my head, I told him, "Just like she was a big part in your life, I know you played a part in hers."

His phone went off before he could say anything back to me. I could hear him saying, "Oh shit, I forgot about the shipment we had coming in, I'm on my way." Another call came in right after. He rolled his eyes before pick up, "What's up?" He walked around and said, "If they come back to the city and they like my words. I might think about getting on stage for a word or two."

When he got off the phone, I asked, "Who was that?"

He looked at his watch and said, "Oh shit I'm late for this meeting, I'll tell you about it later Ray."

Looking at him confused I asked, "What meeting?"

He picked up his phone and grabbed another joint. He then made his way out there door. Stopped and said, "Ray, I definitely needed that talk, just lock up when you leave." then closed the door.

Chapter 29

Heading back home, I start thinking about how everything would be different if they had kept their love, not only his life but my life would be way different that's for sure. Got home and Jasmine heard the door close, she wanted to know everything. She damn near slammed me on the couch. Looking at her crazy I said, "If you don't relax and let me breath maybe I could tell you."

She sat up and looked at me, "Okay, go ahead and start from the top."

I laughed and said "Okay." Told her about the convention Aiden and I had. She was in disbelief that Kidd and Cherilyn almost had a child.

She asked me, "What made them make the decision to not keep it?"

I looked at her as I put my head down. I told her, "It was the hardest thing Kidd had to face when losing her, he almost let depression take the best of him and sometimes I feel like it did and he's just hiding it really good."

She had a sad look look on her face, I could tell she was feeling for him. She asked me very lightly, "What happen?"

I knew it wasn't my position to tell but I also know she is my soon to be wife. So, I began to tell her the story. "Kidd and Cherilyn were no longer together going into the summer of our senior year. Kidd was in the gym crazy, before school, during lunch and at night until midnight or later. He felt like he needed to prove to Cherilyn that he made the right choice in chasing his dream. I was in the gym with him on the day he found out. His phone had nine miss calls. Five from Cherilyn and four from his mom. Kidd looked at me and showed me the phone. I shook my head and said, "Damn bro, you might want to call both of them back." He called Cherilyn back first, she pick up and told him she was sleeping and would call him back when she woke up. He then called Mom she pick up and said, 'Aiden come pick me up now!'

He looked at me, "Bro, I think Mom ain't having a good day or something." He went to pick her up from work.

Right when she got in the car she asked him, 'Aiden, you got something to tell me?'

He turned looking her in the eyes. 'No, I'm good.'

She said, "Cut the bullshit! Aiden! Do you have something to tell me?"

Still looking at her, he responded, 'I mean it was cool hooping today, I put in a lot of work today."

Mom got pissed off, "Aiden! I said cut the shit and tell me what you got to tell me."

Aiden got loud and put his hands up, "What the fuck do you want me to tell you the sky is blue? I told you I don't have nothing to tell you."

Mom looked him in the soul and asked, "So you don't know Cherilyn is pregnant?"

Kidd's mouth dropped and his heart dropped. He turned and asked Mom, "By who?"

She almost smacked him, "By you!"

Kidd was in disbelieve, all he could think about was being with her and his future is going to change. He put the car in drive, told Mom. "No why, we're going to her house right now." As he drove off. They got to Cherilyn's house and Kidd walked over to the door and each step his heart dropped a little more. Before he could knock on the door, Sahara, Cherilyn's mother answered the door. Kidd and Mom stood there, Kidd looked in the house and seen Cherilyn laying on the couch. Kidd walked in she looked up and their eyes locked and you could see nothing but love in both of their eyes. They stared at each other for a while.

Mom yelled out, "Aiden… Aiden… Aiden!" She had to call his name three times before he looked.

Kidd looked over, "Yeah, what's up?"

Mom told him to sit down. He sat down and they began to talk and discuss what happen and what the next plan was. Come to find out Cherilyn was eleven weeks pregnant. She was still in her first trimester and that meant they needed to make a decision quick. Both mom's asked Aiden. "So, what do you want to do?"

Kidd sat there and looked at Cherilyn like it was his last and first time seeing her. Heart breaking out of his chest, he said. "All my life I have felt pain and when I'm with you I feel the happiness, I knew the chance and still took it, so if that means college is out of the option then so be it but I will be there for my child." Mom looked at him in shock, everyone in the room was in disbelieve. He finished with, "But at the end of the day, it's her body and whatever she decides to do, I stand behind her a hundred percent."

All eyes shifted over to Cherilyn. When her mother asked her the same question. Cherilyn screamed out, "I don't want it! Get it out of me!" As tears ran down her face. Once Kidd heard that it broke his heart and tears began to fall from his eyes. Both moms stepped outside to give Aiden and Cherilyn some time alone. Kidd dropped down to his hands and knees, tears continued to run down his face. He told her, "Please let's talk about this."

She turned to look at him and told him, "No! Aiden I'm not bringing a child into this world, when we're not even together."

Kidd grabbed both of her hands, "Cherilyn there is no life, I want to live in, If you're not right next to me each step of the way."

She turned to her other side, putting her head down. "Aiden, you broke my heart, it felt like i couldn't breath and it didn't seem to matter that much to you then."

He responded back with. "Cherilyn your my everything, you're the only reason getting up in the morning is needed, just the thought of being able to see keeps my heart pumping.'

She rolled her eyes then said, "Aiden, don't think this child is going to bring us back and cancel all the hurt you brought to my heart." She looked at him whipping her face and added, "Plus I'm talking to this guy already and his really nice to me." Tears still coming down both of their faces, as their mothers came back in.

Jasmine of course cut me off and asked, "What ended up happening?"

Looking at her side ways, I told her, "Relax and let me finish maybe you'll find out."

She said, "I don't know who you think you're talking to but figure it out before there's a part two to this story."

Smiling as I continued the story, "So, the next day they went and got a abortion, Kidd spent the whole day with her because her body was very weak after the abortion. He would pick her up take her to the bathroom, cooked for her, the whole nine."

Before her mother came home, right before Kidd was leaving. She told him, 'Kidd, I never stopped loving you and that feeling will never go away but I can never be with you again and that shit hurts more than anything.' After she said that tears came down her cheek.

Biting his lip and putting his head down, 'I know and that's why it hurts so much because I will never give another woman my love, the way I gave it to you.' He then walked out the door.

Jasmine looked at me, her eyes getting watery. "So, that's why Kidd is the way he is…"

I looked at her. "What does that mean?"

She closed her eyes and said, "That's why he goes through women so fast and never really gives anyone a chance."

Leaning over as I gave her a kiss on the head. "Yeah, it suck but Kidd will find love or Cherilyn again whichever one comes first."

Chapter 30

Life moves so fast and I hate that I would even think to blink when I was with you. The last time I seen you, you told me I deserve someone special. How could that be when you were the one that was special to me? I'm a fool for saying what I said to you and for the way I acted. Never did I imagine living my life without you. Each day is a struggle when I watch people walk with their lover and I think about how I let the best part of me walk away. Loving you was the best thing I could have done in this lifetime. You made me want more, to do better but not just for myself but for you because you're someone who deserves the stars and the moon. You seen me push myself to the max, I just wish I pushed myself to be the best man for you. Trying to build the best future for you was the only thing I wanted to be good at. You're still the reason I push myself today, hoping when we meet again our dream lifestyle will be sat...

Love. Kidd – xo

Before my meeting with The Shop, I stopped and read a letter. The craziest thing happen right after reading it. I ran in Philip, a old friend of ours from Cherilyn's old high school.

He seen me and said, "Yo! Ray how you been man?"

Putting the letters away in my bag I answered. "Good, just running these businesses Kidd got going up."

He looked around said, "Damn I haven't seen Kidd since high school."

I looked at him and, "Shit, I haven't seen you since high school."

He smiled, "Yeah, I know been overseas playing ball and living the dream with my sons."

My mouth dropped, "You got Kids?"

He smiled, "Yeah, man I ain't that little boy from the hood no more, we grown now."

I laughed out and said, "You ain't never lie, shit I'm about to get married and shit."

He stepped back and laughed, "Say what? To who?"

I answered back, "To Jasmine, I don't know if you know her." As I pulled my phone out to show him the pictures of us.

He told me, "Bro she is beautiful and these pictures are amazing, who took them?"

I smiled and told him. "Kidd, took the pictures."

As he was handing me, my phone he said, "Kidd definitely has a eye for a great picture."

I said back, "Yeah, I know he has his own gallery in the city, you should stop by and check it out sometime."

Philip then asked, "So how is Kidd, I see he still has his hand in everything."

Smiling I responded, "Yeah, tell me about it, he has an art gallery, him and his step dad own this restaurant food is bomb and everything started because our Dispensary/Coffee shop blew up."

Philip looked at me in shock and said, "Kidd was always the golden one, we knew he would make it and be successful." He looked at the ring on his finger then said, "I know Cherilyn is loving each moment of her dream life."

I looked at him sideways. "New life? What does that mean?"

He looked at me funny and responded, "Yeah I know Kidd was so in love with her, I just assumed she was still in his heart as he made it to the top and everything…"

I cut him off and told him, "Kidd and Cherilyn haven't seen each other in years."

He looked surprised and confused. He asked, "So, they never got back together?"

Looking at him as I sat down, "Nope, they're paths didn't bring them back."

He sat down and said, "Man, out of everyone I thought they would still be together for sure." Shaking his head he added, "I knew they broke up and everything but I never seen people love each other the way they did."

I looked at him and smiled "Yeah, I know and I'm pretty sure the whole world never seen any kind of love like theirs. They were the perfect couple."

He agreed with me, "Yeah, I know that's why I'm surprised their not together no more." His eyes got big and he said, "I mean the head cheerleader from my school and she is hands down one of the prettiest girls I have ever seen and then Kidd the city's golden boy, man that's crazy they're not together."

Shaking my head, I said, "I know, if anyone should be together it's them two."

He said, "Now that I think about it, it's her fault we lost to you guys senior year."

I laughed, "How do you figure that?" As I put my hands up.

He said, "Because if she didn't boo Kidd and bet his mom, he wouldn't of had the kind of game he had that night."

Looked up and replied, "Damn, I remember when she did that and Kidd going off would be a understatement. He had something to prove to her I guess."

It was our senior year and Kidd was now in the top twenty-five on the west coast. He was having a great year. We were playing Cherilyn's school to secure our spot in playoffs. We get there and Kidd immediately starts searching the gym for Cherilyn. He saw her cheering before our game. When it was time for us to get changed for the game, he stood there and waited to talk to Cherilyn. He didn't care about getting in trouble with coach or anything. He wanted to see and speak to his girl. Kidd ran over to her and grabbed her arm, she looked back quick.

She look up at him, "What Aiden!?" As she pulled her arm away.

Kidd stepped back a little, "I just wanted to tell you hey and also how beautiful you're looking right now." As he bit his lip looking at her.

She rolled her eyes, "yeah, whatever Aiden I know you."

He stepped once more, "What does that mean?"

She replied, "That means I know you and I know what your about so you better get ready for this lost my boys are about to give you."

Kidd smiled as he turned to go to the locker room, then yelled out, "I still miss when you cheered for me."

He came in and got ready for the game. He didn't really say anything when he came in, it was easy to see Cherilyn was on his mind. Coach even told him, "Aiden you better be read and not let that girl out there fuck up what we been working on."

Kidd looked up and smiled, "Coach I'm ready, just make sure you tune in to the Kidd show."

Coach said, "Yeah, I hope so because I seen you talking to her when you should of been in here with your team but you'll run that late."

We all got up and took the floor, getting into warm up lines. I asked Kidd, "Bro you sure, you're ready?"

He got the ball and shot it, went straight in and he looked at me. "Ray, I'm Kidd which means I'm always ready. So don't worry about me."

It was game time now and they were starting to call out the starting lineup. Kidd was the last one to be announce for our team. "Last, but not least number twenty-three Aiden 'Kidd' brewing."

The crowd was showing him so much love. Kidd turned and blew a kiss to Cherilyn. The one thing they did before each game last year. She caught the kiss and started booing him. The way Kidd's face dropped. I knew seeing her do that broke him on the inside. He turned to me, pulled me close and said. "Give me the ball."

I looked at him crazy, "Kidd, that ain't part of the play."

He then came closer to me, "Fuck the play, I'm about to go off, so give me the ball."

I never seen this look in Kidd's eyes, it was like anger, sadness and love all in one. We won the tip off and I kicked the ball to Kidd. Coach yelled out, "Ray!"

Kidd then went baseline and put on a show, jumped up and dunk it hard as hell. Running back on defense, I looked at coach and said, "He wanted the ball." Then shrugged my shoulders.

Coach looked at me and said, "Good read."

It was a real conference battle point for point. Kidd was having a amazing night, hitting everything he throw up. It was two minutes left, I passed it to Kidd on the wing. He immediately got double teamed. I called for the ball back. Kidd looked at me then slit the double team and came right down the middle of the lane, cocked back and dunked it with authority. They called a timeout and Kidd stopped in the middle of the court, looked at Cherilyn and said, "Can't nobody on this court hold me!" then pointed at her.

Coach yelled out, "Kidd bring it in!"

The game came down to the last minute we went up by three, with Kidd's free throws. We got a steal before they could get a shot up and ended up winning the game. Kidd being the high point man finished with twenty-two points and twelve rebounds. That win put us second in our conference. Everyone was hype and going crazy in the locker room after the game. Kidd was sitting with his headphones in getting dressed. I came over to him, "Kidd you good bro?" as I gave him a little push.

He turned and smiled at me, "Bro I'm good, we're number two in the city and I'm on fire, yeah I'm straight."

I just walked back over and got hype with the team, let Kidd do his own thing. We walked out of the locker room to get on the bus. Kidd stopped and starting talking to Mom. It wasn't odd for Kidd to talk to his mother after the game, she was more than his mom but his coach also. After their conversation Kidd looked kinda upset. When he got on the bus, the team was going bananas. Kidd put that fake ass smile on, jumped up and down a couple time before sitting in his seat and putting his headphones on looking out the window. I went over to sit next to him, "Yo what's good? For real and don't give me that bull shit that it's nothing."

He turned slowly and put his head up to look at me. "Ray, she booed me and bet Mom we were going to lose." His head slowly went down and he finished with. "I remember when she cried because she missed the first five minutes of our game."

I remember how it crushed him, knowing that she wasn't by his side anymore. As I got stuck looking back at the game and that night. Philip said, "Ray! You good or just in deep thought?"

I shook my head, then looked at him. "Nah, I'm just thinking about this meeting I need to be at right now." As I laughed lightly.

We shook hands he said, "Tell Kidd I said what up and that I hope all is great with him."

Gave him a thumbs up as I walked to the car.

Chapter 31

Headed to the meeting with Kidd and our other investors at "The Spot". It's at the restaurant Kidd and his step dad opened up a year ago. When I came in, all eyes turned to me then Jay said, "Boy, I thought you would never show up."

I looked at the clock. "I'm only like five minutes late and plus Kidd ain't even here yet."

Looking around Jay said, "Yeah, I know but Aiden never on time for anything, he just like his momma."

We laughed and decided to start the meeting without Kidd because there was no telling when he would get here. Thirty minutes later Kidd walks in. We stopped in the middle of our decision and looked at him then looked at the time. Jay asked, "Boy where the hell you been at? The meeting started damn near an hour ago." As he pointed at the clock.

Kidd rubbed his head, "I know but I had to meet with the growers, to figure out how we're going to get new stains to The Shop." Kidd looked at me then his phone, "Why y'all worried about me, I know our spot is damn near running itself, with all these people talking about our food."

Jay knotted his head in agreement and said, "I know but it would be good if the person that owns *The Spot* would stop in, here and there."

Kidd put his hands over his mouth, then moved them and said, "That's my bad, I'll try and do better to be here." Then whispered to me, "Damn this ni**a still on my ass I thought that shit ended when I was young."

Almost laughing out loud and responded, "Yeah, you should've known that wouldn't happen."

He laughed, "Yeah, you right Ray."

Jay looked over at us "Now, what is it?"

Kidd put his head down, "Nothing but are we almost done with this meeting?"

Jay asked, "Why, what you got going on?"

Kidd give him a little side eye, "It's just Me and Money have a meeting about the club soon, that's all."

Jay rolled his eyes and said, "Yeah it's almost done."

When the meeting came to an end I told Kidd, "Bro I have to get back to the shop but tell that ni**a money I said what up."

He pulled me in as I give him a handshake, "Ray, you be at the shop a whole lot these days, what's up with that?"

I looked at him and said, "Trees and Beans was the dream and plus that's the spot to be at. Not only that, but with you always out of town, one of the owners has to make sure shit is running smoothly."

He smiled and put his hand around me, "Ray that's why I put you there insures of everything, I knew you would love it and run that shit better than anyone else."

We started to walk out, Money pulled in and hopped out the car quick. Kidd yells out, "Money! About time you get here a ni**a starting to get hungry."

Money walked over to us, "What's good boys, sorry for being so late but I had to make sure the club money was right before I left."

Kidd shook his hand, "It's cool I know how it goes and that shit better be right." He then added "Shit I wouldn't be out here if Ray didn't want to go back to the shop and get high with his latte." They began to laugh.

I told them, "You know me, I just be chilling."

Money laughed, "Nah, you just a white boy deep down." Laughing once again.

I said, "Yeah, whatever and that's why I'm leaving now."

Kidd threw up the peace sign, "Go ahead and leave but just remember, to text me about the ideas you had for the shop."

Looked at him and shook my head okay, as I turned to walk to my car I heard someone bumping their music loud at the light. I looked at Kidd and Money they also stop turned their heads to see who the hell was blasting their music. Kidd froze and his eyes didn't move, I turned to look who was in the car. It was Cherilyn signing a song moving her head sideways bobbing with the beat. Money started pushing Kidd, "It's Cherilyn!"

I put my hands up, trying to wave her down. She turned her head and made this confused look, she could tell someone called her name. Just as the light turned green she noticed Kidd. They locked eyes and it was like they were seeing each other for the first time again. She didn't move until the cars behind her began to honk their horns. Kidd shook his head as he rubbed his eyes. When he looked back up she was already gone.

I came over and pushed him, "Yo! Why you freeze up?"

Kidd looked at me and Money, "I never thought, I would lay my eyes on her again and for her to remember is even crazier."

Money pushed him again, "That was you chance!"

Kidd looked at him sideways, "How was that my chance, she was in the car on a busy street?" I could tell he was upset, he kept going on saying. "What was I supposed to do run out there and make a fool of myself? "

Money looked at him then looked at me, "Ray, why ya boy let his future drive away like that?"

I put my hands up and shrugged, "Shit your guess is just as good as mine."

Kidd pushed both of us and, "Fuck both of y'all."

Money quickly responded back, "Don't get mad at us because you let her drive away."

Kidd was frustrated I could see it in his eyes, he then went off again. "What the fuck was I supposed to do, she probably already forgot she seen me."

Me trying to be funny said, "I guess it wasn't true love then."

Kidd turned his back to us, started to walk back in the doors. He stopped with his head down, "I loved that woman more than anything in this world. You guys would be lucky to feel something like that." He walked inside the door slowly closed behind him.

Money put his hand out, "I see how this meeting is going to go but already Ray I'll get with you later." We shook hands as I got in the car. Driving to the shop to relax, I thought about the way Kidd looked at Cherilyn, it was like he was at peace when his eyes were on her. Just to think some people search for that feeling their whole life, trying to find that one person that takes all the pain away and make them feel at peace.

Chapter 32

After watching Kidd freeze up like he was back in high school I rushed to the shop to get my nose back in them letters. I got to the shop order a latte and a nice indica joint. Sat down at my table in the back and brought out the jar.

I ask myself every day why I let my pride get the best of me, when you were the one thing that was the best for me. I don't know if you know this but I'm a poet now and I perform often, each time I'm about to get on stage I laugh a little and think about my first poem. The one I wrote on the first Valentine's Day not having you. We were still talking and texting about everything, I guess when you're best friends it's kinda hard to let go. Funny thing was sometimes it felt like you were still mine. All I wanted was to be your man again, for you to be in my arms, because every time it felt like my heart was telling you all my secrets. Remember telling myself I need to do whatever it took to have you back in my arms. Truck told me you have to put your pride aside for the one you love or watch them drift away like you didn't want them. All I know is I definitely put pride away that day, that's for sure. Even when it blow up over social media and everyone tried clowning me. I didn't care because your cousin told me, that was the happiest she seen you in a long time. That's all I ever wanted to do was make you smile and it didn't matter what anyone said because it made you happy and that was good enough for me. Maybe one day our love will bring us back for one more hello and I can make you the happiest girl in the world again…

Love.Kidd - xo

The day everyone found out Kidd still had a heart and was still in love with Cherilyn. It was Valentine's Day and Kidd wasn't messing with no girls, but somehow he was still talking to Cherilyn. We got to school and everyone was coming up to Kidd, laughing and shaking their heads. Girls were coming up to him saying how sweet he was. Our boys were running up clowning him, talking about he's soft. Some were saying, "Give me your card, you are no longer in the game player." Each time Kidd looked at me confused and I looked right back at him with the same confused look. It wasn't until Pop came up.

"Bro! No way, you went out like that?" As he pushed Kidd.

Kidd looked at him and put his hands up. "What the fuck are you talking about?"

Money walked up behind me and said, "Aiden bro, why you go out like that? You could get any girl and you're still trying with Cherilyn?"

Aiden was getting frustrated. "If someone don't tell me what's going on, then somebody getting knocked the fuck out!"

Money twisted his face, "Yeah, I doubt that Mr. Lover Boy."

Kidd tried to grab him, Money stepped to the side then got behind me.

Pop grabbed Kidd, "Relax go look on Cherilyn's page and see what she posted on her Valentine's Day morning." He then handed Kidd his phone.

Kidd put everything aside and showed the world just how much he loved Cherilyn. He put a card on her doorstep, with a note, rose petals in shape of a heart and keychain with both of their initials engraved on it. The note read: *"How could one be so foolish to let someone as special as you walk away. I know you said I hurt you, those words alone kill me a little each day and not having you is the worst thing to live with. You were the one who made me believe in love, who made me want more out of life, the one who made me believe in myself. If I knew I had to live my life without you, I wouldn't wake up but knowing your somewhere out there give me hope. I only smile now because I know God made someone as incredible as you. I love you and no matter what I do, this shit won't go away, you're my missing puzzle piece...*

Love. Kidd - xo

The caption on her post read: "Haha look what my ex did." Everyone knew they were a couple so the comments below up. Aiden's name was in one after another. It was clear everyone knew it was him. Kidd read each comment with a blank face, he wasn't trying to show what she did hurt him. He gave the phone back to Pop and said, "Yeah, so what I did that and now what?"

Money shook his head, "Did you not read the comments because they're letting you have it big time."

Kidd looked up to the sky, "Let them say whatever they want. At least I know Cherilyn will forever know I love her." After that, Kidd was back to being a player and now lived by the statement, "That he doesn't do relationships anymore."

Sitting here looking at this jar of note and thinking about that look he had in his eyes when he saw her. I couldn't image losing the only one I was meant to love.

Chapter 33

Damn when I sit here reading these letters and I think about how life would be if he had her right now. I grabbed the next letter and put it to my head then opened it.

When you ran into my arms, it felt like nothing changed for us, like you were still mine. The world froze again and I felt my heartbeat your name over and over for the next couple of days. It was a feeling I hoped lasted forever, not just for a moment. I close my eyes and can see you running right towards me, my heart beating a thousand times per second. I can still feel you in my arms. Me holding you tight because I knew letting you go meant losing you again. It was more of my heart holding on, it needed to feel your touch one more time. Told Money I didn't want to run into you but deep down, you were the only reason I went to the graduation. They said your name and you walked across the stage I heard your family cheering and I knew I wanted to be at all your special moments. You ran in my arms and that was the only thing worth having in this world. I miss your touch a little more each day, it kills me that you're not in my arms. I know you're somewhere out there making the world beautiful. You'll forever hold a special part in my heart, hopefully life brings us back for one more hug...

Love. Kidd - xo

It was Cherilyn's graduation night and Kidd was now dating Amber. A girl that just happened to go to the same school as Cherilyn. Not only did she go to the same school but they were both graduating that night. It was the night of their graduation and Kidd asked me and Money to go with him. We got there, Kidd has these roses in his hands for Amber, which didn't surprise me because Amber was his girlfriend and she was graduating which was kinda of a big deal. They called Cherilyn's name first. Kidd smiled so big as he put his head down. Money pushed him when she made her away across the stage. "Look there goes your girl."

Kidd turned with that same smile on his face. "Yeah I know. I'm proud of her."

Soon followed Amber's name, we cheered and everything but it was different. Even though we didn't cheer when Cherilyn walked across, his energy said it all. Graduation was over now, everyone walking around looking for their families and friends. We're walking through the crowd looking for Amber, then Kidd stopped us. Me and Money looked at him, "Yo, what's up?" Money asked.

Kidd looked around then at both of us, "Whatever y'all do don't let me run into Cherilyn."

We both looked at each other and smiled, "Yeah we got you, just try and find Amber." As I waved my hands for him to find her. We started making our way out to find Amber and out of nowhere we hear someone scream out "Aiden! It was loud but Aiden's name was called out clearly. Each of us looking around, trying to find out where the voice came from. Kidd turns all the way around and Cherilyn was in a full sprint running towards him. She was looking like a track star. With how fast she was running. Kidd's face was in total disbelief and he was froze, he didn't know what to do. The closer she got, the more his arms raised up. Right when his arms were up she jumped right into his arms, it was like she knew he would catch her. He held her tight, as his eyes were closed. They both looked into each other's eyes, I thought they were going to kiss. Kidd put her down and she looked up at him, as he shared at her. It felt like they were sharing at each other for a lift time. Her mouth ran over.

She was screaming out, Son! Oh my god it's good to see you." As she came over to give him hug. They hugged and I could see her mother whispering something in his ear. She starts to push them together, telling them, "Get together take a picture, please for me." They were next to each other and her mother said, "Oh Aiden are those roses for Cherilyn?" smiling as she asked him.

Kidd put his head back a little with a smile on his face. "Nah you know, I can't do that." He turned and looked at Cherilyn. I don't know what is was but when he looked at her those roses went right to her. Who ever said pictures are worth a thousand words, is absolutely right because they were amazing together. In the picture with her holding the roses it looked like they never broke up. They talked for a little and we went back to looking for Amber. I remember grabbing him as we turned to walk way.

"Kidd, where the hell are the flowers?"

He smiled as we made our way to the parking lot, "The flowers are where they belong."

I stopped and looked back at Cherilyn, as she put her head down to smell the roses. I grabbed Money and asked, "What the hell is Kidd talking about, don't he know he gave the roses to Cherilyn and not Amber?"

Money smiled and laughed a little, "The roses were always for Cherilyn."

Putting my hands on my head in disbelief. Money raised his eyebrow. "Why do you think Kidd wanted to come to her graduation?"

I paused for a moment and put one hand on my chin. "Wait hold on!" I screamed out as I ran to catch up with Money. "I thought he got the roses for Amber, shit I thought we was up here for Amber." As I throw my hands up in the air. Kidd was still walking and on the phone, looking for Amber. I pulled Money back a little. "How you know?"

He turned and looked at me. "How do I know what?"

I told them, "How do you know that Kidd came up here to see Cherilyn?"

He shook his head at me, "Ray, really? Kidd went out and got roses Cherilyn's favorite flower. Plus, Kidd has never looked at anyone the way he looks at Cherilyn. Yeah he says Amber might be the one or whatever but he don't mean that shit."

The only thing that was on my face was confusion. Money looked at me and said, "Ray, the only thing I know is when Kidd looks at Cherilyn the whole world knows it's true love and with Amber is forced love."

After he said that Kidd walked back over to us. "What the fuck are y'all doing over here?"

I looked at him eyes squinted. "We doing the same shit you doing and that's looking for Amber your girlfriend." I added 'girlfriend' because I wanted to remind him that he was still in a relationship. Now that I think about it Cherilyn's boyfriend was there the whole time, he watch the way she ran to him and watched them take pictures. We ended up meeting Amber in the parking lot and Kidd took her to dinner. She never got the roses or even knew anything about them. I remember after that night thinking and analyzing Kidd's relationship. Even though Amber kicked it with us each day, it was nothing compared to the way Cherilyn made Kidd feel.

I put the jar in my bag and headed home.

Chapter 34

Couple weeks go by and still no word from Kidd. I wasn't worried because Kidd always disappeared when Cherilyn came up but that was the way he handled the pain of living without her. I'm back in the shop and Aiden's cousin Taylor comes in. I knew it was her by her voice. She was loud and had no care in the world who heard her. In the middle of trying to put one of the letters back in the jar she came up.

"What's that Ray?" As she tried to snatch the letter out of my hand but I moved it back. I knew she wasn't going to leave me alone until I told her or gave her the letter.

She looked at me sideways eyes real low. "Ray, let me see what you got." She put her hand out. You know I ain't leaving until I get that or you tell me because the way you moved look real suspicious."

I looked at her as I reached for the letter. "Yeah I know." I gave her the note.

She looked at who it was to and said, "Oh shit, Kidd is still writing to Cherilyn?" She asked me.

Looking at her crazy, "What do you mean still, you knew he wrote to her?"

She smiled, Yeah he told me, he had this jar full on letters he wrote for Cherilyn."

My eyes got big and I asked, "How long ago was this?"

She looked at me weird, "Like before everything blow up for him. I mean with all Kidd's success I'm pretty he forgot about all about Cherilyn."

Still looking at her in shock. So this was more than a couple of years ago right?"

She was handing me the letter back. "Yeah long time ago, I honestly didn't think he really wrote anything to her."

I shook my head a little, with a little sign of relief.

She then asked me, "Why the hell are you acting so weird Ray and how did you get that letter?"

I looked around to make sure Kidd didn't pop up outta nowhere. I grabbed the jar out of my bag and showed her all the letters. Her mouth dropped and she shook her head.

"Ray, you better hope Kidd doesn't find out you got that jar."

Took a big gulp as I looked at her, "Yeah I know." I then asked her, "Please don't tell him anything."

She looked at me and said, "If he asks me anything about it, I'm going to tell him that's family and Kidd is one you don't cross in any way."

I put my head down and my hand on my head. I know, I fucked up but I was almost done with the jar and I couldn't resist but to keep it and read more. She looked at me as she got up.

"Just know you're playing with fire Ray." She shook her head and turned to walk out the door.

I called her back. "You really think Aiden would take it that far?"

She had this small smile on her face, "Remember when Big Jay and Big Aiden got into it?"

I looked at her crazy, "Yeah, what does that have to do with anything?"

She shook her again, "I'm saying that because unlike Big Aiden, Kidd won't stop and you know that Ray. Especially when it comes to Cherilyn." She then turned around and said, "You reading his love letters, what would you do Ray?" Then walked out the door.

Sitting here thinking about that night and how crazy it got between him and his father.

Chapter 35

It was the day of our graduation and we were going to go out with a bang. Kidd's father was flying in from the east coast. Aiden was never a real big fan of his father. His father not being with him, when he was younger still runs in his mind. We're in the back of the stage clowning around getting hype because this was our big day. Once Aiden's name was called and he made his way across the stage. We seen both Big Jay and Big Aiden get up and head to the door. So, as we're in the back getting our diploma, taking pictures and celebrating our accomplishment. Big Jay and Big Aiden were fighting outside in the parking lot. They both ended up leaving before the cops could showed up. The whole time we were outside taking pictures with our families nobody told Aiden what happen. The whole time he just thought they left. We got to the restaurant and Mom went off after finding out why Big Jay and Big Aiden weren't in none of the pictures because they were to busy fighting. Kidd looks at me confused, I shrugged my shoulders with a blank face. He got up and went over to talk to Mom.

"Hey, what's up?"

She looked at him pissed off. "Your fucking father, he really knows how to fuck up everything."

Kidd looked at her confused. "What happen?" he asked.

She shook her head. He only came out here to fight Jay." She put her hand on her face. "When you were in the back after walking, your dad called Jay outside to talk and they fought in the parking lot."

Kidd's eyes got big and he asked her. "So, who won?"

Mom looked at him with a side face. "Aiden that doesn't matter, all that matters is he fucked your day up."

Kidd never liked to see his mother upset. "It's okay ma, the day is still great, I got you." As he pulled her in for a hug then kissed her on the forehead.

Kidd came back and sat down next to me. "Ray I hate when I see my mom like that."

I put my head down. "Yeah I know I can see it in your eyes."

After I said that Cherilyn came walking in and showed up to dinner. The crazy thing was Amber wasn't there because of some car trouble. When she walked through the door Kidd's eyes lite up and the attitude he had went away. He got up fast as hell to greet her and it was easy to see she still had his heart. The whispers began, we were all looking at each other asking, "Did they get back together?", "How did she know where to come?"

Mom smiled and said, "I told her she was invited to come to anything we have and that's she's still apart of this family."

My eyes got big and I looked at Taylor, she said. "It never mattered what happen, Kidd was always happy with her."

We watched them laughing and enjoying each other presence like nothing changed and they were heart to heart again. They came to the table.

Kidd said "Look who blessed us with her presence."

As he step to the side and showed off Cherilyn as if we didn't already see her. She stepped closer to the table. "Hey fam bam…"She paused for a moment then continuing saying. "I don't know if I'm still able to say that?" As she looked at all of us.

We all sat there for a second just looking at her. TT broke the ice. "Girl you in the family for life, forget what Aiden got going on." As she air pushed him. "Girl come over here and give us so love, stop standing there looking lost."

We all got excited and laughed offering her the chair next to us, of course she sits next to Aiden. The night was going great, until Big Aiden walked through the door. Mom's eyes locked on him and instantly she got up and walked over to him before he could get to the table.

She got right in front of him. You mother fucker, you fly all the way out her to fuck up your son's day." He was about to say something but she cut him off. "You could have done that shit tomorrow or yesterday but on his day, you're still selfish always trying to make everything about you, you ain't shit Aiden!"

Big Aiden stood over top of her and got loud. "I told you, when I see that ni**a it was over for his ass!"

Mom went to say something and Big Aiden put his hand up to cut her off. When Kidd saw that, he grabbed Cherilyn's leg. "Hold on, I gotta handle this ni**a, he got my mom all the way fucked up." He stood up and told her. "Don't leave just yet, I'm not done looking at you."

She smiled and told him. Don't worry I'll be right here."

Big Aiden was still talking with his hands. "I told you I didn't want that sorry ass ni**a around my son."

Kidd came over and stepped in between him and Mom. Wrapping Mom around him so that she was behind him now. Kidd told Mom, "go sit down, I got this." Mom was still trying to say something to Big Aiden, when Kidd turned and looked at her. "I said, I got this go back and sit down."

I remember Cherilyn leaning over to me saying, "I miss how protected I felt, when I was with Kidd." I looked at her as she stared at Kidd arguing with his father. She said to me, "He always made me feel safe."

I looked at her in total shook because they were both dating someone else. I turned my head and looked at Aiden. He had his fists in a ball when he stepped in to talk to Big Aiden. Kidd looked at him but it was like he was looking into his soul or something. Kidd told him, "Aye don't ever raise your voice at my mother, didn't nobody ask you to be here." Big Aiden was about to say something but Kidd quickly cut him off. "If you going to be here, none of the bullshit or you can turn around and hit the door right now." He turned pointed at Mom. "That woman raised me to the best of her ability and now I'm here graduated with a scholarship to play ball in college. With no help from you."

After he said all that, he stood there looking him eye to eye straight in the face. Kidd turned and came back to sit next to Cherilyn. He pulled her chair closer to him. "I'm sorry but I couldn't have him talking to her like he was crazy or something."

She smiled, "Kidd it's okay, I know how you are already and it's cute."

Big Aiden walked over to the table, Kidd looked at him and he said "Harleen I'm sorry for the way I acted but you did more than a great job of rising Aiden and I thank you every day for him." He looked at Kidd. Call me when you're done here."

Kidd shook his head in agreement, we continued eating and talking about all the great times we had in high school. Cherilyn got up shortly before the food came out. "Thank you guys for always making me feel a part of the family and showing me love. I wish my family was like this." After saying that she looked at Kidd. "Congratulations again Aiden, you're going to do great things I can feel it." She blew him a kiss and headed to the door.

We all looked at Kidd and I blurted out. "If you're going to do something, right now is the best time."

He shot up and went after her in the parking lot. Grabbing her before she got to the car. "So I only get a kiss blown to me, no hug or anything?"

She leaned against the car looking at him as he stood over her. He looked right into her big brown eyes. She looked right into his eyes and said, "I didn't want to overstep my boundaries." As she placed her hand on his chest.

Kidd looked down, "There's never no boundaries with you, I told you as long as this thing in my chest is beating, it will beat your name." As he held her hand, their hands laid on his chest for a second.

She pulled his head down and kissed him on the forehead. "Maybe in our next life time things will be different." She then got in the car.

Kidd stood there and watched her drive off. He came back in with this one of a kind smile on his face. Seeing her changed the whole night, we almost forgot that Big Jay and Big Aiden were fighting not too long ago. We were now on our way to his house when he told me. "Ray, loving her is going to be the death of me just watch."

I looked at him. "Yeah whatever, that shit going to change when you get into college."

Mom was silent worried about getting home, to see why Big Jay wasn't know where to be found. Kidd asked Mom. "So they really fought?"

Mom looked at him, "Yeah, your dad told him, he wanted to talk to him outside."

Kidd and I were both ready to hear the story of what happen. Come to find out Big Aiden had some jeans and sneakers on. Big Jay on the other hand dress pants and dress shoes on. So they get outside and Big Aiden said. "Remember all that shit, you was talking. I don't hear you saying shit now."

Big Jay said, "This ain't the time or the place and I'm not ready to fight look at my shoes. I'm here to celebrate."

Big Aiden told him. "What the fuck, your shoes gotta do with your hands." As he flinched at him. That flinch caught Big Jay off guard and he throw his hands up. Big Aiden looked at his cousin and said, "I'm about to whoop his ass."

That's when Big Jay pointed at both of them and said, "You a bitch and you a bitch."

After that was said fists went flying. It was said that Big Jay got beat down but no one really saw the whole thing. They both left before anyone could show up. Kidd was hoping Big Jay won. He said, I hope Big Jay got off on his ass."

I looked at Kidd, "Yeah from looking at your dad, I doubt Jay won."

Kidd put his head down, "Damn Ray just kill all the hope I have."

I shrugged my shoulders. "I'm just saying from what I saw, it didn't seem like Jay won that's all."

We pulled up to the house, Mom got out real quick heading to the door. We got in the house and all the lights were off, the only thing that on was the TV in the back room. Mom walked back there to see what happen. Kidd and I followed right behind her. She got to the room and Jay was sitting down in the dark back turned to us watching the sports channel. Mom hit the light and throw her hands up. "Jay, what the hell happen? Where were you? What went down?" She was asking him a lot of questions, not even giving the man a chance to reply.

He throw his hands up quickly and said. "I got my fucking ass whooped, what do you want me to say?!"

We looked at him and his eyes were black, it just was not a good look. I remember that night like it was yesterday and it's crazy how life moves so fast one moment we're young chasing success and waiting to live out our dreams. Then the next day we're actually living what we dreamed. Unfortunately for Kidd success came but it made he lonely.

Chapter 36

The next week came around and everything was going pretty good. Sitting at the shop, I looked at the jar in my bag. Taking it out I looked at it and put the jar to my head. I then told myself. "Ray, are you thinking right now. Don't like curiosity get the best of you." I put the jar down on the table. Five minutes later Money shows up.

"Bang!" as he put his finger on the side of my head.

I jumped a little, looked up at him. "Shut ya ass up we in the shop a place of peace. Not your club."

He sat across from me. "You right, my bad, my bad."

I put my hand up and asked. "What brings you by anyways?"

He looked at me funny. "My bad if I want to get a joint, latte and relax." He leaned over the table a little. "The better question is what you are doing here, in the back…" He grabbed the jar before I could get to it. "What are these?" I reached back for the jar and he moved it to the side of him. He pulled a letter out the jar. Oh shit… Ray are these letters from Kidd?"

I snatched the jar back. "Yeah, it is and I already know. So you don't have to tell me."

He shook his head real slow as he looked at the jar. His eyes stayed on the jar. "Ray, I'm not even going to ask how you got them or why you have them. All I know is I don't want to be apart of none of that shit."

I put my hands on my head, then placed my head on the table.

He looked at me then the jar. Ray, you know how Kidd gets over Cherilyn." He went on to say. "Just think he was ready to kill for that girl, even when they weren't together. That's all I'm saying man."

I put my head up, hand rubbing my face. "Damn I see your point."

Money smiled, Remember how that night could have went a lot different?" As he tilted his head and looked at me. He then got up and said. "Kidd isn't one to play with and especially when it comes to Cherilyn. Just remember that Ray."

I guess I been getting lucky that Aiden hasn't walked in here and saw me reading the letters. Maybe it was the universe's way to tell me to stop reading because I'm cutting it close.

After Money left I thought of the night and it felt like I could still see everything. We were about to head off to college and one of our closes boys was having a big party. We decided to show up, one last time before good friends become strangers. We're in the party having a good time and we see a few of our friends circling up. Kidd and I go over there being nosey trying to figure out what's going on. We get over there and go to the front.

Kidd asked, "What's going on?"

James our boy said. "Shhh, let him finish the story."

Kidd looked at James then asked. "What's the story about?"

He told him, "I guess he almost knocked out this dude a couple of nights ago."

Louis was the one telling the story. "So, my best-friend Cherilyn came over and she was…"

Kidd cut in and asked. "Real quick did this Cherilyn go to upper East Side High?"

He looked at him. "Yeah so…"

Kidd quickly asked him another question. "Does this Cherilyn work at A & F?"

He look at him. "Yeah, man you done? Let me finish with the story."

Kidd shook his head a little. "Okay, finish." As he put out his hand.

Louis proceeded to tell the story. "So, Cherilyn my best friend comes over and she's crying, so I asked her 'what's wrong?' She looked up at me, with tears coming down here face. She tells me Karl her boyfriend hit her. I lost it because this my girl for life and I wasn't going to let it fly. I was ready to clap this ni**a."

The whole time Louis is telling the story I could see the fire continue to grow in Kidd's eyes.

Louis keeps going with the story. "The only thing from keeping me off that little ni**a was her. She kept talking about That's my baby." So I let her stay the night to get away from him.

Kidd looked at me. "Come on let's go. Call everyone tell them to get ready."

I'm walking behind him to the car. "Who is everyone and tell them to get ready for what?"

He opens the car down. "Don't worry about it Ray but are you coming or am I riding without you?"

I looked at him as I opened the passenger door. "If you going anywhere I'm riding with you."

As soon as Kidd started the car, he got on the phone. "Aye, get locked and loaded, I'm on my way to you." I was looking at him all types of crazy now. He's then said, "I'll explain when I get there."

James came to the car before we could leave. "Kidd, you good? I know that was your girl but don't mess up your future."

Kidd looked at him eyes low. "Nah, he messed up when he put his hands on her but don't trip and thanks for the invite to the party it was cool."

James put his head down. "Alright Kidd just be safe."As they shook hands.

Kidd drove off and I asked. "YO, what's good? What we doing?"

Looking straight ahead he said. "Don't worry Ray, this ni**a Karl really thinks he could do something like that to my girl."

I never seen him this upset before. Like I've seen him mad but this type of anger he had right now was unbelievable. We picked up Money, he asked Kidd. "What's good? What happen?"

Kidd said. "First you got that thang for me?"

Money looked at him sideways. "Yeah, you know I got you."
Then handed him a backpack. We pick up Pop and Truck, they asked
the same question. Kidd told them what happen and how Karl hit
Cherilyn and everyone in the car was hot and ready to knock this
dude out. Kidd tells our homeboy Brent to tell Karl to come outside.
Brent was the only one we knew that knew Karl and how to get to
his house.

We pull up to Karl's house and Kidd told Brent. "Tell him
you got something to give him and you outside."

Brent then asked, "What do I have to give to him?"

Kidd said. "Shit I don't now, some shorts or something."

Brent called him and told him exactly what Kidd wanted him
to say.

Truck pulled Kidd back in the seat. "You sure about this
Kidd, I think you need to maybe rethink it a little."

Pop looked at Truck. "You serious right now, this ni**a put
his hands on Cherilyn

Truck looked back at Pop. "All I'm saying is that she's really
not his girlfriend no more and he got a lot going right for him right
now."

Them two kept going back and forth on what Kidd should do
when Karl comes out the house. I was silent the whole time didn't
know what to say or what Kidd should do.

Money saying. "We better not get caught, that's all I know."

It was not to time to figure out what Kidd was going to do. Karl walked out the door, looking around for Brent trying to see where he was. As soon as Kidd's eyes locked on Karl, he reached in the backpack and hopped out the car.

Kidd rushed at him walking in the yard. Karl looked at, "Yo, what up?"

Kidd had a gun in his hand, cocked in back and pointed it at his head. "So you think, you could just put your hands on my girl like that!" It looked like Karl shitted on himself or something. Kidd got closer. "I should blow your fucking head off right now, for what you did."

Cherilyn came running out the house yelling out. "Aiden, don't do it! That's my baby!"

Kidd looked at her sideways. "What you say?"

She looked him in the eyes. "Aiden if you ever loved me, you wouldn't do this."

Kidd pushed his head with the gun. "You got some angles up there that's for sure." He then put the gun in his pants and came back to the car.

Pop pushed him. "Yo, what the hell? You was supposed to pop his ass or shit let me do it!"

Money looked at Kidd. "It's cool don't trip shit happens but you should have at least pistol whipped his ass."

I sat in the back still scared as shit, Kidd really had a gun and everything. I remember thinking to myself love could really make us do the craziest things. If that would have went the other way Kidd would not be in the position he is in today.

Chapter 37

Once again Kidd was out of town, catching up with Shevy and seeing how things were going up at the grow site. I always think about how close we are to the ones we went to Junior College with. Mom always told us these would be are lifelong friends but we didn't really believe her. College was something else that's for sure. We both ended up signing to this Junior College in Oregon. Crazy how that worked out because Kidd had just signed his letter of intent to go to FSU earlier that summer. The reason he didn't end up going was because they claimed he wasn't NCAA approved.

I remember Kidd coming there and really getting the shine like he did in high school but now it was a little more. We were playing every night and just being dumb like we were in high school.

When I look back at it now, I'm glad we went through the things we went through. It made us who we are today and I love to watch us succeed. We went from the city to this little town and Kidd was bringing life back into the town. Kidd decided to redshirt for the first year, he was still young only seventeen. I remember him saying to me. "Bro if they think I'm good now imagine me next year bigger, faster, stronger and that also means the next three years will be at a University. Come on Ray think about it." As he pointed to his head.

The next year came and he was better than ever. We were more than just the best team in our region. We were the team picked to win the tournament and everything. Kidd was balling out during all the preseason games and workouts. He was doing so good, that he had four of the top programs offering him a full ride scholarship. Wild how I always flash back to the old days, when everything was crazy but just right.

As I sit here reminiscing, I look up and Philip walks in. Philip was our first roommate in the dorm room life. He walked right past me. I grabbed him, "So you don't know anyone, no more?"

He looked at me and got hype. "Yo, Ray! What's good bro?"

I looked at him as I put my hand on the seat. "Sit down. I been good just chilling and enjoying life. What about you how's everything? How's the wife?"

He sat down and rolled his eyes. "Man, Nicole is driving me crazy, always wanting some shit or trying to figure out where I am, you know crazy girl shit like that."

I laughed as I said. "That's what being in love with one girl, will do to you."

He shook his head. "It's like she drives me crazy and everything but all I want is to be with her, like when I'm with her life is worth living." He looked at me with a confused look. Does that make sense?"

I smiled. "Yeah, that makes sense, Jasmine makes me feel the same way all the time and I'm marrying her."

He looked around. "What? Ray the big dreamer is getting married?"

I rubbed my face. "What can I say I been in love with her damn near my whole life."

Philip had a big smile on his face. "Congratulations bro that's a beautiful thing."

Smiled right back at him. "Thank you bro, just make sure you're at the wedding."

He shook his head. "Oh you know I'm going to in there." He then looked around. "Where's Kidd at?"

I looked at him confused. "He went to the O for a week or two, catching up with Shevy and Dre making sure our plants are growing the best." I then asked him. "Why, what's up?"

He rubbed his hands together. "I just wanted to tell him, I ran into Cherilyn last night at the club."

My mouth dropped. "No way!"

His eyes got big. "Yeah, bro I bumped into her and let me tell you, man she is beyond gorgeous."

I smiled and replied, "I bet, I mean I seen her at the grand opening of the club but it was dark and she was still fine as hell."

Philip looked at me. "Man I still don't know how Kidd let her go."

I shook my head. "Yeah I know but you live and you learn." I kept going on with, "for all I know, he pushes himself to the limit to prove that it was a good decision to leave her."

He looked at me sideways. "You really believe that, Kidd is that main one preaching about how we should love. And how we were made for that one person." He Finished with. "I know Kidd would give up all this bullshit to have the girl he fell in love with, in his arms one last time. I bet you that."

I laughed a little. "Philip, you would win I know Kidd is still in love with her. He puts on that front like he don't care about her but he still loves her deep down." I put my head on the table looking at my bag and said. "That's why he hasn't really gave himself to no other woman since."

He smiled as looked at his ring. "It's crazy how we thought it would be Kidd and Cherilyn that would be in love and married by now."

I laughed, "Your right, hurry let's get him back with Cherilyn."

We both laughed and looked at each other. "If it was that easy, it would have been happened by now." He shrugged his shoulders. He then started to laugh a little.

I looked at him sideways and asked. "What's so funny?"

He looked at me, hands went on top of his head. "I still remember the day, he burned the pictures of them two together and just to think I hyped him up to do it because I thought it would make him stop thinking about her."

I shook my head. "When was this?"

He told me. "We were living in the dorms and all I remember is he use to sleep with her picture under his pillow but he didn't want no one to know."

Sitting here in total shock I asked. "So how did you know about it?"

He put one of his eyebrows up and told me. "We were going out of town to meet with some overseas coaches. Before we left he told me to grab his pillow for the trip and when I grabbed it, her picture fell out. I put it on his bed. When we got back he tried to hide it but I told him I seen it already and that she was beautiful."

This was my first time hearing this story. "So what did he say?"

Philip then told me Kidd said. "I keep this with me, because it reminds me I still have something worth fighting for in this life."

I looked at Philip. "Kidd said that?"

He looked at me. "Honest to god bro. Kidd told me she's the only reason to stay alive in this cruel world." He kept going saying. "That's how I knew he would give any and everything up for that girl."

I shook my head in agreement. "Back to the story. Why did he burn their pictures?" I asked.

"Oh yeah, so Kidd told me that he keeps her picture in his wallet. So this way she's always with him. I told Kidd that she's something of the past and he needed to let her go."

Shaking my I asked him. "What did Aiden say after you told him that?"

Philip went on to say. "Kidd asked me how do you let someone go when they're the reason the sun and moon come out each day? I then told Kidd, 'First you need to delete anything that reminds you of her. So let's start with these pictures.' I then gave him a lighter."

Putting my head down. "Why would you give him a lighter?"

Philip looked at me. "So he could burn the pictures." As he rolled his eyes at him.

I looked at him sideways and said "I know stupid but that was his everything. That you told him to burn."

He looked right back at me sideways. "I know that and that's why when I seen her I knew I had to tell Aiden. Maybe he still had some hope or maybe somehow they can get back, shit or at least just see each other one more time."

I laughed and said. "Who knows, maybe they will get back together if their love is really that true."

He looked down at his watch. "But, that's why I came over here, to tell Kidd who I ran into but this dude ain't never in town."

Agreeing with as I shook my head. "Your right, I remember when everything was sample."

Philip got up. "Yeah the good old days were the best. Alright Ray, I gotta get back to the life I choose."

Shaking my head, "Already know man be safe out here. I'll tell Kidd to give you a call when I see him."

He throw up the peace sign as he walked out the door. Snatching my bag off the floor and looking at the jar. I tell myself I know it's wrong to read the last few letters but I'm almost done with the jar. I sat here and looked at the jar, I slowly reached in jar and pulled the next letter out.

Chapter 38

Cherilyn, I never knew when seeing you would be the last time and that kills me because I always wanted to start and end each day with the woman of my dreams. Not knowing when I will be able to watch the prettiest thing in the world breath, breaks my heart a little more each day that goes by without you. Maybe that's why I hold you a little longer and tighter each time. I'm scared I won't see you again. I know we lost time and the pain might still hurt but my heart will forever beat for you. When I'm dead and gone away my soul will search for you with no permission. The thing is I was made for loving you and no matter what in each lifetime, in each sense of reality I will look for you, our love is the only thing worth having close to my heart. I just pray I didn't already live the last time seeing you and if I did that moment I saw you in the store putting clothes away will hold a special place in my heart. I can still hear your voice when I'm in the mall and I can still feel your fingertips on my chest. Each night I pray you're the happiest and you feel no pain...

P.S. I'm a man of my word and I told you I will always love you.

Love. Kidd - xo

We were in our second year of college and at this point Kidd was the town's hero. We were back in city before going to our holiday tournament. Aiden kept asking Truck and I to go with him to the mall. Truck was a little older than us but he was like our big brother, he really looked out for me and Kidd. He also trained Kidd and it always seem like they had the same love problems going on. I always found that to be funny. The thing with Truck is he is one of the realest guys. He tells you how it is rather if it was ugly or not. I remember him coming with us to the mall.

Truck asked Kidd. "Why the hell we here anyways?"

Kidd smiled, "Damn, I can't just go to the mall with my boys and chill?"

Truck leaned his head back, eyes went low and he looked at Kidd. "Nah, fuck that Aiden I know you. What's the real reason?"

Kidd smiled again. "Just wanted to come to the mall that's it."

I step in and said. "You know Kidd he probably got some girl, he came up here to see."

He turned and looked at me with this grin like smile. We're walking around going to each store. Just looking around and clowning with each other. Kidd stopped and went into Tiffany's, me and Truck looked at each other sideways.

Truck pulled me back and asked me. "Yo, who is Kidd messing with up there at school?"

I put my hands up in confusion because Kidd was running through girls. He didn't have just one he kicked it with all the time. So for him to stop in this store left my mind there to wonder. We walked in behind him and to our surprise he was looking at engagement rings. The lady that was helping him knew Kidd by first name bases and everything. So we knew Kidd was in here more than once.

She asked Kidd. "So, Aiden you brought your friends in this time?"

He smiled. "Yeah I wanted to see what they thought of the style of the ring."

Truck grabbed him. "How many times do you come in here?"

Kidd looked at him. "Aye, y'all don't need to know everything I do." And then laughed a little as he pull his arm back.

We sat there and looked at each ring that she brought out of the case. The ring Kidd picked was beautiful, just absolutely stunning. She asked Kidd, "Aiden, when are you going to bring this special girl in?"

Kidd took a deep breath, "Time tells the best stories and this love story is still becoming perfect."

I looked at him lost for words from what I just heard. I pushed him, "Shut that shit up, who you getting this for anyways?"

He looked at me sideways with a grin on his face and looked at the lady. "Thank you so much for everything. I'll let you know if I ever get the chance to ask her the big question."

She smiled as she put the ring back in the case. "Whoever this girl is most be more than special."

As we were walking out, Kidd responded. "Being special would be a understatement for what she is to me."

Truck and I looked at each other and Truck grabbed Kidd. "Man what is it that you're not telling us, who are you planning to marry?"

Kidd brushed him off and smiled. "Just know if I ever get married, you'll be at the wedding."

I laughed, "Kidd you ain't getting married. Where we going now?"

Kidd looked at us and kept walking. We walked behind him and he then went into A & F. It's this clothing store, mainly for girls. Me and Truck looked at each other again.

Truck asked me. "What the hell is Kidd doing over there?"

I looked at him with a confused looked. "Probably trying to get at one of their models or something."

We walked in and seen Kidd sharing into space or at least that's what it look like. I ran up behind him and put my arm around him. "What the hell you thinking about?"

His eyes still looking forward. "Every time I see her, I feel the same fall over again and that's how it's been since the first time day."

After he said that I turned my head to look at who he was looking at and it was Cherilyn. I froze and Truck walked up on the other side of Kidd. "Yo, go say something to her." As he pushed him in her direction.

He turned to look at us. "Nah, I'm good she ain't worried about me."

I'm not sure how life works but when he said that she turned her head and seen us looking at her. She walked over with a big bright smile. "Aiden, oh my god how have you been? I've missed you!" As she gave him a hug, she half waved at us.

It was like right when she looked at him, this smile found it's way on his face like it was made to see her. As he hugged her, he picked her up and squeezed a little, eyes closed taking the moment in like he was going to lose it. He put her down. "Thank you for that, you cracked my back."

Kidd smiled. "You know me always trying to look out for you." They both laughed.

She asked him. "What brought you in and why are you on the girl's side anyways?"

We all looked at Kidd, waiting for the million dollar answer, right before he said anything Cherilyn said. "Oh let me guess you're in here for Amber?"

Kidd stepped back a little. "Nah, me and Amber ain't together. I came in here for Mia."

Me and Truck looked at each other sideways.

Cherilyn said, "Oh my little Mia, I miss her so much tell her that."

Kidd shook his head. "I got you but yeah I'm trying to win the best big brother award and why would I come to your store shopping for another woman?"

Me and Truck slowly made our way to the back to let them talk.

She said. "Oh my store, so you knew I worked here?"

Kidd stood there with a little smile. "I mean it might of just been a lucky guess. Cherilyn you know me."

She folded her arms. "Luck really Aiden? I thought you didn't believe in luck?"

He stepped back a little with a smile on his face. "Okay, maybe it was fate."

She laughed as she rolled her eyes. "Whatever Aiden, I see college ain't change you to much, still that funny smooth guy." As she was still smiling.

They stood there talking for about ten minutes. They were talking about their past and each other's future. Me and Truck were sitting, letting them have their moment. The crazy thing was I heard this couple behind us talking and the women said. "Remember when you use to come to my, job all the time trying to ask me out?"

The guy said, "Hey it worked, didn't it? I mean I have you now."

We got up and went back over by Kidd and Cherilyn.

Kidd asked her, "when's your lunch?"

She looked at her clock. "I took my lunch already but I'm about to go on break in five." Whipping her face she said. "This five minutes need to speed up, I need a snack."

Kidd asked her. "Where you planning on going?"

She looked him up and down. "JJ's they have my favorite drink and snack there."

Kidd told her. "Don't trip I'll go get it for you."

She told him. No, Aiden don't spend no money on me."

Kidd told her. "Getting you a snack or lunch really is nothing, I got you." He turned to walk out.

She yelled out. "You don't even know what I want!"

Kidd was by the door and he turned to look at her. "You want a berry topper layered with granola and bananas."

Her mouth dropped because that's exactly what she wanted. Truck and I looked at each other. Truck leaned over. "Yo, Kidd is good." We laughed.

I said. "Yeah the best."

Cherilyn ran to the door and yelled out. And I want a straw!" She laughed and said. "He's really the best." Under her breath.

I looked at her and asked. "What was that?"

She looked at me surprised. "Nothing, I just said Kidd was great that's all."

I made a smirk. "Yeah I bet that's all you said."

She giggled as she punched me in the arm. "Whatever Ray!"

Truck looked at me. "Aye, I'm about to go catch up with Kidd, I'm hungry as shit."

I looked at him and said. "You right my stomach is touching my back."

We turned to walk out when Cherilyn pulled me back. "Wait hold up Ray, let me talk to you."

Truck kept walking. "I'll be with Kidd."

I said. "Okay, I'll be there just give me a minute." As I turned to look at Cherilyn. "What's up? What you trying to talk about?"

She smiled a little and asked me. "What's wrong with Aiden?"

I put my hands on my head and said. "Nothing's wrong with Kidd, you know Kidd he just as cool as the other side of the pillow."

She giggled again. "Nah, there's something wrong with Aiden I know it. He can't pull that shit with me. Maybe with everyone else but not with me. I can see and feel pain in his heart."

I couldn't believe she was really considered about Kidd right now. They both knew how to show little emotion to the world. I always envied that about both of them.

I asked her. "Why does it matter, if Kidd is okay or not?"

She looked at me sideways with a mad look on her face, one eyebrow raised. "Because Aiden is amazing and shouldn't feel anything but happiness."

I was in total shock just hearing her say anything like that to me.

She looked me up and down and said. "It's because Amber wasn't me huh?"

Looking her in the eyes I told her. "Cherilyn, nobody will be you. You made Kidd truly happy, he never talked about anyone the way he talks about you and I never seen him look at anyone the way he looks at you."

She blushed and said. "I know and believe me I miss him."

Putting my hands on my head. "Then give him one more chance."

She turned her shoulder. "I can't. He hurt me and it feel like I was dying."

Putting my head down. "I get that but you two were just young. All I know is, it was the real thing when it came to love with you guys."

She bit her bottom lip. "Maybe but I don't know if I can take that chance again." She then looked at her watch and told me. "Go see what's taking Kidd so long." As she pushed me towards the door.

I still couldn't believe what she told me. Walking to JJ's I see Kidd and Truck walking back to the store.

"Yo! Kidd!" I ran up to him. Told him what she told me and Kidd couldn't believe it either.

Kidd stood there and then leaned over the rill. "What should I do?"

I didn't have answer for him. Truck looked at him and said. "Tell her what you tell us. Keep it real with her."

He looked at both of us. "Your right, it's time to man up and get my girl back." He started to walk.

Truck pulled me back. "Nah let him do this alone."

He smiled at her right when he walked in. She looked at him then her watch. "Dang it took you long enough." As she reached out for her snack.

Kidd pulled her snack back."If I knew you were waiting on me I would have ran over here." Then headed her the snack.

She rolled her eyes and they sat down. "Thank you Aiden. And nobody was waiting for you, just wanted my snack and wanted to know what took you so long."

Kidd laughed. "Cherilyn you don't see me complaining."

Cherilyn leaned back. "What would you complain about?"

Kidd licked his lip then told her. "Shit I mean I been waiting for you my whole life and somehow we're here and I'm still waiting for you."

Cherilyn smiled and shook her head then told him. "And somehow you're the reason why we're apart."

Kidd put his head down. "Yeah let's not get into that. I just wanted to stop and make sure everything was going good with you." As he turned around to walk out.

She pulled him back and asked. "What's wrong Aiden?"

He stood there and looked at her with a blank facc. "Nothing, I'm chillin but I gotta leave." He then walked out.

He walked up to us and Truck ask him. "So what happen? What she say? Ni**a tell us what you said?"

Kidd put his head down. "I couldn't say anything. My heart was beating like crazy and I couldn't find no words to explain to tell her how I felt."

Truck grabbed him and looked Kidd in the eyes. "If you don't go in there and tell that girl how you feel, I don't want to hear shit about her ever again and if you say anything about her, I'm going to knock yo ass out."

Kidd's eyes got big. "Your right. Fuck it I don't got shit to lose. I mean I already don't have her and that's the worst thing already."

I pulled him towards me. "Don't hold nothing back, leave it all out there. Shit if you can give her that thing in your chest then do it."

Kidd was hyped now. "I got this! When the game is on the line who do you want to have the ball? That's me Kidd, I got this." He turned around and went back in the store.

Cherilyn was talking to one of her coworkers when Kidd walked back in. He walked up behind her, he then tapped her on the shoulder. "Cherilyn can I talk to you real quick?"

She turned and looked at him. "Yeah, what's up Aiden?" Her coworker walked off.

Kidd stepped a little closer to her. "I couldn't leave here and not be honest with you."

She looked at him. "I knew there was something wrong with you." She looked him in the eyes. "It's because Amber isn't..."

Kidd cut her off. "Cherilyn it doesn't matter who it is, they won't be you and nobody will ever be you. You're the reason I believe in love. When I didn't have nothing to smile about, I still smiled because I new I had you and not having you is the worst thing to live without."

317

She cut him off. "Kidd you can have any girl and your in college being the star, everything you ever wanted."

He told her. "That's wrong, you're the only thing I ever wanted and I promise, I would always keep it real with you and that's the real reason I came in here. It wasn't to shop but to see you one more time."

She stop him there and put her hand on his chest. "Aiden, you can't keep doing this to yourself. You made us like this."

His eyes getting watery. "Your right, I just wanted you to know the truth." As he pulled her in for a hug then kissed her on the forehead. "I will always love you Cherilyn. Don't forget that." He turned around and walked back out the store.

His eyes red when he walked out. I ran over to him. "Yo, what's good?"

Truck asked him. "Yo, what she say?"

Kidd kept walking right pass both of us straight to the car. We ran over to him. "Bro, what's good talk to us."

He turn to us before getting on the escalator as a tear ran down his cheek. "Nothing happen, just know she don't love me no more."

We both stood there and looked at each other. "What, that doesn't make no sense." I told Truck.

He said. "Yeah, I don't know what just happen."

We started making are way to Kidd, he was going straight to the car. We got to the car and he was sitting inside shaking his head with the music playing. We got in the car with him, Truck put his hand on his shoulder. "Bro, it's cool at least, you know you tried."

I put my head on his head. "Man you good, there's someone better out there."

He put his head on the steering wheel. "I get that but y'all don't understand she takes me to a place unimaginable and trying to live without that is hard… I just thought maybe something was different in the stars for us, ya know."

I remember looking at him after he said that and I told him. "Kidd you gotta move on now and get ready to ball the fuck out when we get back to school."

He looked at us and said. "I guess its welcome back to the real world." As he shook his head and drove off.

Chapter 39

Kidd was back in town, for his First Annual Art in the Clouds event. It was a event he put together with a couple of people he knew from the poetry, photography and music sense he became apart of over the years. It was a way to give back, where anyone could live out their dream and show off their art. He said it was the best way to allow people to still catch their dreams. It lets them know their goals aren't out of arm's reach. He always had some type of event on December first. He said it was because that was the night that changed him forever. It was a night that took his life and made him realize the true beauty is all around us.

We were at the gallery setting up for the night to come. With this being his first big event and all the people expected to come. Kidd walked up on the phone. "I'm still thinking about getting on. I haven't decided yet."

I looked at him and put my hand on his shoulder. "Who is that?"

He paused and looked at me. "It's Dre and Shevy they wanted me to spit something tonight."

Kidd was a poet or use to be at least, he hasn't written or performed anything in a while. With everything going on in his life, I guess he doesn't have time.

He got off the phone. "So, Ray how's everything going?"

Looking around at the whole set up. "How does it look like everything is going? You know, we going off you Kidd." As I put my arm around him.

We were now looking at how everything was coming to together. "Man look at this." As Kidd waved his hand. "A Kidd from nothing is really inspiring people to follow their dreams. Now that's some crazy shit." He laughed a little looking at the stage.

I responded. "You always been the one Kidd and I thank you for the journey through this thing we call life."

He patted me on the chest as he laughed. "Oh so now you're the poet?"

I laughed. "Nah, just learned a few things, ya know." I looked at him then asked. "So you're getting on or what?"

Snatching his head back rubbing his neck. "Who knows I might say a word or two depends how I feel at the moment."

I pushed him. "Yeah, yeah whatever I know you and you got something up your sleeve I can feel it."

He smiled. "Maybe I do, maybe I don't, you going to have to wait and see." He then walked off to talk to the other artist that were here.

Watching everyone come together and feel nothing but joy was amazing. But I couldn't help but to think about the night we almost lost Kidd. It's crazy no matter how many years go by, I can still feel that night all over again.

After we go back from break, it was like Kidd had something to prove. We had just got back in town from the holiday tournament we were invited too. Kidd was the most valuable player at the tournament. He was the only freshmen starting and he was leading our team in points. Also he was up to be the caption. Before the season even started, Kidd had already had big schools offering him a scholarship. After winning the tournament Kidd sock the world with a verbal commitment to ASU. Our school at this time was in Oregon, so we were nowhere close to our home. We get back into town around midnight. As we're getting off the bus, coach stopped Kidd. "Aiden, make sure you go to sleep."

Kidd looked at him smiling. "You know me coach, I'm just going to be chillin."

Before Kidd could walk away coach grabbed him. "Your right I do know you. That's why I'm tell you to go to sleep."

Still smiling Kidd said. "I'm probably going to rub on some booty." He then laughed.

Coach started to laugh. "I don't need to know everything Kidd but get out of here and get some sleep." Kidd started to walk to his room. Coach grabbed me. "Ray make sure Kidd doesn't do anything stupid."

I told coach. "I got you don't worry about anything." I then ran over to catch up with Kidd. I got on the side of him. "Yo, so what you got planned for tonight?"

He looked at his phone. "Shit I don't know yet. Some of the guys are going to this party and want me to come with. Might go don't really know yet though."

I told him. "Didn't coach tell you to stay in and go to sleep?"

He looked at me weird. "Man, coach says a lot of shit but does that mean I do what he says… No didn't think so."

Shaking me head. "Yeah, whatever you say Aiden."

We go to the room and within ten minutes, it was three of our teammates running in our room telling Kidd he needs to come to the party.

Kidd looked at them. "Nah, I'm just going to chill here and play the game ya know some chill shit."

Anthony our point guard told him. "You have to come, nothing but girls there and they all want to see Kidd. So get yo ass up and get dressed."

Kidd looked at him sideways. "Bro I'm chillin."

Sean our other teammate pulled a bottle of Hennessy from his hoodie. "Kidd we turning up tonight. Come live a little."

When Sean did that Anthony pulled a bag of some bug out and said. "Bro come on now you know it's going up tonight."

He got up and started getting dressed. I looked at him sideways now. "Bro coach said to stay in and get some sleep."

He looked at me as he was putting on these ripped bleach jeans. "Yeah, I'll get some sleep when I'm dead but until then, I'm going to enjoy being young."

They were all dressed and looked at me, Kidd asked. "Ray, you coming?"

I looked at my phone and it was one in the morning already. "Nah, I'm just going to go to Jasmine's."

Kidd laughed."He gets one little taste of some ass and falls in love." He shook his head as everyone laughed.

I said." So you got jokes I can see. Sorry if I still believe in this thing called love."

He brushed me off and waved his hand. "Yeah, you missed me with that shit Ray but I'm going to hit you when we get back."

Told him. "Okay cool and if I don't answer I'll get with you tomorrow."

He gave me a handshake and walked out. Little did I know that was almost our last hand shake. When he got in the car, our teammates gave him a six pack. Kidd was drinking one after another while our boys rolled up a blunt. They got to the house and at first there was hardly anyone there, by two o'clock in was packed. Shoulder to shoulder everyone enjoying themselves. Kidd was on the beer pong table and was not losing. Talking shit after each shot he made.

"Who's next? It don't matter because I'm giving out buckets to everyone all night." Then put his hands in the air.

Anthony came over to the table. "Aye, Kidd let's go down the street and kick it with some more girls. It's getting too packed in here."

Kidd looked at Doug who was one of our other teammates that also was his partner on the table. Kidd told Anthony. "Alright, we're going to meet y'all outside after this game. I'll make it fast don't trip."

Anthony told him. "Okay make that shit fast, we got females to get too."

Kidd and Doug laughed. "Yeah, we know that's why we'll make it fast."

Anthony turn to walk out. "Whatever you say Kidd just hurry up."

They started the last game and as they were playing these girls were eyeing Kidd. One of them walked up to him and pull him as she put a paper in his pocket. Kidd looked at her and bit his lip. "Okay beautiful I got you."

"As he rubbed his finger on his chin, then hit the next shot. They were down to the last cup on the table, when Kidd started talking shit again.

"Y'all don't understand, the Kidd can't be stopped!" He then shot the ball into the last cup.

Everyone in the party went crazy yelling and everything. Doug looked at Kidd and told him. "Let's meet the team outside."

Kidd responded. "You right it's time to blow this spot."

They headed for the door. The girls and her friends were smiling at Kidd. He winked at her as she smiled and giggled at him. As they made their way out the house. Kidd bumped shoulders with this guy. The guy pushed Kidd and said. "Watch where the fuck you're going Nigger!"

Kidd looked at him fire filled his eyes. "Nah, fuck the bullshit! Let's take this shit outside, since you can't watch your fucking mouth."

They both made their way to the door and the whole time they exchanged words until they got outside. When Kidd got to the porch, the guy's friend ran up and punched Kidd in the mouth. Doug right away hopped in and got the friend. Kidd shook the punch off and started fighting the guy and whooping his ass. They beat both of the guys up and the guys ran back in the party. Now Kidd was beyond on pissed off, everyone was grabbing him trying to get him in the car. He was to upset and pushing everyone off him saying.

"Fuck that everyone out the car they got us fucked up. Get back to back these ni**as don't know where I'm from!"

He then walked in the middle of the crowd and yelled out.

"It don't matter, anyone can get they ass whooped who's first!"

The guy who he was agreeing with ran out first and Kidd punched him twice and dodged his punch. Then another guy ran over swinging at Kidd. Kidd stepped back dodged his punch then got hit by another guy from the back. Now everyone was out of the car trying to hit someone, punches were flying everywhere. There was only seven of our teammates at the party and one of them ran off as soon as the fight started. Punches filled the sky and out of nowhere a loud smash goes off everyone looking around trying to figure out what just happen. Sirens rang out loud, everyone running trying to disappear into the night. Looking around they seen Kidd laid out on the ground, head bloody, eyes struggling to hold on to conscience. The team ran over trying to get him up and into the car. A police officer showed up trying to help and when he seen Kidd,he paused for a second. Kidd was taking his last breaths. The officer held Kidd in his arms blood everywhere, put two fingers on his neck and didn't feel no pulse. The officer picked him up when the sirens of the ambulance came closer. They put him in the back right away, the EMT's started working on him. They pronounced him dead, no sign of a heartbeat. Thirteen minutes later his heart started to beat again and they rushed him to the hospital. Kidd was now in a coma fighting for his life. I remember my phone going crazy in the morning. I picked the phone up when I seen my coach's name. Hey what's up coach?'

He said. "Ray, are you sitting down?"

I had just woken up so I was laying down. "Yeah coach what's up?"

He took a deep breath and a long pause. "Were you at the party last night?"

I told him. "Nah, I was sleeping." As I turned and looked at Jasmine laying right next to me.

Coach then took another deep breath. "It's Kidd."

I shook my head. "What did he do?"

Coach said. "He was in a fight last night."

My first thought was he was in jail or something because I knew how Kidd could get when he gets mad.

Coach's voice got low and he said. "Kidd is in a coma."

I jumped up, Jasmine looked at me crazy. "Ray, what happen?"

I was putting my clothes on in a rush not saying anything to her. She got louder each time. "Ray! Talk to me!"

This was my first time snapping at her. "Kidd is in a coma! And I should have been there!" Then walked out her house.

I ran into Shevy's room, he looked at me in total shock. "Yeah, I know coach just called me."

We both sat there and looked at each other. After about five minutes to let everything set in, we got on the phone trying to find out what happen last night. We end up finding out that Kidd was fighting three guys, one of them hit him in the head with a glass bottle. This lady who was the next door neighbor hit him in the head with a crowbar. I remember walking into the hospital and seeing Mom in tears as she looked at Kidd with all these tubes running though his body.

I told her. "Kidd is the strongest guy I have ever met, he's going to come back to us."

Every day in that room, people wanted to see him and be there for the family. They had to perform brain surgery in order to save his life. The doctors had to cut a piece of his skull to relieve the pressure off his brain. They said his brain was swelling up at a fast rate. It felt so unreal each day that went by, not knowing if he would open his eyes again or even if he would be the same person when he woke up. Kidd was trending on every social media outlet there was. It was like everyone wanted to show how much they loved him. That's when I found that saying to be true, "everyone loves you once you're gone."

Mom asked me. "Ray, do you think I should reach out to Cherilyn?"

I kinda put my head back and looked at her. I don't know but I do think she should know."

I mean even if Cherilyn and Kidd weren't together she was the girl he fell in love with. Mom got on the phone and made the to Cherilyn.

"Hey Mom." Is all I heard when she answered the phone.

Mom paused a little. "I don't know if you heard but Aiden is in a coma."

Cherilyn paused. "Oh my god!" She started to cry on the phone, I could hear her voice get low and trickle a little. She asked Mom to do her a favor. "Can you do me one thing Mom?"

Mom looked at the phone. "Yeah anything, what is it?"

She told her. "Can you kiss him on the forehead and tell him, he promised no matter what in each lifetime we would be together. So I'm going to need him to keep that promise."

Mom put her hand over her mouth then said "Cherilyn don't worry, I'll tell him."

They then got off the phone. Mom looked at me. "I think, I just broke her heart all over again."

I looked at Mom confused. "Why would you say that?"

Mom put her head down on Kidd's bed. "I could hear it in her voice."

I looked at Aiden then the Mom's phone in her hand. "Come on bro you need to wake up, Cherilyn still needs you, shit I still need you."

I remember those three weeks he was in a coma was the worst three weeks of my life. Not knowing if I would be able to laugh with my boy again was the worst feeling. Kidd woke up and that had to be the happiest day. For him to open his eyes was super big for us. Everyone going crazy just happy to see his eyes one more time. It was kinda funny when he woke up, he had all these girls saying they were going to marry him and all this extra stuff. It still blows me away because he had to start from the beginning with everything, learning how to read, write, walk and talk all over again.

Chapter 40

I still can't believe he went through all that and now he's here giving others a reason to follow their hearts. Kidd walked back up to me and put his arm around my shoulder. "Man, Ray how this day could be so much different right now."

I put my arm around him. Yeah, I know who would have thought, I would still have to put up with your shit all these years." I then squinted and asked him. "So, do you still remember that night?"

He looked at me with a straight face. "Remember that night? On some days I can feel my body reliving each step and it scares the shit out of me."

Right after he said that Money walked up. "Yo, Kidd this some fancy shit, I still remember all the open mics we went to over the years."

Kidd looked at him and smiled. "Yeah, those were the days. Where leaving it all out there was the only thing to do because we knew we were leaving something behind."

Money looked at him. "So does that mean you going to get up there and give us a little something? We haven't heard you in a minute. So give us some new shit."

Kidd took a deep breath. "I guess we're going to have to just wait and see."

I looked at Money. "You know them so called artistes always trying to be secretive and shit."

Money laughed. "I know, either that or he doesn't have nothing else to give us."

Kidd stepped back in and said. "Nah, I got something to give y'all. It just might be to deep for y'all hearts that's all."

I looked at Money. "Yeah right, I guess we'll just wait and see."

Kidd smiled and as he walked away he said. Just wait and see because Kidd doesn't let down nor does he disappoint."

I responded. "Yeah, yeah, whatever we'll believe it when we see it."

Kidd laughed and walked off to get ready of the event. It was getting closer for the event to start. Kidd was on stage now. "People! people! come closer bring it in."

Everyone made their way closer to each other and closer to the stage. Kidd began to speak. "Somehow life brought you here and that means for some reason it knew you needed each other and that allows us to make the world beautiful again. So I welcome you to The Art In The Clouds where artist from anywhere can come and show their art off. Tonight we'll have painters, musicians and poets bless the stage. Remember to enjoy yourself and also to allow yourself to take all the beauty in because there still so much beauty in this world."

I was standing with Money, Dre, Shevy and Truck. I leaned in and said. "I'm guessing he practice that shit."

They laughed Dre said. Yeah, I know he did but those were still some nice words."

Money added. "Shit I know how we can get Kidd up there to spit something."

I looked at him sideways. How you going to do that?"

Money looked at his phone. "I'll get up there and show off some word art."

I looked at him. "Is it going to be some new shit? Or something on one of your songs?"

He looked at me. "Some shit that hits the soul and makes life meaningful again."

I smirked my mouth. Okay, Money let's see what you got."

Money called Kidd over. "Aye, if I get up there and spit something, you gotta spit something also."

Kidd looked at him. "Okay but it has to be something only the heart can hear."

I looked at both of them. "So is that a yes?"

Money looked at me. "Nah, that's a hell yes!"

We sat back and watched different artist get on stage and show of their art. There was an amazing painter that painted a masterpieces of a beautiful broken heart. Then there was a violinist who had everyone lost for words. The show and event was going great, then the poets came and rocked the stage each with a different flow and story.

I always thought it was funny how life worked out. They took a ten minute intermission break to talk to each other about the artist who blessed the stage. Kidd was on the other side talking to a couple of photographers about different shots and lighting. It was amazing watching everyone from different backgrounds vibe together and enjoy each other's art. I looked to my right and froze Cherilyn was moving her hair to the other side of her face. My mouth dropped, I was now looking around for Kidd but he was already back on stage about to start the closing of the event.

Kidd grabbed the mic. "I hope everyone is enjoying the night and all the art around but more than anything I hope it makes you believe in that thing beating in your chest and I hope that beat is telling you to follow your dreams."

I turned and looked to make sure Cherilyn was still there and to my surprise she was sitting down smiling at Aiden. It made me smile and laugh a little because she was looking at him like it was her first time seeing him. It was a couple people ahead then it was Money and Kidd right after him. I got up and walked closer to Cherilyn, I was on her left side now.

I leaned over and asked her. "Do you still believe in love?"

Cherilyn quickly turned back and looked at me, got up and hugged me. "Hey, Ray!"

We sat down and I laughed. "So, you're not going to give me an answer?"

She smiled. "Love is all around us and it makes me smile each day, so yes Ray I still believe in love."

I asked her. "So, what brought you all the way down here?"

She smiled again. "I don't really know, I guess it was just the art in the clouds that brought me to the beauty." She gave out a light giggle.

"You always had ways with those words." I quickly said back to her as I was shaking my head.

She asked me. "Is Kidd performing? Because I heard he was something to watch."

I looked at her then up at the stage. "Yeah, that's what he said but I never know with Kidd."

She squinted her eyes and asked me. "Was he going around the question?"

I told her. "Yeah he was never giving a set answer."

She smiled once more. "He's going to get up there don't worry."

I looked at her sideways. "How do you know?"

She looked at the stage, as Kidd came back on. "Because I know Aiden."

Still looking at her I said. "I know you do… Probably the only one who does."

Kidd got on stage. Beautiful people the night is coming to an end but we still have one more performer, who is a good good friend of mine. We started everything when were young and foolish but somehow life kept us together and somehow it's allowing us to reach people's heart by giving them our art. Please give it up to one of my best friends Marc 'Money' Mills."

We all clapped and Cherilyn said. "I wondered if he was going to get up there and spit something."

Looking at the stage and wondered if Cherilyn kept taps on us or something because Kidd hasn't spoken to her in seven years now. Before I could ask her anything Money got on the mic.

"Thank you all for being here. I feel we as people keep a lot of emotion hidden but tonight we let all those emotions out because being vulnerable is perfectly okay."

He took a deep breath and started. *"Sometimes I dream about that perfect love. The love you read about the kind you watch on a big screen. The love the songs print in the lyrics...."*

We all clapped and were blown away, it was just like Money to keep it short and sweet. Kidd was back on. "After that how could someone top that. Now that was the best way to close this event. I hope everyone had a great night with all the art around you. Make sure to spread the love."

I couldn't believe it, Kidd wasn't going to perform anything. I looked at Cherilyn and she was in shock as well.

She looked at me. "I guess I don't know Aiden like I thought I did."

Money came back on and grabbed the mic. "Wait, wait, wait my good friend the one who brought us together tonight would love to share a beautiful word or two before we call it a night. So give it up for Aiden 'Kidd' Brewing."

Kidd turned around shaking his head no. Cherilyn stood up and headed for the door. Kidd's eyes locked on her. "Okay, I'll give you beautiful people a piece I keep close to my heart."

Cherilyn frozen and turned around, then came back and stood next to me. Kidd didn't want the mic but for everyone to hear the emotion in his voice. He stepped up.

"I always imaged running into her, what would I say when my heart sees the one who made the beat in my chest something to listen to, what words world my lips form when they speak to the one who made the phase I love you a feeling, and what feelings would my body want to feel when her name comes back with every emotion known to man. The crazy thing is I come up with three different scenarios on how I could run into her each day, so that's about 21 different ways a week and about 84 different ways a mouth and it's only been around 18 hundred days, since the last time I seen her. I only know that because my memories won't let the thought of her leave my mind. If it was written for us to cross paths one more time but the catch was loving her was going to kill me just as fast as a bullet could. I would give her both my heart and the gun to let her know, as long as there was US in the word trust she would have me, the same way she had me at hello when we met years ago. I just wished someone told me how this love thing worked out before I let my soul suffer without her…"

His eyes stayed on her for each word. She whipped her face turned and walked out shaking her head. Kidd jumped off the stage and went after her. Everyone sat there lost of words, then claps filled the room once everyone realized it was her that the poem was about. Money came back on. "As you can see and feel the love in the air, make sure to take the art and keep it in the sky for the world to see. Thank you and goodnight."

Kidd caught up to Cherilyn. "Cherilyn, where are you going?" He yelled out as he pulled her back.

She moved her shoulder. "Somewhere, out of here!"

Kidd turned her around so she could see him. "Why are you leaving?"

She looked up at him. "Because I can't feel this way no more Aiden! You don't understand you never did!"

Kidd put his head down to look at her. Then help me understand please, because I been lost even since I let you go."

She pushed him and he grabbed her hands and pulled her in closer. "You have to stop it Aiden! You mean to tell me you knew you loved me after you let me go? Save that shit for someone else."

Kidd put his head up looking at the sky, trying to hold his emotions in. His head went down. "Cherilyn, I loved you from the moment you pulled up at my house on Halloween." A tear ran down his face.

She said, "Aiden I don't want to love you, this shit hurts." She stepped back as Kidd let her go. "It's like when I see you, all these feelings come running back to my stomach and then you say that shit up there on stage…"

Kidd whipped the tears coming from her eyes. "I needed you to know all I ever wanted and needed was me and you. Because love is something you don't give up on."

She cut him off. "Aiden, I can't do this." She turned to walk off.

Aiden pulled her back once again. "Can't do what?"

She looked at him, both of their eyes red and watery. "I can't love you." She turned around and walked to her car.

Kidd stood there and watched her drive off. I came up behind him. "Kidd is everything okay?"

He turned and looked at me. "She doesn't love me. She never did."

Putting my hand on his shoulder, lost for words I asked. "So, what does that mean now?"

Whipping his face. "That means no matter how much time goes by, it will always feel like I'm losing her all over again." He looked at me. "The crazy thing is, everything feels better when she's here. Rather it be for five minutes or five seconds." He put his head down once again then ended our conversation with. "I never really knew, something so beautiful could bring so much pain."

With his head still done he made his way to the car. I stood there lost and confused. Shevy came up on the side of me. "Where's Kidd going? Is he cool?"

Dre, Money and Truck walked up. We all watched him pull off. I rubbed my face and said. "It was like they broke each other's heart again."

Money added. "I knew something like this was going to happen, I could feel it in the air but I would have never guessed Cherilyn would came. And that Kidd would spit the one poem, he keeps close to his heart. Now that shit lost me."

"How long has it been since they seen each other?" Truck asked.

I told him. "They haven't seen or spoken to each other in seven years today actually."

Dre said. "Damn that's crazy, just to think with all the girls Kidd's been with, Cherilyn is still the one who holds his heart. Who would have thought?"

I told them. "It's always been Cherilyn, it will forever be her and I guess that's how love works."

We ended up calling it a night and all went back to our lives, I knew everyone would check up on Kidd. So I decided to let him think.

Chapter 41

About a couple of days go by after the whole running into Cherilyn. Kidd was held up in his house, didn't want to talk or see anyone. I was at the shop getting ready to go over some paperwork and bills that needed to be handled before our shop gets closed.

Right when I open my bag, Jasmine comes up. "Hey babe? What are you doing?"

Stop zipping my bag. "About to handle these bills, so we can keep living our beautiful life."

She smiled. "Always working. I like that Ray." She rubbed her hands together then asked me. Do you know if Kidd is okay?"

I looked at her then at my phone. "The last time I talk to him, he said he wanted to be alone and not to worry about him."

She put her head down, then it went right back up with a smile. "So, that was Cherilyn at the gallery?"

My smiled quickly went away. "Just know Aiden checked back into the heartbreak hotel."

Her eyes got big and mouth dropped. "Did she not hear what he said?"

I smiled. "Yeah, I'm pretty sure she heard what he said, but sometimes love only hold people together for so long."

She looked at me sideways. "Not if it's true love."

Putting my head up to look at her. "Some aren't this lucky babe." I then leaned into to kiss her.

She kissed me and got up. "Ray, I love you so much." She then kissed me on my head. "I'm going to let you finish up." She turned to walk out the door. "Just call me when you get done."

I told her. "Okay, I love you"

I went back to unzipping my backpack. Seen the jar and there was one letter, that I didn't get a chance to read. Something told me not to open the jar but curiosity is a bitch. I reach in my bag brought the jar out and sat it on the table. Opening the led grabbing the final letter.

So I know it's been awhile since we talked and it's been even longer since I see your beautiful smile. I still have yet to met someone who could bring that same beat and emotion to my heart. I know you would say I need to do something to be happy and stop hurting myself by thinking about us but it's kinda hard to forget about you. When I see your reflection in a glass window or how I hear your voice singing each song that plays. I still remember you placing your hand on my heart and telling me I needed to be happy. Until this day I can feel your handprint when I stop and touch my chest. That's why I still hope when October comes around and a leaf lands on you. It reminds you how I fell for you because it was nature to fall in love with you. Sometimes I still carver our names in tables and chairs, then hope one day you'll see it and remember all our conversations. Cherilyn all I know is you'll forever be my favorite walk down memory lane. It's funny because I never believed pain would last this long, but it would kill if you left my thoughts. I believe this is why my eyes trick my heart into seeing your smile each day because it knows, not having you would bring death faster than any illness known to me. I wrote this to tell you thank you for allowing me to fall in love with you. Even though I know we might just be hopeless hearts passing by, loving you was the best decision I made...

P.S. Someone somewhere is dreaming about our one

of a kind love and somewhere else a couple

is living out our what if's...

Love. Aiden Brewing – XO

I hear a voice behind me say. "I remember writing that and telling myself no matter what, nothing I say or write will ever bring her back to my arms."

I turned to look and seen Aiden standing there arms folded. Eyes locked on me and I could see the fire growing in his eyes. Not only that, but the whole vibe changed in the room.

Aiden was now rubbing his hands. 'The crazy thing is I never sent a letter off to her. So please tell me why the fuck I find you here reading one of the letters I wrote for her eyes?" He then snatched the jar off the table. He looked at the jar then back at me. "Not only that but you got the whole fucking jar!"

My eyes still big and in shock I tried to say. "Sorry…"

He slammed the jar on the table. "Sorry, that's all you got to say is sorry? Nah how about this fuck you and your sorry!"

My face in confusion. "Kidd it's not even like that." He turned to walk out and I got up. "Aiden, you're really about to do this over some letters?"

He stopped back still turned towards me. The jar in one hand and the other hand on his head. When he turned around the jar came flying out of his hand. I ducked the glass jar hit the wall behind me. Glass and letters filled the floor, I heard each letter land on the ground. Kidd's eyes red and watery. "Those weren't just letters Ray, those are the only way I find peace. The only thing that brings her back to me when I need to believe in something bigger than myself." He clenched his jaw, then looked me in my eyes. "Ray I trusted you!"

I stepped in a little closer. "Bro I know it was wrong to read it but…"

He cut me off. "But nothing! Ray I should break your fucking mouth right now but I'm not. Just find a way to delete yourself from my life." He turned and walked out the door. I stood there speechless, looking at all the mess caused from these letters. I started to clean up, works wanted to help but this was my mess and I didn't want anyone to see these letters from Aiden. The whole time all I could think was I never seen Aiden that upset and disappointed all at once.

As I continued to pick up each letter, I found there were even more letters I didn't get a chance to open. Heard the door open but I didn't pay too much attention to it. A soft voice spoke to me. "Ray, slow down you don't want to get cut by the glass or even worst a paper cut." Little giggled followed.

I turned around and it was Cherilyn standing with a smile on her face. She looked at the mess on the floor. "Who the hell did you get mad? And what happened?" As she was kneeling own picking up a letter. "I didn't know you wrote Ray?"

Still looking at her in total shock I replied. "These are your letters Cherilyn."

She looked at me sideways and looked at one of the letters. Opening the letter and out loud read. "*Hey, Cherilyn as you know living without you is the hardest thing to do…*"She went quite reading the rest in her head. After I picked up the last of the letters on the floor, I heard her read.   *"Don't give up on me, there was never no love lost. We were just lucky enough to meet the perfect soulmate…"* Her eyes then went on me.

Standing in front of her with all these letters in my hands. I reached out my hands giving her all the letters. She handled the letters in her hands as she stared at each one curious to find out what Kidd wrote to her. I turn to find her something to put them in but she grabbed me. "Ray, sit down. Have a joint and a latte with me."

I did just what she asked me to do. I could tell she had many questions by the look she had in her eyes. We order our drinks and joints, than began to get reacquainted with one another. Smile still on her face as she looked around then asked. "Where is Aiden?".

Putting my head down in shame, I said. "I'm surprised you didn't run into him."

She quickly looked at the door. "Why you say that?"

Putting my head up with a grin on my face. "He kinda caught me reading one of those letters in your hand."

Her eyes dropped down to the letters. "Why would you be reading one of these letters?"

Shaking my head, as my hands laid on my face. "Because they take me back to when Aiden was happy and reading those letters put you back in his life in my mind."

She smiled as she gripped the letters tighter. "Ray, you mean to tell me Aiden isn't happy? All his dreams came trues. How could he not be happy?" As she waved her hand to show me the shop.

I looked her in the eyes. "Because he doesn't have you." Before she could say anything I explained. "Cherilyn, I have never seen anyone make that man any happier than you did. Everything he had done, he hoped you would you like it and it would bring you to him."

She sat up straight. "Yeah I bet, I'm guessing that's the same reason he's been with so many women."

Rubbing my neck. "Yeah, you kinda are the reason for that as well." As I let out a little chuckle. She rolled her eyes before saying anything. I told her. "Every girl Aiden has been with, he looked for you in them, whether it was the way she laughed, to the way she walked."

She looked at me eyes big. "So, you're telling me he pretended that girl was me?" Eyebrows went up.

I laughed a little then said. "Not necessarily. All he ever said was nothing felt the same with any other girl."

She leaned forward on the table. "Okay, whatever you say."

Still looking at her I shook my head. "I can see you still hard headed it." As I smiled.

She asked me. "So where did Aiden go?"

I shrugged my shoulders. "I don't know probably to his house."

She still had this smile on her face. "So where does he live now? Last time I heard he was living in Oregon.

I leaned back. "How did you know he was living up there?"

She told me. "I ran into his aunt some time ago and I remember her telling me he was up there." She brushed her hair over her shoulder. "Don't worry Ray I got eyes and ears out here." Letting out a little giggle afterwards.

I sat up. "Oh okay I see I see." Putting my hand on the table I told her. "He just moved into this beautiful house in the hills. Trees around for the getaway kinda of vibe and the view is amazing."

Her eyes got big. "I still remember pulling up to his house. Dang that seems like forever ago."

I sat there watching how she went back to that night they met it was as if she missed him. Looking around at the shop. "So I have to know how the hell did you and Aiden ge a dispensary and one like this. It's a coffee shop also?" As she was still in total shock, taking everything in.

She sat there waiting for me to tell her more about Aiden and their time apart. She put her hand on her chin and asked. "How did all this happen?"

I leaned on the table. "After the coma Aiden was just different."

She made this confused face. "Different? Different how?"

I took a deep breath. "It was like he knew life was more than just chasing the fame and riches."

She smile as she rubbed the letters. "I believe it. I seen some of his artwork. Aiden is really good."

I continued saying. "Yeah and that coma made Aiden beyond friendly with everyone and he was all about showing love and support."

She made another confused face and ask. "So why is he not in the league?"

I put my head down to look at my hands and told her. "As he pushed himself in the gym and with all the life goals. He started having flashback of that night. He said it was like he was battling his memories and that was causing him to have major headaches."

She leaned back, face in shock. I was surprised she was even asking questions about Kidd, let alone feeling compassion for him.

I told her. "Kidd had this really good relationship with our sociology teacher and he told her about the memories. And how he felt like each day was his last. She told him to look into the medical marijuana program."

She leaned back on the table. "That doesn't tell me how you two got here." As she put her hands up looking around.

Laughing as I was shaking my head. "If you let me finish I'll tell you how everything became to be."

She smacked her lips. "Hurry up and get to the good parts then."

When she said that I put my hand on my head then shook my head once again. "Shit give me a chance. I can see your still inpatient."

She laughed putting her hand out, waiting for me to finish.

I told her. "Kidd was dealing with all the headaches and it got worse as school and the season went on. That made him do all the reading on medical marijuana and he found the benefits that the plant was offering. Amazed on how it was helping tons of people in different ways."

She shook her head as she was smiling. "So you mean this stuff really helps him."

I looked at her. "Helps him? This stuff brought him back to dreaming and believing in himself again."

Her eyebrows went in and the right one went up. "What the hell does that mean Ray?"

Closed my eyes putting my head back down. "It just means, Kidd was in a dark spot when he realized he wasn't the golden one anymore. This plant brought him back and even made him feel life a little more."

She asked. "So, he found all this love as he was in school and coming back to being himself?"

I smiled. "Yeah, when we were in school Kidd was high all the time, but it just made him do everything. It gave him ideas and you know Aiden when he puts his mind to something he does it. That's half of the reason why we're in the position we're in."

She looked at me confused. "How the hell did he do everything high?"

Looking at her I explained. "It was like he was drawn to everything. He had this strange craving for knowledge and his crazy ass wanted to know what the 'what if's' in life were like."

With a crazy look on her face she said. "So, Aiden got here because he wanted to know what the 'what if's' was like?" Smiling as she finished.

I had my eyes low. "Yes, so with him being around the marijuana so much. He became a patient and started to learn even more about the plant with the help of his grower Green."

She looked at me, head tilted to the side. "Grower? What does that mean and his name is Green? Either I'm high or you're fucking with me right now Ray."

I laughed and said. "Let me explain and it will make sense I promise."

She sat up straight and waited for me to start telling her. I cracked my neck then started to tell her. "When Kidd became a patient he was able to have a grower. That was someone who grew all his cannabis for him. The guy's name is George but he preferred to be called Green and Kidd promised if he got in a position to do any good he would build with the ones he started with."

She looked down at her phone. "What does he have to do with anything you guys going here?"

Rubbing my hands. "If you give me a chance you'll understand."

Rolling her eyes again. "Okay, Ray."

I took a deep breath. "So, he had on this knowledge when he came back. Aiden, being Aiden with his friendly ass he started to meet all the right people in the medical marijuana field out here in the city. He knew marijuana was going to be a lucrative market once the law changed a few years ago."

She put one eyebrow up again. "Where did Aiden come back from?"

I smiled. "Aiden was overseas for two years."

She looked at me surprised and asked. "When did Aiden go overseas?"

Smiling I began to tell her. "After Aiden came back and played JC in Oregon. He got a scholarship to Vermont played a year there and balled out."

Her eyes got big. "I still remember watching Aiden play in high school, that was one of the things I like about him so much. He was so competitive and confident it was sexy."

I leaned back. "Yeah, I don't know about all that but he definitely did his thang on the court." I continued, "He caught the eyes of some overseas coaches and they wanted him the following year. Aiden signed his contract and went to Greece where he played for two years."

She brought both eyebrows in then asked. "Why only two years?"

Put my hands up looking at everything around us. "He said he had more to offer this world than just dribbling a ball. He wanted to inspire young people to believe in themselves. I believe that's why he's always taking risks."

She smiled I could tell hearing that made her happy. She looked at her phone again. "So, Aiden left playing ball to do this?"

Looking at her ways I told her. "He just wanted to be remembered for more. All this is just a plus."

She leaned back looked around. "How is this a plus?"

Shaking my head I answered. "Because Aiden just wanted to be a writer."

She raised that one eyebrow again. "A writer?"

Biting my lip because I knew I was the only one who he told but this was Cherilyn. She was still looking at me confused. "Yeah, Aiden always said maybe if he finished that book he was working on. It would have brought love to so many hearts." I let out a little laugh.

She smiled and asked. "What are you laughing at?"

Told her. "Because the book he was writing was a love story. He said when he was in the coma, he relieved his whole life and seen everything. He said right before he woke up, his brother told him maybe if he tried a little harder to get the one he loved. His life would be a whole lot different and it's funny that I'm actually telling you, the one he fell in love with."

Her smile got bigger. "When did he say his brother talk to him?"

Shaking my head again because I knew I shouldn't have said anything but I told her anyways. "He said that's who came to him when everything went white." Her eyes big and hand over her mouth. I opened my eyes more. "He said he asked him is this what happens when he dies. His brother told him almost and went to hug him, then Aiden woke up out of the coma." Hand still over her mouth.

She looked at her phone once again then back at me. "I'm so glad Aiden woke up, I was scared when I found out what happen. I remember wanting to fly out there but I couldn't see him for the last time like that with all those tubes in him."

Closing my eyes. "Yeah, your right I hate that I will always have that picture of him stuck in my head." Opening my eyes I asked. "Why do you keep looking at your phone? You need to be somewhere?"

She bit her lip. "Kinda but he can wait. I want to hear more about Aiden and how he changed." My eyes got big when I heard that. She asked. "So what else does Aiden do?"

I smiled a little bigger. "Well other than Aiden being a poet, he's a photographer with an amazing. He also just opened his first art gallery with all these dope shots. He's part owner of The Spot with Money. Him and Big Jay opened his own food joint, the food is off the hook. Jay still knows how to throw down."

She smiled. "I miss his cooking." She looked around looking at everything and how peaceful Kidd made it in here. With the pictures, music and lighting Kidd knows how to make people feel at home wherever he is.

I said. "Oh yeah and he's part owner of this beautiful establishment."

She smiled again. "Dang Aiden really made a name for himself. I'm proud of him but I knew he was going to do great things." She looked down at the letters and smiled even bigger. "Honestly Ray I just wanted Aiden to be happy."

I looked at her. "It's funny you say that because none of this brings happiness to Aiden's life. He told me he would give all this up to have you back for one second."

She looked down gripping the letters as she put them over her lips, then put them down on the table. "Just tell Aiden I wish I could have seen him." As she stood up.

I watched her hold the letters tight in her hands as she looked at me. "I'll make sure he gets the message."

She turned and made her way to the door. After a few steps toward the door she stopped and turned around. "Oh, yeah tell him, he promised he will find me in each lifetime and I don't want to see him break any promises." She smiled, holding the letters close to her body as she walked out the door…

To. You <3

Loving you was the best thing I did in my life and not having you is the hardest thing to live with but knowing your still out there gives me a reason to wake up. One day we will run into each other and we might not talk or even wave at each other but knowing there's a chance I can run into you gives me a smile. I hope your enjoying all things life has to give you because no, matter how much time goes by you will always hold a special part of my heart...

Love. Hoop - xo